Shasta Beckons

Chronicle of Ceres, Book 3

CL LaVigne

For permissions, contact:

CL LaVigne

cindy@cllavigne.com

Cover Designed by MiblArt

Shasta Beckons

(Chronicle of Ceres, Book Three) - 1st Edition

www.cllavigne.com

www.facebook.com/CLLaVigneAuthor

ISBN (paperback): 978-1-7322933-9-7

ISBN (eBook): 979-8-9884845-0-9

For those who follow their journey despite the adversities.
You may be fearful, but your determination to find the truth propels your forward.
You may be doubtful, but your faith sheds light on the darkness.
Clarity, peace and joy await you.

Contents

Chapter 1

The Vision

Keeper of the keys, a warrior stands.
Shasta beckons the mystics and the shamans.
Electric, magnetic and balanced, the vortex opens.
The time is nigh. The battle approaches.
Gather the troops and reclaim the forgotten throne.

KAI STOOD ON CRIMSON soil bloodied by the those killed in battle. A tortured scream pierced the darkness and drew Kai's attention to movement a few feet away. He recoiled. A corpse crept forward. Its rotting flesh sloughed off as it pulled itself along the rocky soil. It shrieked again and strained to touch Kai, pointing at him with a bony finger dripping with decaying gore. Paralyzed by fear, Kai's face twisted in horror as the grisly cadaver advanced. It first gripped his boot, and then clutched his pants as it dragged its rotting remains upward.

Kai bolted awake and screamed a primal howl. He slashed the air around him, battling the invisible enemy with his imaginary broadsword.

Jeff jerked awake and pulled Kai into a bear hug, calming him with gentle kisses and soft words while Kai thrashed against the phantom attackers. Jeff engulfed Kai in his strong arms and held him close, rocking and soothing him. Eventually, the warrior yielded to the warm embrace of his husband.

"It was just a nightmare, my love," Jeff soothed bowing his head low and cooing into Kai's ear. His breath fluttered wisps of his husband's dark, curly hair.

Kai snuggled into Jeff's chest and relaxed to the steady thrumming of his heartbeat.

"I witnessed her death this time," Kai whispered. "I felt her pain and anger as if we were the same person."

"Take deep breaths." Cradling Kai's head, Jeff rocked him, smoothed his hair, and assured him with soft words and caresses. Jeff wished this torment would leave Kai alone—leave them both alone.

The carnage had visited for the previous three mornings. Each time, a different scene unfolded. Each nightmare delivered disturbing images of death, and upon waking, Kai's ghostly adversaries dissipated. But this morning was different.

This morning, the vision of his sister's death flickered in his mind like a strobe light. The crisp image blinked, taunting him with his sister's final moments. Kai stared head, his eyes wide as if he could still see the corpse drawing nearer. "I'm losing my mind, Jeff."

Jeff sighed a long, weary breath. "The nightmares are getting worse." He gritted his teeth and hugged Kai harder. "We'll get through this, hon. We'll get through this together."

Kai believed he shared a psychic link with his sister, Hilly. Through this supernatural connection, he could feel and see everything she experienced. After the Revelation at The Nine Muses, three months earlier, Kai and Hilly had developed an intense telepathic bond—a psychic awareness of each other's movements and emotions. The dark, disturbing dreams were psychically spawned snapshots projected from Hilly.

Recently, a sense of foreboding darkened Kai's thoughts, and escalated his anxiety. While supervising his current art installation, he collapsed to the floor screaming. Mental images of Hilly battling evil in a blinding blizzard atop a snowy mountain flickered through his brain like a vintage movie reel. Kai had squeezed his head between his hands hoping to squish the graphic images from his mind.

He feared losing his sanity and realized it had become increasingly difficult to separate his emotions from Hilly's. He recalled his mother describing the torment of the friends she called empaths—sensitive souls who connected with the energy vibrations of others around them. Like emotional whirlpools, these empaths possessed the ability to collect the emotional baggage floating around others. But many empaths succumbed to the overwhelming spiritual tidal wave washing over them without filters to allow incoming feelings to pass through harmlessly.

Kai knew it was a serious problem, which was spiraling out of control. If he didn't find a way to manage the influx of Hilly's energy, he'd either go insane or take his life. He wondered if psychic mediums experienced the same problem. Were their incoming messages from ethereal spirits or just random thoughts bumping around in their own heads? How did they know the difference? How did they stay sane?

Kai needed to contact Darrius for advice. But that call would have to wait. Today demanded his full attention. It was opening night for his much-anticipated abstract exhibit. He needed to oversee last-minute placement adjustments for some of the paintings and touch base with the event coordinator. Although he was excited about the show, Hilly's psychic pokes were interfering with his concentration.

Jeff and Kai pushed through the throng of early guests. Still wearing the exhaustion from that morning's nightmare, Kai held Jeff's hand and slowly followed him through the crowd, averting his eyes from stares. Usually art openings excited him, feeding him with a positive energy that bolstered his confidence. But, tonight, he desperately wanted to be anyplace else, even Denali's desolate, icy slope with his sister.

The bartender approached the couple. He carried Kai's traditional opening-night vodka tonic. "Not tonight, James. I'm too tired," Kai said while dismissing the bewildered server with a wave of his hand.

"You're distracted," Jeff observed as he tugged Kai toward Beatrice Bradley, the local art critic.

Beatrice used her title proudly even though she couldn't tell the difference between a Pollack and a Malevich, much less identify an abstract from a realism painting. But her wealth granted many privileges, and she fancied herself a critic of everything in Sedona, including art.

Like many, she had her own demons. Not even her money could disguise her excessive drinking and inebriated skirmishes. Local artists affectionately called her Beatrice Brandy because of her love for the mellow liquor, but none dared to use that nickname directly to her face.

Beatrice stood back, adjusted her glasses, and grimaced at Kai's painting *Mental Bondage*. She took a long sip of her brandy and stumbled closer.

"Hi, Beatrice!" Jeff hailed cheerfully as he pulled his reluctant husband along. "That's one of Kai's most important works. As a matter of fact, the trip back to his family estate inspired the entire collection." Jeff smiled at Beatrice who sneered back. She slurped her drink and glared at Kai who looked away, his thoughts lost in snow and ice atop a mountain.

Noticing his husband's rudeness, Jeff smoothed over the rough edges of his behavior. "Kai, say hi to Beatrice. You know...the *esteemed art critic*, Ms. Bradley?" Jeff jabbed Kai in the side with his elbow.

"Hello," Kai responded in a distracted manner.

"I have never been treated so rudely!" Beatrice proclaimed.

Something deep inside Kai snapped. The emotional pressure he had suppressed for the last three days raced upward, demanding to be released, and he couldn't—no wouldn't—stop the explosion. Kai whirled to face her. His expressionless face cloaked the rage brewing inside.

"Really? That surprises me. I'm sure I was rude to you last month when you ripped my *Faces of Battle* to pieces, proclaiming in your holier-than-thou manner that it 'lacked imagination,' and that it was 'a sad attempt at capturing reality through an abstract lens', and—"

"Please excuse us, Beatrice," Jeff interrupted. He scowled at Kai. "Kai hasn't slept well lately."

Jeff seized Kai's elbow and wheeled him around, leading him through the gallery as guests and art groupies gawked and whispered nasty comments. Throwing the back door open, Jeff shoved Kai into the alley.

"What the hell are you doing? Are you purposefully sabotaging your exhibit?" Jeff's face reddened with anger.

The Sedona night air swirled cool and refreshing, the citrusy sweet smell of angel's trumpet wafted on a gentle breeze. The tranquility of the scent scattered as Kai screamed at his husband, "Jesus, Jeff, give it a rest! That inebriated old cow won't make or break me!"

Jeff grabbed Kai's arms, yanking him closer. "No? You think Beatrice won't blab about your inconsiderate behavior to everyone in Sedona? Despite being a lush, that woman is one of the richest people in this city. And, even if she has no idea what an abstract is, people fawn all over her opinions. That's just the way it is, hon."

Kai jerked away. "Son of a bitch, I hate Beatrice Brandy!" Clenching his fists, he turned in the alley, scanning the area for something he could hit. Finally, his raged exploded as he kicked the dumpster.

"Your shoes!" Jeff wailed. "Not your new Ferragamos!"

The kick was not well-placed and the tip of the shoe caught the reinforced edge of the metal container, crushing against Kai's big toe. "Shit.

Shit. Shit!" Kai cried, hopping around on one foot while holding the injured one. "I think I broke my toe!"

"Forget your fucking toe, you paid almost a thousand dollars for those shoes," Jeff said as he grabbed Kai's foot and carefully inspected the Ferragamo. "You creased it, but the leather isn't torn. Thank goodness. I think Tim can fix this."

Kai stared at his husband as he fussed about the leather shoe. His styled locks bounced up and down as he scolded Kai. At forty-eight, Jeff still had a luscious head of dark brown hair, so thick, one could get their hands stuck in it.

Jeff gazed up at his husband.

A cry caught in Kai's throat as he met Jeff's stare. Those eyes led to a beautiful soul. Fifteen years ago, when they first met, Jeff ensnared Kai with his hazel eyes. Gold flecks swam around the edges, and when the sunlight glinted, just right, the gold flashed like a beacon. Even after ten years of marriage, Kai's heart hammered at the sight of their unique beauty.

A single tear rolled down Kai's face.

"Babe, what's wrong? It's okay. You didn't mean to scuff your shoe. I'm sure Tim can fix it."

Kai pulled Jeff up and engulfed him in a huge hug. He softly kissed his neck and whispered, "I love you no matter what happens."

Jeff pushed him back. "Honey, what's wrong? Is it the shoe?" Kai shook his head. "Is it Beatrice Brandy?" Kai chuckled and shook his head again. "What is it, babe? I can't make it better if you don't tell me."

They held hands and stared into each other's eyes. The tender moment was shattered by an abrupt opening of the back door. A bag of garbage sailed over their heads into the dumpster. Kai smiled, welcoming the break in the tension.

"Oops, sorry fellas. I didn't know anybody was back here." The janitor stared at them a little while longer before shutting the door and leaving them in peace.

"Jeff, I'm afraid I need to leave you," Kai announced as his bottom lip trembled.

"Wh—what?" Jeff stammered. His eyes widened in disbelief.

"Something's been nagging me since The Nine Muses."

"You mean your quest," Jeff said quietly.

"I don't know how to explain it, but there's a weird energy pulling at me, luring me to Mount Shasta. It won't leave me alone. It's present when I'm awake and lurking when I sleep—or try to sleep."

"Your psychic link to Hilly, no doubt."

Kai cradled Jeff's face and kissed him, full and warm.

"What's that for?" Jeff asked, squinting suspiciously.

"This is why I love you so much. It's as though you can peer into my soul and know what I'm feeling and thinking. Yes, it's those crazy dreams and the visions of Hilly. I know in my heart that I need to join her. She needs me right now."

Jeff slipped his arms around Kai's waist and pulled him closer. "I'm so glad you shared everything about your family with me. I don't fully understand all of your powers but, frankly, I think it makes you sexier than ever. You're my enigmatic man." He kissed Kai quickly on the lips and continued, "You once told me that you would leave for Mount Shasta and walk the shaman's path. Are you telling me that time has come?"

Tears welled in Kai's eyes. Jeff was the strong one in their relationship, and Kai relied on that strength to keep him grounded. Jeff lifted him when he was at his lowest. Jeff guided him into the future and encouraged him to focus on his art and to pour his emotions into the paint. Jeff used his business connections to establish Kai in Sedona's smaller galleries where his natural abilities flourished, and he quickly developed a following.

Kai loved his husband so much. And yet he yearned to leave him and embark on his quest. He gazed into Jeff's eyes. "Yes, I feel that if I don't leave soon, I may implode."

Jeff tousled Kai's hair. "Well, we can't have that, can we? Who would clean up the mess, not to mention pay the astronomical bill to clean your silk suit?"

Kai laughed and hugged Jeff tight. "Thank you. Thank you for being exactly who you are."

"Come on. We need to go inside and deal with Beatrice. You have a lot of sucking up to do after the way you treated her."

Jeff took Kai's hand and gently led him back into the gallery. It was ten o'clock in the evening, and the crowd was just getting started. A dull roar grew in the main hall where thirty guests had gathered to sip drinks and critique the exhibit.

"It's three blobs of color. Red, yellow and black," an elderly man complained. "That's not a painting. My granddaughter can do better." He emphasized his opinion with a martini, which sloshed and spattered the tile under the abstract in question.

"Did you see Beatrice?" another woman whispered to her friend as she held her hand discreetly in front of her face. "That dress makes her look like a human glitter ball." Hushed giggling followed.

"Here comes Kai," a young man gushed to his friends. The group rushed to greet him, and to pay homage to their idol in the hopes that he would choose one of them for his traditional painting giveaway that night. They screamed at him as he passed.

"Kai, I love what you're wearing tonight."

"Kai, this painting literally screams my name."

"Kai, are you still married?"

Jeff frowned at the ingratiating young men fawning over his husband. He steered Kai away from them and toward a diminutive woman leaning on the bar in a silver-sequined gown and much-too-tall silver pumps.

As they approached, Beatrice tottered while turning to greet them. "Well, hello there, fellas." Jeff caught her elbow as she fell against him. "Whoops. I'm a little unsteady in theesh shoes," she slurred.

She spoke directly into Jeff's face, the acrid blast of alcohol forcing him to look away in disgust. He coughed politely before speaking, "Beatrice, Kai has something to say to you."

Guiding Kai in front of the swaying art critic, Jeff pressed, "Kai, don't you have something to say to Beatrice?"

Kai stared at Beatrice who swayed as though she stood on the deck of a ship in a hurricane. Back and forth, back and forth. Soon, Kai began rocking in sync with her, giggling as he mimicked her. "Beatrice," he began. The woman leaned forward to stare at Kai through her thick glasses, and the movement caused her to lurch forward. Kai caught her and swept her into his arms as if they were dancing partners. With her mind swimming in alcohol, Beatrice didn't notice her clumsiness and continued fiddling with her glasses, squinting at Kai as he spoke, "Beatrice, I want to tell you that you won't have me to fuck with much longer."

Jeff silently cursed and glared at Kai.

"WHAT?" she bellowed. The inebriated woman strained to hear and see the man holding her.

Kai cleared his throat. "Let me put it this way you inebriated art hack—FUCK OFF!" Grinning, Kai tossed Beatrice into Jeff's arms and strolled into the main hall, leaving his husband to deal with the tottering old woman reeling from her brandy binge. Jeff glared at Kai.

"Who was that? What did he say?" Beatrice asked as Jeff held her and motioned to the bartender to call a taxi.

"Nobody, Beatrice, nobody." Jeff gazed toward the gallery where Kai stood in the middle of the main hall, smiling and twirling in circles with his arms outstretched like an excited little boy spinning in his first snowfall. "Just a man who's made an important decision about his life."

Chapter 2

Alaska Homecoming

DENALI RISES INTO THE sky like a magnificent diamond in the Alaska Range's crown. A granite cloak flocked with snow falls gracefully over rocky ridges and drapes her slopes with ice crystals which sparkle like jewels in the summer sun.

The great earth spirit reigns over her realm with severity and mercy.

Unpredictable ice storms, avalanches and blizzards await those souls who attempt to conquer her peak, while the wild creatures thrive in the valleys nourished by her snow melt.

As Denali rises into the azure sky, the sprawling Mat-Su Valley stretches before the great mountain like a multi-color tapestry of golden foothills, deep blue lakes, and lush green forests. A peaceful, reverent space, visitors trek into this wilderness to bathe in Denali's positive energy.

But Denali is not always generous with her magic.

A subtle vibration rippled through the tranquil air. Soft as a butterfly's wingbeat, the gentle disturbance was the only indication that a portal opened nearby. The gateway's maw churned with black air currents spiraling clockwise in the inky void—a noiseless obsidian opening.

Hilly, Jake, and Benedict exited the portal near the Sentinel Boulder which stood guard over the magical lupine meadow. Once the travelers had cleared the entryway, the portal closed with a hiss.

"I don't think I'll ever tire of portal jumping," Jake admitted. "Seconds ago we were in North Carolina and now we're in Alaska."

A weary, bored expression flashed across Benedict's face. As a Cererian, he was accustomed to traveling via energetic highways—portals, vortices and, his preferred method, teleporting. While each method varied in technique, their efficiency for journeying great distances was unparalleled.

Hilly faced Denali and pressed her palms together. "Oh, Great Mother, by your grace and power, I have returned home." Hilly closed her eyes and continued her conversation with Denali telepathically—a soundless homecoming between mother and daughter.

Benedict and Jake remained silent as Hilly performed her sacred ritual but observed her actions with concern. Changes had occurred in their friend since the battle on Denali's summit days earlier. She had grown progressively subdued and introspective, abandoning her fiery behavior for an atypical quietness. They attributed her emotional shift to her recent and unexpected separation from her husband, Curtis.

Hilly bowed toward Denali and opened her eyes. A wistful smile graced her lips as she gazed at the snowy peak in the distance. She whirled toward her companions. "There's much to be done. I know Darrius wants to meet with us, but I must first seek the counsel of Mother Denali." She flinched and squeezed her eyes as she clutched her side.

"Are you okay?" Jake asked, his eyes squinting with worry.

"I'm fine," she blurted as she regained her composure and clenched her fists like an injured athlete determined to finish the race despite the pain. An emotional storm brewed inside her—there were frantic screams of over one thousand magical souls. Their constant anguish eroded her mental strength.

Everild's spirit was the loudest. He delighted in torturing her with evil thoughts: *Kill Jake. Consume his magic. Better yet, behead Benedict and his Cererian powers are all yours.*

Since the battle on Denali, her moods churned from jubilance to melancholy, switching between the two with no warning. Pain was a constant companion. It initially began as a body ache as though she was developing a cold, but grew into an annoying stabbing pain that could appear anywhere unexpectedly. Emotions—hers and those of the souls—flooded her brain. She was constantly distracted and unable to concentrate. Besides the tormented spirits swirling inside her, she carried the fresh sting of being rebuffed by her husband.

Hilly hadn't wanted to separate, but it was the only solution. They both needed time apart to battle their demons.

How could Hilly explain to Curtis that her body was now the vessel to thousands of spirits, pushing and shoving to escape their human prison? How could she describe the suffering she endured as they screamed inside her head while their magical powers swirled in her blood, exciting her and making her feel omnipotent?

Hilly wrestled with her demons in silence, choosing not to tell anyone. She recalled Curtis' disgusted look when he'd discovered she was related to Stygian. His repugnance had shocked her. Since the battle, Jake had scrutinized her every move. When she confronted him, he had said 'he was just concerned about her wellbeing', but she couldn't help wonder if Jake worried that she was transforming into something evil like Stygian.

Mother Denali was right. For that split second during the battle, Hilly changed the face of the future, but at what cost? Despite the restlessness of the souls inside her, their combined magic expanded like an inflating balloon, which created a pressure that begged to be released. She wondered if the Yfel Brethren had also changed over time, becoming increasingly brutal as they struggled to adapt to the intense magical energy building within their bodies.

She felt compassion for those soldiers. She understood their cruel and rabid behavior. For she, too, experienced negative thoughts—wielding her magic in destructive ways so she could release the spiritual pressure. She hadn't adjusted to the enhanced psychic abilities as a descendant of Stygian, and now her power had increased almost a hundred-fold because of the spiritual community churning within. She hoped she appeared normal to her companions, but feared Benedict's Cererian abilities would allow him to see the subtle changes occurring within her body. The intensity overwhelmed her. She would soon go insane or on a murder spree if she didn't find relief from her predicament.

There was only one place that might remedy her torment: Denali. After all, it was The Great One who foresaw the events unfold on her summit. Denali understood her child would play a pivotal role in The Cererian Prophecy and was destined to follow a treacherous path into the future.

Hilly stood quietly in the presence of her friends. She absently twisted her fingers together and stared into the distance, toward Denali. Her thoughts pulled her far away as she reflected on her past and worried about her future. Jake tried to lighten the mood.

"Let me accompany you to Denali in case you need an extra set of battle daggers." Grinning, he withdrew Cathal and Cadmar, and wiggled them in front of her face.

He broke her concentration, but she frowned at him, perturbed with his childish behavior. As she gazed into his brilliant blue eyes, which always touched her heart in a gentle way, she suppressed the urge to punch his throat—an order ripping through her brain from Everild. Jake would never know how close he came to death that day.

A puzzled look on Jake's face alerted Hilly of her unusual demeanor. She relaxed her face, scattering the frown lines. "No, thanks. I'll be fine. It's a personal issue, and I'd rather handle everything myself."

Hilly gazed at Jake. His eyes were like twin pools of blue water, cool and inviting. His pupils widened and red flecks flashed in the irises, something she hadn't seen before. She yearned to tell him everything. She longed for him to pull her close and console her.

And then the voices returned.

She clenched her fists as a distraction.

"Hilly! Easy, you'll break my hand," Jake groaned. She hadn't noticed that she had gripped Jake's hand and was now strangling his fingers.

Hilly dropped his hand and looked away. She wouldn't let Jake see her suffering. Hilly was a strong, confident witch with incredible powers. But she couldn't control the discord within her own head. It was vital that she see The Great Mother as soon as possible.

She sucked in a long, deep breath and faced her companions as though nothing had happened. "As I was saying, I need to take a short trip to see Denali, and then I'll join you in Aningan. I won't be long. Benedict, I'm sure you don't mind teleporting Jake back with you, do you?"

"My pleasure," Benedict replied calmly.

"Good. I'll message Darrius when I'm ready to return to town."

"Don't be long," Jake added. He stared into Hilly's eyes and raised an eyebrow.

Hilly felt Jake trying to mentally messaged her and slammed the door to her mind, an action she thought best to prevent unwelcome replies from the souls inhabiting her body. Jake frowned, but she flashed a quick grin and nodded at him as she replied confidently, "I'll be back before you know it."

Hilly gazed into the distance, toward Denali, and raised her hands to cast a spell. She invoked the elemental spirits of the north, east, south, and west until a portal materialized. The magnetic energy buffeted her as she stood in the entranceway and faced her companions. Benedict returned her stare stoically. Jake forced a smile to his lips.

She nodded at Benedict and turned to Jake. She sensed his anxiety and the concern he had for her. She winked and leapt into the portal's gaping maw. The minute she penetrated the membrane, the gateway closed with a hiss.

Buoyed by Hilly's playful gesture, Jake grinned to himself. It was an excellent sign that despite whatever troubled her, she was still in control.

"Hilly is brave," Benedict noted. "Nature's spirits can be unkind if undue demands are placed upon them."

"What do you mean?" Jake asked.

"Your friend seeks relief from the tortured souls that are now a part of her, but Denali cannot interfere with The Cererian Prophecy."

"What tortured souls?"

"Your friend is no longer the Hilly you remember. She is now a preternatural being who walks in the shadows. She doesn't yet understand her full potential or realize the importance of her journey."

"What is it with you Cererians? Can't you speak plainly? Give it to me straight," Jake grumbled. Benedict's cryptic ramblings annoyed him.

"I don't understand your angry outburst, but I will speak plainly, as you put it." Benedict paused to gather his thoughts before continuing. "Hilly is no longer fully human. She continues to undergo a massive transformation as detailed in the Prophecy."

Benedict changed the subject. "We must hurry, Darrius is contacting me telepathically. I've made him aware of Hilly's situation. It's urgent. So, unless there's something keeping us here, in the middle of the tundra, I'll teleport us back to Aningan."

"Let's go." Jake's clipped response didn't faze Benedict. Jake disliked the odd Cererian. His straightforward manner was off-putting. He possessed a cold, robotic personality and wasn't shy to speak his mind even if others might get hurt, but Darrius believed in him so Jake would wait before passing judgement on his new associate.

"This might feel odd," Benedict warned as he placed a hand on Jake's shoulder.

Instantly, the two men disappeared.

Chapter 3

Mother Denali

THE PORTAL OPENED ONTO a snowy glacier. Hilly stepped from the gateway and smacked into a wall of frigid air. The Mat-Su Valley flourished under warm summer temperatures, but on the mountain it was below freezing, and Hilly was poorly dressed. Uncontrollable shivering rattled her body, and her eyes teared from the biting cold. She hugged herself for warmth and hopped in place.

She considered traveling back to the warmer valley, but the souls inside her body urged her to stay. They knew why she came here. If Denali could free them from their human prison, they would do everything within their power to ensure the meeting with the earth spirit took place. They pleaded with Hilly to stay.

Hilly agreed. She needed to meet with Denali, not only for the magicians' spirits, but also to find answers to the questions she had about her heritage.

She looked upward, marveling at the granite cliffs covered in icefalls. Above them was a cloudless sky the color of forget-me-nots. The vivid blue reminded her of Jake's eyes but she shook her head, scattering the thought of her friend. She was here for a selfish reason and didn't need distractions.

A flurry of light snowflakes drifted about her head, coating her hair like a lacy winter scarf. Despite the chill, she began to feel safe and warm. The sensation one feels when they've reached home after many years of wandering.

But Denali's child was far from feeling secure.

Since the influx of magical souls, and since the mental assault by Everild's spirit, Hilly had not rested. The agitated voices of the countless magicians demanded to be released into the ether and to join their ancestors in the heavens.

They pounded on her heart, begging for mercy. Their constant pleas eroded her willpower. Hilly feared she would snap and release her fury on the world. She needed to know if there was a way other than suicide to release the tormented souls.

Suicide.

The word fluttered through Hilly's mind like a frightened bird, and it shocked her. She would never consider taking her own life but it was a solution. She wondered if Everild introduced the sinister idea into her mind.

Abruptly the ground heaved, catapulting Hilly onto the glacier. She watched in horror as ice boulders bounded down Denali's rocky cliffs, ricocheting past her as she struggled to regain her footing. Dislodged snow and granite from the higher elevations formed an avalanche that roared toward Hilly. She raised her hands, palms forward toward the advancing gray wall and conjured high magic to halt the catastrophic rockslide.

"STOP!"

"Mother?" Hilly replied, unsure if the entity was Denali.

"Cease your magic, you belligerent child." The words arrived as whispers on the wind.

Hilly obediently lowered her hands and nervously watched as tons of rock and ice raced toward her. Although a glimmer of doubt pulled at her sensibilities, complete faith in Denali comforted her as she closed her eyes against the impending doom.

"I hear you Mother, and I believe in you," she said calmly. The avalanche roared in her ears as she tensed her body against the rockslide. She resigned herself to whatever fate Denali dealt. Even if it meant death.

Hilly squeezed her eyes and held her breath.

Silence.

Moments passed. Hilly stood still, her body stiffened in anticipation of the impact that never came.

The rumbling and violent shaking ceased.

She peeked at her surroundings, first squinting, and then her eyes rounded in disbelief. There were no gigantic boulders nor was there a monstrous snowpack. The snowy glacier was pristine as the moment she had first arrived.

"How dare you even think about taking your own life," Denali admonished. "That is forbidden. Life is precious. You bring shame to your family considering such an action. I should have let the avalanche consume you, and then, perhaps, you would understand."

Hilly fell onto her knees and raised her hands to the rocky cliffs. "Mother, I am in despair. How can I release the souls from my body and restore peace to my own spirit?" she cried.

A gust of wind buffeted Hilly and pierced into her chest like a frozen knife as it sent waves of chilled shivers throughout her body. Gales blew down the cliffs and dumped fresh snow upon the glacier. The icy tempest descended upon Hilly, churning in a frigid white-out that covered everything, including Hilly, in a white, snowy blanket.

The weight of the snowpack crushed her body.

The heaviness halted her breathing.

Her heartbeat slowed.

Thump. Thump.

Hilly lay embraced in the arms of hypothermia as she lapsed into a coma.

Hilly awakened to an intense burning on her skin. No longer on the glacier, she leaned against the rocky side of a massive cave. Her skin was blistered from scorching fumes wafting from thermal vents in the floor. A steaming trickle of orange-red magma zigzagged by her feet as it followed the cracks in the crust. The searing lava slithered away, carrying energy to the bowels of the great mountain.

"Hilly?"

Hilly jumped, startled by the unexpected voice. "Is somebody there?"

"Hilly."

A tone of familiarity plucked at Hilly's senses. She recognized this voice, and her pulse quickened as she realized Denali had brought her into the safety of her rocky home.

"My child, come to me."

"Mother? Where are you?"

"Follow the sound of my voice, and you will find what you seek."

Hilly carefully navigated the steaming river of lava, following the disembodied voice down a long, dark corridor. Noxious sulfur fumes thickened the air, making it difficult to breathe. The rocky passageway narrowed to a channel barely wide enough for her to shimmy through. The last few yards tested her resolve as she squeezed past hot, jagged granite which slashed her chest. Bleeding from several cuts on her upper body, she emerged and found herself in a cavernous chamber.

Soaring more than twenty stories tall, the large room shimmered with brilliant sunshine which filtered through massive quartz crystals jutting at angles throughout the room. Numerous lava tubes snaked up from the floor to the domed ice ceiling. The sun's rays reflected through the crystals, and cast a shower of brilliant light onto aquamarine pools covering the floor.

Hilly shielded her eyes against the intense brightness and gasped at the beauty of the underground oasis surrounding her. A small waterfall formed from the mountain's ice melt tumbled from the roof to the floor and disappeared through an underground hole. Gnarled, black tree roots protruded from the ceiling and walls like twisted fingers reaching for unseen hands.

In the middle of the cavern by the cerulean water stood an old woman leaning on a wooden shepherd's hook. Without looking at Hilly, she raised one hand, curled a knobby, arthritic finger, and beckoned Hilly to join her.

Hilly hesitated. Although Mother Denali had appeared as an old woman to her in the past, this woman was bent and crooked, like the gnarled roots pushing through the ceiling and walls. Her long, tangled hair hung around her face, and her ragged clothes dangled from her emaciated body. The threadbare rags were not the fine clothes one might expect on a supreme spirit of Nature.

Hilly cautiously approached. The woman stared at the ground and avoided her gaze.

"Mother?" Hilly's voice quavered. Surely this specter was not her earth mother but some other creature sent to deliver a message.

"You ask as though you are unsure of whom stands before you? Do you not recognize me, my child?" The old woman replied in a raspy voice which screeched like a rusty gate.

"You have appeared as mere whispers of the wind and elements of the weather. Only once have you taken human form—an old woman in the sky, but not as a wretched hag. I don't think you are who you claim to be."

"Close your eyes and listen to your heart. What do your instincts tell you? Remove the veil from your mind and see clearly with the gifts you possess."

Hilly inhaled deeply and closed her eyes. Her mind flooded with cascading images of snow, ice, and rock. In the middle of the icy montage stood a young woman with long brown hair and large brown eyes. A dusting of snow covered her hair and eyelashes. Ice crystals formed a magnificent gown that shimmered and sparkled in the dazzling sunshine. Quartz crystal rings dangled on each finger and a crystalline crown sat atop her head. The woman smiled warmly at Hilly and stretched her arms forward as if to embrace her.

Hilly opened her eyes and found the old hag standing a few feet away. Her gnarled and bent arms stretched forward as if to snatch her. She gazed at Hilly through sightless eyes, white orbs floating in a scrunched, wrinkled face. Bewitched by the entity, Hilly couldn't move her legs nor could she blink. She stood mute as the old woman slowly advanced with shuffling steps. The witch grinned a collection of jagged and broken teeth as a black forked tongue slithered between them, and arched toward Hilly.

Repulsed, Hilly turned her face away. A shiver raced up her spine as she recalled the moment Everild had also tormented her with his long, black tongue. Was this wretched creature an associate of the dead Cererian?

"Hilly." The witch murmured as she stumbled closer. An odor of rotten meat wafted. Hilly's stomach lurched from the putridness and tossed bile into the back of her throat.

Earlier, Denali had challenged her to close her eyes and use her instincts. But the obscene specter before her had stolen her gaze and forced her eyes to remain open.

Hilly needed to regain control.

Trust your intuition. Close your eyes. Hilly repeated the words in her mind like a mantra until she freed herself from the witch's spell and was able to squeeze her eyes shut.

An image of the young ice queen returned in her mind. The woman spoke softly, "Your eyes can betray you, my child. Always trust your intuition. Open your eyes."

A joyful cry escaped Hilly as she found the old hag had disappeared and had been replaced by the beautiful earth spirit, Denali. The Great Mother stood before her in a body fashioned from white, faceted granite. Two eyes carved from blue opals sat serenely above her sculpted nose and delicate crystal lips. Her angular, icy-white arms extended gracefully down her side. In one hand, she held a slender, selenite wand.

"You see, my child, in our world, not everything we see is reality. But our intuition is always true. If you listen to it."

"I am humbled by your presence," Hilly said as she bowed. She kept her head lowered until Denali spoke again.

"Rise, child." The earth spirit smiled. When her crystal lips bowed upward, they captured the sun's rays and projected miniature rainbows across Hilly's face.

"Mother, am I dead? Did I die on the slope? I remember the weight of the snow pinning me to the ground and taking my breath away. I recall becoming very sleepy."

Denali chuckled. The rich, melodic giggle sounded like windchimes blowing in a gentle breeze. The Great Mother wasn't ridiculing Hilly. Her reaction was a gentle response to Hilly's innocent naivety of the supernatural world.

"Your heart still beats strong in the outer world. Your physical body has plunged into a deep meditative state. Here, in this world, you stand in the realm of spirits. I invited your soul to join me in my rocky kingdom. All living things embrace the duality of existence—the physical and the spiritual. Those who embrace their magic can easily float between the two worlds."

Hilly nodded. Denali's words struck a chord. She astral traveled regularly allowing her spirit to escape her body and journey to other places. Her soul had taken flight when she participated in her vision quest with Jake, but, in those instances, she was quite aware that she was out of her body—she felt lighter as if she was a phantom. Standing before Denali, Hilly felt the physical weight of her body.

"I understand, Mother, but when I astral travel, I feel light like a shadow. Why do I feel heavier in this world?"

"You are evolving, my child. There will be a day when you no longer notice the difference in energy between the worlds."

"Evolving?" Hilly frowned at the use of the word. It prompted her to envision herself as a monster. A beast that had pushed Curtis away.

"That's all I can share right now. Be patient. Allow yourself time to explore your magic and learn from your encounters. You have many exciting adventures ahead of you."

Hilly chewed her lower lip in frustration. It upset her when Denali dodged her questions and answered with placating rhetoric. But she knew better than to push for more information. She couldn't risk enraging the great earth spirit. She'd be patient for now.

Denali observed Hilly with interest.

"You trusted your intuition today and now you will be rewarded." The granite queen moved forward and embraced Hilly, caressing her hair and stroking her face. "My beautiful child, I feel the chaos churning in your body. I cannot release the spirits who reside within. I can only quiet them and make them feel at peace."

Denali reached up to her face and gently plucked out one blue opal eye. She held it before Hilly. "Behold, the jewel of intuition. It is the gemstone of calming energy and harmony." The sunlight glinted off the facets and radiated powerful energy around and through Hilly, making her disoriented and drowsy.

"Walk in your world and be at peace, my child," Denali said softly. Abruptly, the Great Mother thrust the opal into Hilly's throat, directly into the jugular notch.

Hilly staggered backward from the brutal assault. She clutched her throat and cried out, "Mother, why?"

The action was vicious but compassionate. With that one movement, Denali initiated a chain reaction of transformations within Hilly. All she could do was observe the process as Hilly completed the metamorphosis.

Hilly lurched forward and gasped for breath as she clawed at the stone securely fastened in her throat. Her lungs swelled with fluid and foreign matter. Hilly coughed violently to dislodge the material stuck in her throat and spit up blood-stained phlegm and shards of granite. Seeing the stone fragments tumble from her mouth, Hilly panicked. Staring wide-eyed at her earth mother, she gestured for Denali's help.

"All will be okay, my child," Denali soothed.

"Mother, help me!" Hilly wailed as she collapsed to the ground, her arms stretching toward the earth spirit. Her belly swelled to enormous proportions like an overinflated balloon; and Hilly held her stomach, fearing it would explode at any moment. Pain snaked throughout her entire body, pushing her to the edge of insanity. Hilly rolled back and forth, and scrabbled for Denali's granite cloak, desperate for the earth spirit to relieve the searing pain.

Denali bent forward and lightly touched Hilly with the tip of the selenite wand. An immediate burst of warmth pulsed in her heart and spread throughout her entire body on a wave of healing energy that saturated every cell as it raced along the veins and arteries.

The agony vanished.

Calm and serenity engulfed Hilly.

"Behold the selenite's gift of healing," Denali announced as she raised the wand into the air.

Hilly knelt on the ground and caught her breath. The healing energy swirled in her blood like an ocean wave ebbing and flowing. Hilly lightly brushed the blue opal nugget in her throat; and the jewel thrummed a vibrational song which soothed the tortured souls within her body.

"I sense your emotions are calming." Denali observed.

Hilly gazed up at the Great Mother. She couldn't deny the brutal attack had granted her tranquility and peace—feelings she hadn't experienced in a long time. "But how? What did you place on me?"

"Remember during your vision quest when the Sentinel Boulder shared the image of a blue opal? He offered you a glimpse into your future. Jake knew the qualities of the gemstone, but neither of you could understand how significant it would be for you in the future. The blue opal will balance your emotions and calm the thousands of souls swirling inside your body. I placed this magical stone at your throat chakra to allow you to speak without the interference of the spirits that inhabit your body. This stone will bless you with communication, honesty, and empathy."

Hilly felt more tranquil than she had in a long time. The restless spirits had been quieted and their constant barrage of voices had been stilled, leaving her with a void. Tears flowed freely down her cheeks. The dam holding back her emotions had been lifted, allowing authentic feelings to rush forward.

Hilly felt relief.

"Thank you, Mother. Thank you for this amazing gift," Hilly cried.

"You must embark on the rest of your journey, my child. You will travel to lands inhabited by strange creatures. But all of nature's children are equal. No one is better or worse than the other. It's time I take my leave. Remember, my child, always trust in your intuition for there are many veils that may cloud your vision."

A strong earthquake rocked the chamber. Small stones and quartz crystals cascaded from the ceiling and bounced off the walls.

Hilly awoke on the icy glacier entombed in a snowdrift.

Was it all a dream?

Using her psychic senses, she scanned her body and detected a serenity she hadn't experienced for days. The voices were no longer present. With a renewed strength, she pushed up, loosening the hardpacked snow on her back and shook herself free from the bits of snow and ice clinging to her clothes. She reached at her throat and just below her collar was the cold, faceted surface of the blue opal.

It was all real. Denali gave me a precious gift.

The voices of the magicians and Everild had finally been quieted. But, under the surface, her blood pounded with the combined magic of all the spirits she harbored inside. They compelled her and emboldened her to conjure, to perform magic on something...anything.

Remembering the advice of Denali, she reined in her emotions and looked inside, deep into her soul. The lessons of the past few weeks had been patience, reflection and control. These were attributes Hilly didn't naturally possess but desperately needed. She inhaled deeply and then exhaled slowly, allowing the breath to tease any remaining tension from her body.

She lingered in the peacefulness, relishing the quiet and stillness. Standing alone on the glacier, only the strong beat of her heart echoed in her ears. She had been a vessel for so many voices for too long. Now that the souls were quieted, she felt a twinge of melancholy, an unexpected yearning for those who were once part of her. She shook her head, attempting to scatter the sad thoughts, but she couldn't deny the emptiness that gnawed at her.

Moments earlier she couldn't bear to have the screams in her brain, and now she actually missed the tortured souls.

"What the hell is wrong with me?" She posed the question to Denali's cliffs. Her words echoed off the granite.

She smirked. Her upper lip lifted in a twisted grin. "Damn, Hilly, get a grip on yourself. You finally got your life back, and you're *still* not satisfied!"

And there it was. The word that pricked at her mind. She wasn't satisfied. How could she be when her life was in such turmoil? Curtis thought she was a monster, the Yfel Brethren prowled the earth, and she still hadn't figured out the extent of her magical powers.

Time to end this pity party!

Holding her hands in front of her, she spoke the ancient words that came so easily to her nowadays. A gateway loomed before her pulsing with energy. Glancing back toward Denali's peak, she nodded reverently toward the Great Mother before calmly walking into the portal, confident she could now control her disturbing urges.

Chapter 4

Observer & Elder

JAKE AND BENEDICT MATERIALIZED outside the nondescript office building of Aningan Properties in the middle of a block of dilapidated buildings on a quiet dirt street. Vacationers avoided this area, choosing to frequent the more popular tourist areas located in the town's center.

"Damn, that was a hell of a ride!" Jake exclaimed. His arms stretched to either side as he steadied himself against the dizzying effects of the teleportation. Although Jake was accustomed to portal travel, teleporting was more abrupt as though he had been launched by a slingshot.

"I gather that was your first time," Benedict remarked as he mounted the steps leading up to the office.

Jake pressed his hands against his head while the world spun around him. The urge to heave boiled in his belly, and he swallowed the acid fumes bubbling up from his stomach. He growled a throaty rasp, and spat a huge gob of phlegm into the dirt followed by another and another.

"Do you require assistance?" Benedict inquired as he waited by the door to the office. "If not, please hurry. Darrius expects us to be on time."

Jake bent over in the street placing his hands on his hips. His stomach gurgled, and he wasn't sure if there would be an eruption. He peered at the Cererian.

Why is he such an oddball? Jake thought.

Benedict stretched almost seven feet tall and his skin was a sickly white. Gangly arms and legs sprouted from his lean body as if he was made of rubber, and a shock of thick, white hair fell smooth around his ears and down his neck. To Jake, he appeared like a lanky ghost.

"I'm coming. I'm coming," Jake grunted. Holding his grumbling stomach, he staggered up the steps and nodded at Benedict. "I'm ready."

Benedict opened the red and green door—a garish entranceway into what was the despicable headquarters for Aaron Aningan.

"Welcome," Darrius greeted. "Thank you for being punctual."

"Wow!" Jake said as he scanned the front room.

The last time he had stepped into the building, Uncle Aaron was still in control of Aningan. At that time, the office had loomed dark and unwelcoming as if an evil presence seeped into the walls and flooring. Now, the space was bright and airy, featuring new furniture, ample lighting, and lush plants. A sunny energy swirled within the room.

Jake brushed his fingers along a freshly painted wall. "Damn, Darrius. I never thought I would be happy to enter this nasty place. It's like you've scrubbed away Aaron's negative energy and replaced it with a new coating of powerful vibes."

"Thank you, Jake," Darrius beamed. "It was a concerted effort by everyone in the town, and it turned out better than expected."

Darrius had considered burning the wretched building to the ground and erasing all physical reminders of Aaron, but the town's elders convinced him to keep the office as a monument—a foundation upon which peace and balance would be restored to Aningan and its people.

Enlisting the aid of the locals, Darrius removed every piece of furniture and emptied the office of anything that could be carried away. During the new moon, the townspeople gathered around a bonfire and torched Aaron's belongings, watching the fire spit sparks into the night sky—a formal energetic cleansing of all that was bad and evil.

The following day, healers washed the walls and floors with spiritual lavender water. One medicine man told Darrius the walls lapped up the curative fluid, thirsting for relief after many years of abuse and negativity. The final step involved three shamans who spent the night chanting prayers and cleansing the space with sage and spiritual breaths.

Benedict spoke with urgency. "As I mentioned earlier, Darrius, Hilly had a pressing matter and will not join us for our meeting."

Jake sighed and shook his head. Benedict had the personality of a masseur with talons for fingers—always rubbing him the wrong way.

"Thank you for that reminder," Darrius responded cordially. He discreetly winked at Jake, a sign for Jake to relax and play along. "It's okay that Hilly isn't present yet as I need to share information with just the two of you." Darrius guided both of them down the hall and into the back office.

The room exuded a peaceful calm, not at all like the atmosphere when Aaron and Hilly screamed at each other or when Aaron would delight in torturing him. The old man had wielded his discipline in a particularly cruel way by paralyzing Jake and forcing him to endure tremendous suffering while unable to flinch or even blink. Jake had stopped counting the number of times he was the recipient of Aaron's painful punishments in this space.

Four cushioned chairs formed a circle around a small, wooden table. The ensemble sat upon a bright Native American handwoven rug with bold colors of red, brown, black, and white. The gigantic mahogany desk which had served as Aaron's throne was gone, burned in the bonfire and was replaced by a small desk hugging one corner of the room. Simple cotton curtains covered the window peering over the alley.

"Please take a seat," Darrius invited. "Hilly will join us shortly, but before she arrives, let me set the mood for our discussion."

Benedict frowned at Darrius' words.

"Benedict, I see my statement has confused you. My goal is to share information so when Hilly arrives there are no surprises. So, I will be setting the 'mood' if you will."

Benedict nodded and then shrugged. "Seems like a waste of time, but please proceed."

Darrius continued. "As you are aware, Hilly is meeting with Denali regarding the spirits that inhabit her body."

Jake replayed the battle sequence in his mind. If only he had known about that possibility and had been prepared, perhaps he could have redirected Everild's mouth away from Hilly and all the spirits would have soared into the heavens and found the peace they deserved. He frowned, realizing that his actions harmed his friend; and he felt responsible for her unfortunate situation. His eyes darkened with doubt.

"You can't blame yourself, Jake," Darrius comforted. "Nobody is at fault, not even Hilly. The Cererian Prophecy will unfold as it is written."

"I understand what you're saying, but I don't like it," Jake huffed.

"Hilly is a dear friend to both of us. We are powerless to assist her through this personal battle that only she can fight. For a warrior like yourself it's maddening to stand by and watch your comrade in arms suffer," Darrius commiserated.

"Excuse me, but what do his emotions have to do with what we need to understand about Hilly?" Benedict interjected.

Jake glared at Benedict. He opened his mouth to snap a response, but Darrius placed a hand on his knee and squeezed gently.

Darrius dipped his eyes at Jake and then he replied to Benedict. "Brother, you'll find that interacting with humans demands that we learn their customs and nuances, especially if we want to be successful in our collaboration. Humans form close bonds and yearn to help each other if they are in need. Do you understand?"

Benedict interlaced his fingers and raised his hands to his chin. "This is difficult, Darrius. Apparently, I must learn a great deal about human emotions and how they play a role in our future."

Darrius nodded. "All in good time. I know you will succeed."

Darrius paused and closed his eyes which fluttered furiously under his eyelids. Seconds later, he opened them and addressed the room. "Hilly messaged me. She is on her way. So let me be succinct. Hilly is evolving and will continue to do so. The blood of Stygian races through her veins. She will not be able to keep her innate powers at bay. We must monitor her for signs that she is not coping with her transformation."

Darrius turned to Jake. "We must *all* watch for cracks in her armor like destructive behavior."

Jake leaned forward. "What do you mean? Are you saying Hilly may become like Stygian and try to harm us? What does your Prophecy say?"

"Jake, the time may come when you will need to trust your instincts and not your friend."

Darrius raised a finger to his lips, indicating everyone remain quiet.

All eyes turned toward the door.

"Hi fellas." Hilly said cheerfully. "You weren't talking about me, were you?"

Jake bounced up and ran to Hilly, his arms outstretched for a hug. "That was fast. Everything okay?"

"Mother Denali is amazing. I couldn't be better." Hilly grabbed Jake in a bear hug, squeezing him hard until he begged to be released. She turned toward Darrius. "Darrius, it's so good to see you again." She hugged him and kissed him tenderly on both cheeks.

Darrius smiled warmly, noting the change in her demeanor.

Benedict mimicked Darrius and rose to greet Hilly who hugged him lightly. He awkwardly returned her embrace while glancing at Darrius for approval.

"Darrius, you've done wonders with this room. It's so joyful," Hilly said as she twirled around, soaking in the new furnishings and decorations.

"You seem much happier since I last saw you," Darrius replied. He psychically scanned her to see if an unfriendly entity had seized control of her body.

She sensed him probing and scolded him, "Darrius, cut that out. It's me. Denali gave me a wondrous gift. A present that helps keep the voices calm." She pulled her collar down, revealing the blue opal affixed to her throat.

"A blue opal!" Jake shouted. "Like the vision the Sentinel Boulder shared with you during your vision quest." He stepped toward Hilly, his fingers poised to touch the gemstone. "May I?" She nodded quickly. Jake's finger traced the edges of the jewel fused near Hilly's skin. It was as if it was a natural part of her, as though she was born this way. "Is it working? Is it having an effect on your emotions?"

Hilly laughed. "I'll say! Despite the chaos that swirls within this body, Denali's gift has quieted the voices and calmed their fears."

Benedict glanced at Darrius and messaged telepathically, *Did Denali interfere with the mandate of the Prophecy by affixing this calming tool?*

Watching Jake and Hilly celebrate her newfound freedom, Darrius responded to Benedict, *No. Hilly still retains the souls. Events will unfold as they are intended.* Benedict nodded his understanding.

"Hilly, now that you're here, I have a few announcements that I think you'll enjoy. Please take your seat." Darrius gestured toward a chair by Jake. Hilly hugged Jake one more time, and curled up in the chair.

Grinning like an excited little boy preparing to perform a new trick, Darrius turned toward the hallway. "Sammy, please bring us some coffee!" Jake and Hilly's eyes widened. They hadn't seen Sammy since their encounter at the hotel.

A round face peered around the corner into the office. "Hiya! How is everybody?" Sammy ambled in carrying a large urn of coffee. He placed it on the side table and asked, "Who needs cream or sugar?"

"How is this possible with Aaron gone?" Hilly asked as she jumped up.

All smiles, Darrius responded. "Sammy is too important to toss out with his bad master. So, I had 'Aaron' give him new orders." He winked at Hilly and Jake who both chuckled. They understood the true meaning behind Darrius' comment. He had shapeshifted into the likeness of Aaron to give Sammy new orders.

Hilly joined Sammy who busied himself pouring hot coffee into the mugs. She wrapped her arms around the stout little man and pulled him close. Sammy stared at her with his crooked smile. Hilly coached him, "Hug me back, Sammy. It's great to see you again!" Sammy obeyed and clutched her sweater.

"Miss Hilly, it's so good to see you, too! Let me make your coffee," he said, stepping away from her. "Black, right?" Hilly smiled and nodded.

Jake joined them and tousled Sammy's gray hair. "Damn, it's good to see my sidekick again."

"Jake, I really missed you. I haven't taken Stella for a ride in a long time. Maybe..." Jake thrust his hand in the air to stop Sammy from yammering. Sammy shyly gazed at Jake. "Gotcha, Jake. I'm blabbing again. Black coffee, right?" Jake took the mug and sat down.

"Mr. Darrius, do you need more coffee?"

"I'm good. Let me introduce someone. Sammy, this is Benedict."

Sammy extended his hand, eager to meet a new friend, but Benedict stared at it. He politely smiled at the nawiht. Without skipping a beat, Sammy whipped his arm back and said "Hiya! Do you want some coffee?" Benedict hesitated.

Realizing Benedict was unfamiliar with the hot drink, Darrius urged him, "Give it a try, Benedict. Humans drink it all the time. Prasad was not too fond of it. I believe he called it a foul-tasting bean, but I find it refreshing."

Sammy poured a cup and gently handed it to Benedict who stared at the contents while sniffing the nutty aroma. He observed everyone slurping the dark fluid. Following their lead, he brought the cup to his lips and took a sip. He immediately coughed and grimaced and set the cup on the table as though it had bitten him.

"Perhaps it's an acquired taste," Benedict said as he folded his hands onto his lap. "Shall we continue with our meeting?"

Jake and Hilly arched their eyebrows and looked to Darrius who stared at his colleague.

"You'll find, Benedict, that when interacting with humans, it's preferred to exchange pleasantries before launching into business." Darrius spoke firmly but with a gentle tone much like a teacher to a pupil. Although Benedict nodded, his face wore the creases of confusion.

Darrius cleared his throat. "To Benedict's point, let me begin the meeting by welcoming everyone. We've all recently encountered very painful moments in our lives that bring us together today. The point of this meeting is to start fresh. With Aaron returned to Ceres where we hope to rehabilitate him, the town of Aningan needs a strong leader to assuage the concerns and questions left by Aaron's despicable actions." Darrius paused and sipped his coffee.

Darrius continued. "That individual will be Benedict."

"Bullshit," Jake whispered into his coffee.

Darrius glared at Jake. "Do you have a comment, Mr. Pierson?"

Hilly watched the two men. Darrius' formal inquiry indicated he was in no mood for bad behavior. His dignified tone was his method for restoring decorum to a tense situation.

Jake set his mug down and leaned toward Darrius. "Yes, I think it's a mistake." He jerked his head toward Benedict. "We don't know anything about him. Considering that Aaron, another Cererian, exploited my people, I feel we need a member of the tribe to represent our interests."

Darrius touched his fingertips together, politely considering Jake's response. "Yes, I see your point, Mr. Pierson. But it's critical a Cererian Observer is installed in this region, and the perfect choice is Benedict.

However, Aningan needs and deserves balance. To achieve that goal, another person will join Benedict in rebuilding the town. That individual will be *you* as you lead the people in your new role as Elder."

Stunned, Jake's eyes widened and his mouth dropped. "Elder? How? There's a process..." Jake threw a look of surprise at Hilly who leaned over and patted his knee.

"Let me explain while you recover your senses," Darrius said.

"You suggested I meet with your elders and learn the truth about Aaron and his unethical dealings in this town. I took your advice. They invited me to participate in one of their ceremonies—a healing ritual. We sat together, put the past behind us, and looked toward the future and its possibilities. That's when your name was mentioned, not by me but by the collective voices of the Elder Council. You have proven to them through your words and deeds that the time has come for you to join them. Your main responsibility will be as an advisor to Benedict as you work together to heal the town."

Darrius paused. "One more thing. This amulet is yours and must be worn at all times." Darrius handed Jake a pendant carved from ivory and silver. A magical tribal artifact handed down from one generation to another, the necklace was much more than jewelry. The amulet possessed protection powers for the wearer. The medallion and every silver link in the chain represented the hundreds of men and women who proudly served their people as an elder.

Jake cradled the amulet in his hand, admiring it from all angles. Ascending to Elder in the community was a significant achievement. Gathering the chain into his hands, he gazed at the medallion with love and reverence before slipping it over his neck and tucking it inside his shirt. He leaned back in his chair with a satisfied grin on his face.

Hilly reached over and squeezed his hand. "Congratulations, Jake. You deserve it."

Jake beamed. "Thanks, I appreciate that."

"I forgot the best part," Darrius began. "Sammy will be your second-in-command." Hearing his name, Sammy grinned his toothless smile at Jake. "Sammy is like family in this community and deserves to remain with his family. He will serve you well in your new role."

"Sammy, please face me," Darrius requested. "Do you remember our discussion?"

"Yes. I report to Jake now, and I will take care of his needs like I did with Aaron and you."

"And what else?" Darrius said with a twinkle in his eye.

"Oh, yeah!" Sammy lifted the black Cererian crystal from around his neck and proudly showed it to everyone. "I can use this to get things done real quick for you, Jake! No job is too small or too large. I'll do anything—"

Jake raised his hand, halting Sammy mid-word. "Thanks, Sammy. I look forward to working with you again."

"Do I sit with him now, Darrius?" Sammy asked as he glanced between Darrius and Jake.

Darrius nodded. Sammy picked up his stool and placed it behind Jake's chair. "I'll sit here until you need me Jake, okay?"

"Sure, buddy." Jake gave Sammy a thumbs up.

Benedict watched the celebration with intense curiosity. He mentally messaged Darrius, *I'm not sure how to behave with the news Jake has received. Isn't it just a duty he must perform? Why is Hilly so happy, and why is Jake smiling?*

Darrius looked at Benedict through soft eyes. He knew the young Cererian had much to learn. *Remember the times you studied plants with your father? Not every plant was the same. Even those in the same genus had distinctly different behaviors. It is the same with humans. I sometimes find myself in awe of how beautifully they express their feelings and their emotions.*

Benedict nodded and observed Jake and Hilly as they chatted about the news. *I will continue to watch and learn.*

Darrius was confident in his selection for Observer. Benedict was a brilliant young man with a methodical brain for process and procedures. His compassion for others reminded Darrius of Prasad's gentle disposition. Benedict's moral resilience while serving the Yfel Brethren impressed Darrius who saw his resolve as a display of tremendous courage and willpower. Darrius hoped Benedict's determination to do the right thing would help Aningan heal from past misdeeds and flourish under his collaboration with Jake.

But, as Darrius reflected on the disturbing events of the last few days, he questioned his instincts regarding his Cererian brothers. Aaron, an individual he had known and trusted for a thousand years, fell prey to the greed and temptation of power. If a strong comrade like Aaron could willingly plunge into evil's black abyss, would Benedict? Were there other Cererians who grew restless and desired to stray from their sacred mission?

Darrius leaned back in his chair, considering the possibilities. The Prophecy predicted the battle on Denali, but it did not prepare Darrius for the betrayal from his own kind.

Chapter 5

Jake's Celebration

FLANAGAN'S IRISH PUB WAS especially rowdy. The Tundra Trio Plus Todd rocked Irish tunes with a fiddle, flute, accordion, and Todd's bodhran, which he thumped enthusiastically as the party revelers jumped, clapped, and sang along in a deafening roar.

The bartender threw all tap handles open, struggling to keep pace with the beer demand as Jake's friends celebrated his ascension to Elder. Jake sat atop the bar, swaying to the music, lifting his mug high, and singing along with the mob, "Drink it down, down, down!" He obliged his mates by tilting his head back and sucking the beer down in mere seconds. The more he drank, the more the crowd sang and bribed him with more beer.

His buddies pulled him from the bar and threw him into the air yelling, "Hurrah!" Jake knew they intended to make him vomit. That was the purpose of the insane game they'd played since they were old enough to drink. His friends dubbed the hurling match "the chuck-up". The guest of honor would be chucked up in the air in the hopes he would eventually chuck up everything in his stomach.

Jake's inebriated friends threw him into the again but missed as he fell to earth and slammed onto a nearby table. Mugs of beer crashed to the floor. His mates howled with laughter while the patrons cursed their clumsiness. A multitude of hands grabbed Jake to help him to his feet as his friends chanted, "One more beer!"

Steadying himself against the effects of the alcohol, his head swiveled around the room, and his eyes locked with Hilly's. She sat alone by the door sipping her stout. She grinned at his antics. His heart pounded. It surprised him how excited he became upon seeing her.

"Come on, Jake, another round!" his friends chorused as they led him to the bar. He reluctantly joined them. As they yanked him forward, he stole a glance at Hilly to make sure she wasn't a hallucination. Meanwhile, a friend shoved a mug into his hand and began the chant. Jake raised the glass and tossed the beer down his throat like with the ten previous brews. Once finished, his friends threw him into the air again and yelled, "Hurrah!"

The chuck-up game was fun for his friends but not so much for spectators if he did vomit. His boots slipped in the beer sloshed on the floor, and he fell flat on his back. The world around him tilted at odd angles as he eyes spun in their sockets. His buddies hoisted him under his armpits and pulled him to his feet as they cried out to the bartender, "Harry, another beer!"

Movement snatched the group's attention. Everyone stopped and gawked at the vision in white standing before them. With his mouth hanging wide open, even Harry stood transfixed, unaware the frothy beer was overflowing the pitchers and cascading onto the floor.

Hilly blocked the mob's approach to the bar. Jake swayed between his buddies. His head lolled to his friends and then to Hilly as he tried making sense of what was happening.

"I think he's had enough, don't you boys?" Hilly grinned a twisted smile. Jake peered at her through bleary eyes. He struggled to focus on the witch-hunter's hat perched on her head before his head dropped down to her white thigh-high boots. He nodded drunkenly with her statement, and then his head drooped onto his chest.

Hilly stepped closer.

"Jake!" she barked. He lifted his head, and his eyes rolled back as he mumbled a response. "Jake, snap out of it!" Hilly yelled as she slapped him across the face.

His buddies gasped and gripped Jake tighter. Prompted by the unexpected blow, adrenalin surged through Jake's veins, and his eyes slowly narrowed on Hilly.

"Jake? Are you there, or are you drifting away on your beer buzz?" She raised her hand for another strike, but he caught it inches from his face.

"I know you enjoy hitting me, but cut it out," he growled. Hilly smiled, seeing life returning to her friend. Jake shrugged his mates away. "Get off me!" He swayed, hands outstretched, and willed himself to stand on his own.

Hilly chuckled. "Nice. Now, for your next act, you'll impersonate a walking man." His friends howled with laughter.

"Shut the fuck up!" he yelled. His cheeks flushed crimson. He stared at the goddess in white who had captured the attention of the entire pub. He desperately wanted to sober up and make a good impression, but his pride wouldn't stand aside. "Okay, Hilly, what do you want? I'm trying to celebrate with my friends."

Hilly shook her head. "I wanted to congratulate you. If you would rather hang out here with your pals then go right ahead. But I thought you might want to drive out to the Sentinel Boulder for a little magic."

Jake's buddies murmured lewd comments and punched him in the arm. "Shut up, assholes!" Jake yelled. "We're only friends."

Hilly grabbed Jake's elbow and twirled him around. "Come on, Jake, let's take your party outside. I think you need some fresh air."

Jake didn't resist and allowed Hilly to gently pull him toward the door. Once outside, Hilly shoved Jake into the dirt street. He wheeled around twice, staggered several steps, and fell backward onto his butt.

"Your friends are jerks. Do you know that?"

Jake sat in the middle of the street staring at the tips of his boots. "Yeah, I know," he said with a tone of resignation. Grinning wide, he added, "But they are great friends and know how to throw a party!"

Hilly rolled her eyes. Jake was a good friend and a trusted warrior, but his buddies dragged out the worst in him. She reached for Jake, and they grabbed each other's forearm so she could tug him to his feet. "Can you stand by yourself?"

The tip of Jake's tongue poked out of his mouth, and he straightened his shoulders as he focused on standing straight. He casually tried to brush the dirt off his jeans but lurched to the side. He smoothed his hair by running both hands along the side of his head. But his half-closed eyes, lopsided grin, and constant swaying were evidence that he still operated in an inebriated fog.

He cleared his throat. "Yeah, I can stand. Standing still? That's a different challenge."

He gazed at Hilly. His eyes fell to the blue opal fastened in her throat. He lingered on the gem's brilliant color and the sharp angles before lowering his eyes to the bodice lacing. The dangling threads lured his gaze downward, to her breasts.

Hilly huffed at his drunken leering. "Come on, let's go for a walk." She grabbed his arm and pulled him down the street.

Hilly accompanied her staggering escort back to Aningan Properties. Turning onto the dusty, quiet street, Hilly waved at Sammy who sat on the steps dutifully awaiting the return of his master. He hailed her, "Hiya!"

"Hi, Sammy!" Hilly panted. "I could use your help." She jerked her head at Jake.

"Sure thing!" The little man bounded down the steps and loped toward the couple. Jake dragged his feet in the dirt, forcing Hilly to wrestle him under her arm while hauling him forward with each step. "What's wrong with Jake?"

"He's a little sleepy," she lied. "We need to put him to bed right away."

Jake typically slept at his office, Pierson Express Flights, and, fortunately, it was located just a few buildings away. Hilly had seen his bedroom during her astral travelling a week earlier. 'I've got all the comforts of home right here,' he had told her later when she asked why he slept in the office. 'I've got a bed, fridge, and television. What else do I need?'

Sammy slid under Jake's free arm and pushed his head into his armpit while hugging him around the waist. Together, Hilly and Sammy man-handled their friend down the middle of the street as Jake babbled, "I really love you guys. I really do!" Jake belched loud and long and then grinned at Hilly. "That feels much better. Did I ever tell you that you're pretty?"

Hilly stifled a giggle. "Nope. Never did."

"Well, you are! And not because you have big breasts!" Jake lolled his head toward Sammy. "Hi there, Sammy! How's my buddy today?"

"Miss Hilly, is Jake sick? He's acting really weird."

Jake's head drooped onto his chest and a throaty snore pierced the quiet alley. The weight of the unconscious man increased, and they struggled to maintain their balance as he lurched against Sammy. "Dammit, Jake, why couldn't you make it to the office?" Hilly snapped.

"I don't think he heard you, Miss Hilly. He fell asleep again," Sammy observed.

"You think so?" Hilly immediately regretted barking at the naïve nawiht who didn't understand why his master was acting so weird, but Hilly was tired of carrying Jake's heavy carcass though the streets. Her patience had long since departed.

They finally reached Pierson Express Flights, but first they had to drag Jake up five steps to the boardwalk. Hilly silently cursed as they prepared for the ascent. "On my count, Sammy, just pull him up and don't stop. Just keep tugging him no matter what happens."

Following Hilly's lead, Sammy grabbed the back waistband of Jake's jeans, tucking his thumb inside as far as it would reach. "Okay, Miss Hilly. I'm ready."

"One, two, three. Pull!" Hilly and Sammy grunted as they hoisted Jake's dead weight upward. Jake's boots snagged the top step, halting his companions and pulling them backward. Hilly whirled to face Jake. She hooked her arms around his chest and yanked him toward her with all of her strength. His boots dislodged and all three friends fell into a heap on the boardwalk.

Jake lay on top of Hilly who struggled to push him aside. "Sammy, help me get Jake off!" Sammy tugged on Jake's arm as Hilly pushed up on his chest.

Jake's eyes had fluttered open during the violent scuffling, and he found himself inches from Hilly's scrunched face, which flushed red as she wrestled with his almost two hundred pounds pinning her down. He grinned a goofy smile. "Hi, beautiful."

"Get off me Jake! Be useful and roll onto your side!" He blindly followed her orders and began rolling side-to-side. Unfortunately, he rolled to the left as Sammy and Hilly pushed him to the right. "Jake, cut that out. Work with us! Roll to the right. Now."

Jake flopped onto the boardwalk, sprawling onto his back with his arms out to the side. "Why is the sky spinning?" he asked as his eyes slowly opened and closed.

"Sammy, let's get Jake to bed." Hilly grabbed Jake under the armpits and lifted while Sammy pushed him up from behind. Barely conscious, Jake kicked his legs, trying to plant his boots firmly on the planks and stand up. "Sammy, do you have a key?"

Sammy patted the pockets of his shirt and then his pants. He stared at Hilly, his eyes wide with fear. "I can't find it."

Hilly groaned as Jake slumped in a stupor against her. She glared at Sammy. "Sammy, you better—"

"Found it!" Sammy shouted as he pulled a cord from around his neck. The silver key dangled like a jewel at the end. "I forgot Jake told me to wear it around my neck, so I'd remember where it was." Sammy giggled and danced a celebratory jig.

If looks could kill, Sammy would be a pile of smoldering ash. Hilly clenched her teeth and grunted, "Sammy, please open the door." Jake had passed out again and began sliding down Hilly's body. Sammy plunged the key into the lock and turned it. *Click.*

"Great." Hilly gasped. "Now throw the door open, and let's get this bag of meat inside." Sammy grabbed Jake's right arm, helping Hilly pull him inside.

"In the back, Miss Hilly. There's a bed in the back room," Sammy said as they wrestled the unconscious man down the hall. Halfway there, Jake lifted his head and mumbled unintelligible words before chuckling to himself. "Boy, he must be really sleepy. Sounds like he's dreaming."

The dark outline of the bed loomed in the distance. Soon they would be able to unload their drunken comrade. As they struggled into the dimly lit space, Hilly cursed, "Son of a bitch! This room is a shambles. Sammy, shove all that crap off the bed."

Sammy eased out of his embrace with Jake and began scattering the miscellaneous items onto the floor. He automatically provided a verbal inventory as he tossed things. "Jacket, carburetor, girlie magazines, half-eaten sandwich." Sammy paused and sniffed the sandwich. "Smells like tuna, probably three days old."

Hilly rolled her eyes. Her patience and strength had vanished. She reached the point where she'd be satisfied dropping Jake onto the floor, atop his pile of shit. "He's a bit of a slob, isn't he?" Hilly asked.

"He's been busy," Sammy defended. He threw the bedspread aside, revealing ivory-colored sheets stained with spilled coffee and mashed chocolate pieces. Sammy rejoined Hilly and pushed his head into Jake's armpit. Together, they shuffled him toward the bed and threw him down face-first. Jake grumbled a muffled complaint into the sheets.

Free of her burden, Hilly stepped away and stretched her cramped arms while surveying the pigsty Jake called home.

Sammy bustled around—first flipping Jake onto his back, then pulling off his boots, socks, and pants. Hilly didn't avert her eyes, but thankfully, Jake was wearing underwear. Somehow, she had imagined her friend was a commando kind of guy. Facing Jake, Sammy tugged him into a sitting position and yanked his shirt over his head, before pushing him back onto the pillow. Jake snorted and rolled onto his side, sliding his hands under his head like a sleepy child. Sammy tucked the sheets under his chin and covered Jake with the bedspread. "There you go, Jake," Sammy proclaimed. "Nighty, night."

Hilly observed Sammy's routine with interest. Despite Sammy's idiosyncrasies, the two men acted more like brothers than master and minion. Hilly was touched by Sammy's gentleness and commented, "Good job, Sammy. He looks so peaceful."

"Thank you, Miss Hilly." The two stared at their companion as he mumbled between raspy snores.

"Sammy, I'll stay a little longer to make sure Jake's okay."

"Sure, Miss Hilly. You can sit in that chair right over there. That's usually where I sit when I'm here with Jake. I'll sit up front."

"Thanks, Sammy, I appreciate that."

Sammy ambled into the front room and pushed a stuffed chair in front of the large window so he could look outside. People watching was the next best alternative since the television was in the back room with Jake and Hilly.

Now that Sammy was gone, Hilly thought she'd have a little fun with her friend—payback for putting her through all this trouble. Sneaking a glance toward the front room, ensuring Sammy wouldn't see her, she tip-toed to Jake's side. He snored loudly, his lips fluttering with each exhale and spewing stale beer directly into her face.

She grimaced and fanned the air.

Jake mumbled and flipped onto his back. Carefully, Hilly pulled down the bedspread and sheets, revealing Jake's hairless chest. Her eyes widened as she scanned a series of black tattoos decorating the curve of each rib. She recognized many ritual symbols, but other images were foreign, appearing similar to hieroglyphics. Her friend was quite a complicated person, and she yearned to understand more about the ink and their meanings.

Hilly lingered on his chest. She admired his masculinity, but then thought of her husband. She hungered for her soulmate. Tears welled in her eyes as she recalled their last meeting full of anger and rage. He blamed her for the pain he suffered at the hands of the Yfel Brethren; she was saddened that he didn't understand the torment she endured. His words had stabbed deep into her heart, and her emotions still bled from that encounter. She bit her lower lip, wondering if they could reconcile.

Jake snorted, yanking Hilly out of her daydream. Eyes full of mischief, Hilly remembered her plan. She opened a small cosmetic tote and withdrew two tubes of red lipstick and black eyeliner. She parted her lips and slowly applied the lipstick, adding extra coats with each pass. Slowly, she leaned over her friend until she hovered inches from his tanned face and carefully planted a juicy kiss onto his full lips.

He didn't stir.

She pressed harder onto his mouth one more time. Then she moved above his chest, poising over the right nipple before pushing her lips onto his chest, leaving a large red mark. She then kissed his left nipple and stood to admire her handiwork. She stifled a giggle.

A constant buzz filled the room as Jake snored contentedly, oblivious to Hilly's antics.

She reapplied the blood-red lipstick and covered Jake's chest, arms, and face with large red smooches.

For the finale, she withdrew the eyeliner wand and very carefully applied a thick, black coating above and below his eyes.

She silently chuckled at the graffiti covering Jake's body—the bright red marks and raccoon eyes. Satisfied with her artwork, she collapsed into the chair opposite the bed and studied Jake, watching his chest rise and fall with each breath.

Underneath all that makeup was a truly handsome man, a rugged individual who understood honor and friendship. Jake was raw around the edges, but Hilly liked that about him. He was confident and didn't withhold his opinions. Having fought alongside Jake, Hilly admired his bravery. But she pondered the role he would continue to play in her future.

Jake had entered her life like a typhoon—a windbag full of bravado and arrogance—but lately, she witnessed a positive change in his behavior and wondered to what extent he would accompany her as she followed her own journey. She hoped he would be with her for the long haul.

Hilly grew drowsy, and her thoughts raced back to the battle on Denali where she had hugged Everild in a death spiral while Jake flew nearby, ready to strike the lethal blow. Her and Jake had locked eyes. It was a brief moment, but in that one glance, they shared complete trust in each other. Days after the conflict, those feelings still lingered. Hilly trusted Jake with her life. She could rely on him for anything. But she realized there was another emotion pulsing below the surface—stirrings of love bubbled up for the unkempt man, the arrogant soldier who managed to ensnare her heart.

Jake awoke the next morning and stretched long, his feet and hands reaching beyond the edges of the bed frame. He slowly opened one blood-shot eye and then the other. Light from the nearby window filtered into the room, illuminating a white shape in the chair opposite the bed. He lay on his back, the sheets puddled around his waist, struggling to focus his eyes. He propped up on one elbow and leaned forward. Hilly slept peacefully, scrunched in a ball and still wearing her white outfit.

Jake smiled.

His memory was murky, but he remembered his riotous friends and the vision in white who swooped in to take him home.

He coughed, hoping Hilly would awaken.

She opened an unfocused eye and looked at him. After several moments, the sleepy fog lifted, and she recognized her friend. "Good morning, asshole."

"Good morning," he replied. "You sleep in that chair all night?"

Hilly withdrew her long legs and stood. She stretched her arms high above her and then bent forward toward the floor. Her joints snapped and popped. "Yep, I wanted to make sure you were okay. You were in no shape when I snatched you from your pack of pals at Flanagan's. Sammy put you to bed."

"Hi Jake, how ya feelin this morning?" Sammy said, joining them.

Shielding his eyes from the daylight, Jake winced, a raging headache pounding in his head. "Quiet, Sammy. Quiet."

Sammy placed a finger in front of his lips and repeated in a low whisper, "Hi Jake, how ya feelin' this morning?"

Hilly giggled.

"I could be better," Jake said sitting up.

Sammy's clamped a hand over his mouth, hoping to stop the laughter from tumbling out. Instead, a series of gurgles and hisses slithered through his quivering lips.

Jake stared at him. "What the hell is wrong with you?"

Sammy doubled over as he clenched his sides, still holding back the laughter. He pointed a shaky finger at Jake.

Hilly rubbed the sleep from her eyes and stared at Sammy. She followed his outstretched finger waggling at Jake. A breath caught in her throat as she gawked at Jake who was staring back at her.

"Oh my, is that the time? I really must be going. I'm really late for...for...for something," she stammered.

No longer able to contain himself, Sammy roared with laughter and dropped to the floor. "Jake, you look so pretty!"

Hilly quickly gathered her belongings. She trotted to the front door hurriedly saying her goodbyes as Jake protested, "Wait, where are you going? I thought we'd have breakfast together. Payback for bringing me home."

Hilly couldn't suppress her laughter any longer. Opening the front door wide, she bolted onto the boardwalk and released a loud howl. Without glancing back, she shouted, "You've already paid me back!"

Jake sat on the edge of the bed and glared at Sammy, "What the fuck are you laughing at?"

"The funniest...thing...I've ever seen." Sammy gasped. He tugged Jake's arm, urging him to stand and face the mirror. "Get up, Jake. Look in the mirror."

Jake rubbed his eyes and shook his head, trying to shake the cobwebs from his mind. He stared into the mirror and then looked away, not sure of what he saw. He rubbed his eyes again and refocused on his reflection. Taking a step forward, he leaned closer to the image and slowly lifted a finger to the bright-red lip mark in the middle of his forehead. He traced the thick black lines around each eye. Slowly he lowered his eyes and groaned as he saw the rest of Hilly's masterpiece—bright red smooches all over his chest and arms.

"What the fuck!"

Chapter 6

Shasta

A SECOND IS EPHEMERAL but omnipotent. In one quick tick of time, the future can transform, resulting in a beneficial outcome for some and a catastrophic conclusion for others. The moment Jake killed Everild, psychic ripples burst outward, racing around the world, deploying an energetic message to all of Nature's spirits.

Another page of the Prophecy has turned. The sorceress has vanquished Everild.

Fearful whispers murmured throughout Mount Shasta's forested slopes. The mutterings circulated among the communities as a soft buzzing carried on the warm breeze. A human wanderer may have thought the sound was nothing but a hoard of summer insects, but to the tribes of Mount Shasta, the droning formed the nucleus of their lyrical language, composed of many songs and verbal variations.

The whispers carried a warning: *Prepare yourself, our peaceful world is next!*

Located in Northern California, almost two thousand miles south of her spiritual sister, Denali, Shasta vibrated with frenetic energy, turbulent activity churned up by the elementals and other natural spirits reacting to the witch's battle against the Yfel Brethren. These gentle, spiritual entities now feared the magicians would march upon their hidden world to wage war, savage their pristine lands and steal their powers. The fear was palpable.

Shasta, the matriarch of the Cascade Range, shook her rocky crags, distributing tremblers throughout her slopes. A loud grumble rose from the depths of Shasta's soul as the great mountain thrummed calming words to her magical populations.

Be still, my children. The Prophecy will unfold as it has been preordained. The witch is the earth child of Denali. She and her friends will not harm you, but they will penetrate the veil that protects you from the outside world. They will find you. I will never allow anyone or anything to harm you. That is why I moved to this sacred space almost a millennium ago as was directed by the Prophecy.

The great mountain physically moved herself almost fifteen miles to the west of the Cascade Range. While scientists don't understand how the stratovolcano changed her location, the spiritual world knew the truth. Shasta chose to break from the arc of the Cascade peaks and relocate to a sanctuary rife with energetic ley lines. This position connected her to sacred places around the world, and formed a network of intense metaphysical energy. This strategic move was detailed in the Cererian Prophecy. Shasta had understood her critical role in Earth's future.

Looming almost fifteen thousand feet, the behemoth was reverent mother to many magical entities and protecting her children from the outside world was her sacred mission. As the human population expanded, its boundaries crossed into spiritual spaces, hallowed territories that were blindly plundered in the name of progress. The great natural spirits scattered throughout the world warned of these invaders—magicians and the nonmagical Folk who unwittingly pushed into unexplored lands, disturbing the natural balance and disrupting the energetic flow.

Shasta understood outsiders would eventually penetrate her forests—the cloaked home to millions of supernatural individuals. She hoped that if she invited a trusted soul to her slopes to attend the Council of Light, an annual gathering of all tribal leaders, then the human would listen, understand the fears, and carry the message back to the outer world. If her plan was successful, Shasta would maintain control of her realm and the future of her tribes.

Already aware magicians planned to follow the ancient Siskiyou Trail, the old Native American path from Oregon to California, Shasta reached out to her lost son, a soul destined to walk the shaman's path in search of his ancient roots and discover his lineage.

Shasta whispered to her children including the fey, bigfoot and the leohts (an ancient tribe of wisps.)

Heed my words. The future races to meet our world. That which we have expected for years, advances toward us with alarming speed. The pieces of the Cererian Prophecy are falling into place and now it is our turn to perform in this magical play. The future of Earth depends upon our actions as we march forward to the final encounter that will either destroy all life or finally establish the peace we have deserved for a millennium. Among the magicians walks our champion, the soul destined to restore peace to our world. It is your duty to test his mettle, measure his strength, and evaluate his worthiness to join you as a spiritual entity on these slopes.

A great murmuring echoed off the cliffs and crevices as ambassadors of all the spiritual worlds voiced their agreement with their mother. Elementals, nature's spirits, ancient entities, invisible sprites, and everything in between consented to Shasta's plan.

The populations were equal in importance. No community was above or below another, regardless of their inherent powers. For a millennium, Shasta led these diverse worlds in peaceful coexistence.

But now the Prophecy warned of invaders to their land, magicians following their preordained path into the future. Among them walked Shasta's lost son—a human soul born in her shadows and christened in her pure waters. A magician awakening to his psychic abilities; and the champion who will unlock the spiritual markers hidden around the globe, and restore peace to the world.

Almost one thousand miles southeast of Shasta, Kai thrashed in his bed, softly groaning as the nightmare penetrated his sleep. Unlike the other dreams, he didn't see through Hilly's eyes nor experience her battles. This time, he portrayed himself.

He walked through a dense forest, following an animal track up a mountain slope. There was no fear, only familiarity. Convinced he'd been in these woods before, he confidently strode along a path littered with fallen leaves.

The darkness of a new moon swallowed the blackness of the trees and rock-strewn hills, casting unusual shadows upon the landscape. A buzzing filled the air, and he scanned the forest for the origin of the noise. In the distance, six softly glowing orbs advanced toward him, moving easily around the trees and gently rising over the large rocks.

He fixated on the kaleidoscope of colors swirling within each ball of light, mesmerized by the flashes of reds, blues and yellows. The orbs stopped a few yards away, hovering two feet from the ground, evaluating him, and sensing his intentions. Moments passed before they moved forward, slowly maneuvering around him and encircling him in a ring of pulsating light. The hairs on his arm stood at attention, responding to their magnetic energy.

The blood pounded in his ears and he swayed. He swooned from the intense dizzying effects. His eyes slowing closed and he groaned a sound born from pleasure. Intense joy filled his heart, a happiness one experiences when they've finally returned home from a long journey.

A gentle voice entered his thoughts. *My lost son, you are destined to find me and the cloaked communities of which you belong. Trust your intuition while on your journey, for the pathway is full of hardships. I will send you a spirit companion to aid in your travels who will guide you through the roughest sections of your adventure. Until we see each other again, I send you love and light.*

Chapter 7

Decision Made

THE CELLPHONE BUZZED ON the nightstand and threw a soft glow across the bedroom walls. Kai and Jeff slept through the intrusion, exhausted from a late night at the gallery opening. Their black sleeping masks plunged them into a comfortable darkness.

Startled by the vibrations, Oscar, their mixed-breed puppy, sat up and cocked his head.

His black nose twitched, sniffing the air for the intruder that lay on the nightstand a few feet away.

The call ended.

Oscar padded closer to investigate the invader that had grown quiet. He sniffed the device, leaving a wet trail down the length of the screen, and it sprang to life, vibrating and illuminating the room once again. Oscar jumped back and woofed a soft bark, unsure of the creature before him.

The phone continued humming and blinking. At only thirty pounds, six-month old Oscar had the baritone vocals of a fully grown mastiff, and he growled a deep, rumbling warning at the flashing monster. The device continued to taunt him, so the young dog released his full fury with booming barks in rapid succession.

Jeff and Kai yanked off their eye masks and swiveled their heads around the room as they searched for the source of the commotion. The frightened puppy pounced upon the threatening device, viciously shaking it while growling.

"What the fuck!?" Jeff shouted as he bolted out of bed. He grabbed the baseball bat he kept near his nightstand in case of burglars. He hoisted the bat into the air and carefully approached Oscar who wrestled the noisy device on the carpet. "Oscar, what is it?"

The cellphone silenced.

Oscar stopped growling and held the device in his jaws like a chew toy, gazing up at his owner who loomed above him, the bat circling in the air.

"What's going on?" Kai asked, flipping on the table lamp. "What's Oscar got in his mouth?"

Jeff slowly lowered his weapon and reached for the drenched phone cradled in Oscar's teeth. "Oscar killed your phone," he casually remarked, tossing the wet device to Kai. The puppy wagged his tail and looked at Jeff for praise. After all, he had saved them from certain death.

Although his head pounded from the previous night's celebrations, Jeff couldn't resist Oscar's cute face. "You're a good boy," he cooed. "Who's Daddy's little boy? You are." Jeff rolled onto the floor with Oscar and scratched his belly as the happy puppy snorted.

Kai wiped the phone with the sleeve of his pajamas and pressed the switch on the side. The phone illuminated. "Good. It looks like Oscar spared its life." Scrolling through the missed calls, he noticed Hilly had called twice. "Hilly called, but she didn't leave a message. I'm calling her back." Kai envisioned a myriad of mayhem befalling his sister as he anxiously listened to the phone ring. He sighed when Hilly finally answered.

"'Bout damn time, Kai!" Hilly joked. "Please tell me I didn't get you out of bed."

"Um, kind of." Kai gazed at Jeff who glared daggers back at him.

"Oh, damn. I bet Jeff is staring at you right now, isn't he?"

"You guessed it. I'm dead meat." Kai chuckled.

"I'll make it up to him. I promise. I need to tell you something important. I need you to fly out here as soon as you can. I have this odd granite rock called the Sentinel Boulder that is engraved with ancient symbols, and local legend speaks of star visitors using this boulder for their rituals and applying special keys to open it to other dimensions. Of course, I immediately thought of you—The Keeper of the Keys!"

Hilly talked fast, her voice laced with an enthusiastic energy.

"Star people?" Kai asked.

"As far as I can determine, they may have been the original Cererians who visited Earth well before Darrius' exploration party."

Jeff frowned at Kai through slitted eyes. He angrily tapped his watch and glared at his husband. Oscar wrestled in his arms and begged to go outside.

Kai winked at Jeff and blew an air kiss as he talked with Hilly, "The symbols are carved into the surface?"

Jeff hefted Oscar into his arms and marched to the bedroom door. He paused and dramatically jabbed his middle finger into the air toward Kai.

Kai rolled his eyes and blew another kiss at Jeff.

"Yep. When do you think you can come out?" Hilly knew Kai wouldn't be able to resist the lure of the Sentinel Boulder. He loved a good adventure as much as she did.

"I had a gallery opening last night, and we're still suffering the effects of that party. My exhibit runs the rest of the week. So, I don't know, Hilly." Doubt clung to his words.

"Come on, Kai. Join me. Would it be too much to ask Jeff to handle the remainder of the showing while you're away?"

"Hilly, that's not fair. Jeff has supported me through everything in my life. If it wasn't for him, there's no telling where I'd be now. You know I'd do anything for you, but..."

"Is that your little witch sister?" Jeff asked as he leaned against the door jamb. He'd clearly been standing outside the door eavesdropping. Kai nodded and smiled. "Give me the phone. Hello? Hilly?"

"Hello, Jeff?"

"Hilly, I love you like a sister—"

Hilly interrupted. "I love you like a brother, too. That's why I know you'll understand if Kai spends a few days with me deciphering an alien boulder near Denali. It would give him a chance to practice his newfound skills."

Silence.

Jeff held the phone to his ear and stared into Kai's face. He was a sucker for his husband's brilliant blue eyes. He walked to Kai sitting on the edge of the bed and smoothed his tangled hair. He gently traced the edges of his full lips with his fingertip. "Hilly?"

"Yes, Jeff?"

"Promise me Kai will not get hurt, and you'll send him home in a week. Deal?"

"Yes. Yes. Absolutely. Thank you, Jeff. I love you."

Jeff wiped tears from Kai's cheeks and cradled his face. "Your brother is the most important person in my life, and if anything should happen to him, I don't know what I'd do." Kai cried harder.

"Don't worry Jeff. Tell Kai I'll text him the details. Thank you, again! And, I'm really sorry for waking you guys up. I hope you can go back to bed now."

"Sure, Hilly. Thanks. Goodbye."

Jeff tossed the phone onto the bed. "There, everything is taken care of. My warrior will soon embark upon his quest." Kai leapt into Jeff's arms and squeezed him tight.

"I don't deserve you, Jeff. I love you so much." They looked into each other's eyes and slowly kissed.

When they parted, Jeff whispered into Kai's ear, "If you're not back in a week, *all in one piece,* I'll divorce you *and* your sister." Then he grinned a wicked smile. He caught Kai off guard, lifted him up and slammed him onto the bed before jumping on top of him. They kissed long and hard before Jeff pulled away. "Kai, I can't imagine life without you. Please be careful. I need you to come back to me. Promise me."

"I promise," Kai answered as he slipped his arms around Jeff and pulled him close.

Chapter 8

The Mark of the Shaman

THE NEXT DAY AFTER Hilly's call, Kai reclined in his spacious first-class seat on a jet bound for Alaska. He mused about his recurring dream of the glowing orbs surrounding him in a forest. He couldn't shake the nagging feeling of déjà vu, that he'd walk that trail before. But when?

He swirled his vodka tonic and gazed into the drink as if he would catch a glimpse of the elusive answer. After several moments, he took a long sip and leaned back into the seat. The alcohol chased away his fear of flying and dulled the remnants of the dream.

Kai took another sip and grinned, amused by the contradictions in his life. He was a supernatural warrior who could fly. He was descended from a family devoted to the sacred element of air. Yet, planes terrified him. He studied the corridor leading to the cockpit and theorized if he could control the plane—place his hands on the yoke and pilot the jet himself—then he would be fine. He would be in control of his own fate.

But not today.

Today, he'd drink and dream of the adventures ahead of him. An explorer traveling to a strange land to discover ancient relics and follow the shaman's path.

Three drinks later, Kai drifted off to the drone of the engines; images engulfed him once again. But he wasn't afraid. He welcomed the dream with an eager anticipation, anxious to see the orbs as if they were old friends.

The vision began as it always did. It was nighttime, and he walked along an animal track cushioned by fallen leaves. A thick pine forest surrounded him and he struggled to see in the blackness—dark shadows and black shapes. Kai swiveled his head back and forth, searching for the balls of light that always came to him in his dream.

Then he saw them. Pulsating lights descended from the sky and slowly encircled him, showering him with brilliant rainbow colors. Feeling secure in the wash of their positive energy, Kai closed his eyes and hummed a tune, a familiar melody from long ago. The orbs joined him with voices ranging from high-pitched squeals to baritone vocals, rising and falling like the waves of a strong heartbeat. The chorus continued as Kai slowly danced in the middle of the circle, arms outstretched to either side.

A woman's voice gently entered Kai's mind but her words were lost among the musical timbres. The woman spoke again, this time much louder. Kai stopped dancing and searched for the source of the voice. Though he lingered in the fringes of his dream, the physical world crashed through and yanked him back to his seat on the plane.

The jet shuddered violently. He gripped the armrests and frantically scanned the cabin. All of the passengers had disappeared. Food and drink remained untouched on trays. A fork jutted from a piece of steak while the knife rested on the edge of the plate. A pair of discarded slippers lay in the aisle by Kai's seat.

"Hello? Is anyone here?" he called out. Anxiety washed over him.

The jet bucked again. He rose, stumbled toward coach, and shoved the curtains aside. He swallowed the scream in his throat. An audience of empty seats stared back at him. "What the fuck?" he yelled as he raced down the aisle. "Where is everybody?"

He reached the galley near the back of the plane.

Nobody.

He banged on the bathroom doors and yanked them open.

Nothing.

He turned around and studied the cockpit. *The plane is still flying. Somebody must be in there,* he thought.

He sprinted down the aisle and stopped at the door, unsure of what to do. *If somebody is inside, they may think I'm a hijacker, but if nobody is inside, who's flying the plane?*

As he turned the doorknob, he was both relieved and surprised to discover it turned easily and it wasn't locked. He held his breath and slowly opened the door, afraid of what may lie on the other side. For a second, he considered the pilot may aim a pistol at him.

"Holy shit!" he screamed.

An empty cockpit stared back at him.

"What the fuck is going on?" he yelled. The yokes moved back and forth, seemingly manipulated by unseen hands while the jet's nose plowed a straight course through the azure sky. His heart galloped with panic, and his palms dripped with sweat.

Am I still dreaming? Maybe I drank too much and I'm passed out in my seat. This nightmare is fucking crazy. I want out now.

My son. The wispy voice echoed in his brain.

Gripped by terror, Kai bolted back to first class and dove into his seat, pulling a blanket over his head like a child hiding from a monster. *This isn't real. This isn't real,* he repeated.

Moments passed as he trembled behind his thin cover. Gradually, he pulled the blanket down below his nose. His eyes darted around the cabin looking for anybody or anything.

He was still alone.

Hysteria tickled the edges of his brain and Kai screamed, "What the hell is going on?"

My son. The voice echoed in his head, much louder this time, as though it emanated from the cockpit.

The blanket fell to the floor as Kai leaned forward and gripped the seat in front of him. He hunkered behind the headrest and peered toward the front of the plane. A cry caught in his throat as he stared at the door slowly opening and closing as though it was beckoning him to come inside. His mind raced to the edge of insanity as he realized he was all alone on a plane flying itself somewhere over the Pacific. *Am I going insane?*

My son, come to me.

Kai had to investigate. He needed to see what awaited him inside the cockpit. He was getting nothing done hiding behind the seat. Terror had lodged in his throat, and he swallowed the lump. He gasped and drew in a long breath. He hadn't realized that he had stopped breathing. He sucked in another deep breath, held it, and exhaled out his nose. He began to calm.

He inched toward the cabin. He then held the door ajar and peeked inside. "Oh, my god!" he yelled.

Outside the wind screen, hovered an ethereal being made of ice crystals. Its feathery frost stretched across the glass, refracting the sunshine, and showering the cabin's walls with miniature rainbows.

The magical being spoke again. *My son.*

Convinced he was experiencing a drunken hallucination, Kai squeezed his eyes shut and repeated, "I know you're not real. I know you're not real."

He opened his eyes, staring first at the floor before gathering his courage to look upward and out the window. The shimmering specter hovered outside. It expanded and grew larger until the entire six panes of glass were engulfed with glistening ice crystals and a dazzling display of colors.

Use your mind, instructed the pulsating vision.

Kai hesitated. His brain battled his intuition for control of his thoughts. Logic screamed, *Nobody is flying the fucking plane. You're going to die!*

His instinct countered, *There is nothing to fear.*

Darrius had advised Kai to trust his gut feelings because his intuition would never betray him. What did he have to lose? He closed his eyes and engaged his telepathic gifts, mentally messaging the being, *What do you want?*

The diaphanous entity throbbed with energy. *My son, you have forgotten your earth mother, Shasta. Soon, you will walk the shaman's path and return to your natural world, one in which you frolicked as a child.*

Kai frowned. The frosty spirit made no sense. He had no memories from his early childhood. He didn't even remember Darrius saving him from Stygian. *I don't know who you are. What do you want?*

The icy apparition illuminated, brightening the cockpit with such intensity that Kai shielded his eyes from the blinding glow. *Your memories are fragile petals on an ever-blooming flower, but a darkness cloaks your mind. As you overcome each hardship along the shaman's path, a window will open, shedding light on more memories. When you penetrate the veil, you will arrive with the full and complete knowledge of your connection to the Cascades. Until then, I will impart this gift to you, to remember the family to whom you belong.*

The entity pulsed a shaft of light through the wind screen. A long, jagged bolt of energy zigzagged into the room, snaking toward Kai. It momentarily halted in front of his face, mesmerizing him with a shower of colors before it stabbed forward, punching his chest just above his heart. Kai flew backwards and skidded down the aisle into coach. His head slammed the base of a seat and knocked him unconscious.

The plane violently shuddered, jolting Kai awake. He stared up at the flashing FASTEN YOUR SEATBELT sign and realized he was back in first class and no longer lying in the aisle. He frantically looked around the cabin.

Passengers calmly buckled their seatbelts and continued casual conversations, oblivious to the turbulence. He sighed and leaned back in his seat, but his thoughts wouldn't rest. The vision seemed too real.

Kai discreetly unbuttoned his shirt and peeked under the flap toward the center of his chest. He gasped. A red welt had formed and a slight odor of burned hair drifted to his nose. He touched the wound gingerly and flinched from the pain. He glanced around, ensuring nobody was staring at his bizarre behavior, reached into his bag, and withdrew a compact. He carefully slid the small mirror into his shirt, angling it for a better view of the injury.

"Shit," he whispered as he examined the brand seared into his chest. The mark consisted of two horizontal diamonds, the smaller one nestled inside the larger version, and a small dot in the center. He traced the welt with his finger.

He rebuttoned his shirt and leaned back in his seat. He replayed the events—the empty plane, the icy spirit, the bolt of energy that burned an image into his chest. He questioned his sanity. Then he thought back to the early morning hallucinations in Sedona—hiking on a mountain slope surrounded by energetic orbs of light. *Is this all connected?* he thought.

"Excuse me, sir. Would you like another drink?" Kai jerked from his reverie and stared at the young flight attendant pleasantly smiling at him.

"What?"

"A drink. Would you care for another drink?"

Kai studied the empty glass sitting on the tray in front of him. Nothing made sense. "Um, yes. I'll have another. Better make it a double."

"Not fond of flying, sir?" the attendant inquired as she noticed his nervousness.

"You might say that," Kai replied. "I don't like it when things get bumpy. How long have we been flying in this turbulence?"

"Not long. Always seems to happen in this area."

"Why is that?

"I'm not really sure. I've heard rumors that the Cascade Range, especially Mount Shasta, emits strong magnetic pulses into the ocean. Strange occurrences like lapses in time and unusual bursts of light occur regularly. I'll make that drink for you, sir," the attendant said as she quickly left.

Kai mulled over "lost time and unusual bursts of light." He recalled Hilly's tales of Denali—a magical mountain spirit that manipulated the elements and appeared on different occasions as a raven, an icy entity, and a blizzard. Denali spoke to Hilly telepathically like the entity that had communicated with Kai.

After he returned to Sedona from The Nine Muses, Kai focused more on his painting and less on his newly acquired psychic gifts. Between the prophetic dreams and the recent odd encounter with Shasta, Kai realized his life was rapidly changing like it had for his sister.

As the jet traveled to Anchorage, the importance of his arrival finally registered. Although Hilly had been the person who invited him, it was Shasta who had choreographed the visit.

Kai lightly touched the wound on his left breast and telepathically messaged, *I understand Shasta, I will see you soon.*

Chapter 9

Hexmix

JAKE WATCHED HILLY AND Sammy climb into Old Val. "Looking forward to finally meeting the Keeper of the Keys," he shouted after them. Hilly waved as Sammy gunned the Valiant into life. The ancient car shuddered violently and spit black puffs of smoke from the tailpipe.

"Looks like Old Val is ready to go!" Jake yelled over the whine of the engine. Hilly grimaced and flashed crossed fingers. Sammy smashed the pedal, and the car squealed away toward the airport to pick up Kai.

Jake turned his attention back to Lola. He carefully wiped her fuselage with a chamois, massaging the metal skin until it gleamed in the sunshine. As he worked around the aircraft, Jake mentally scanned the body for anything out of order.

She purred her approval as Jake lightly skimmed each blade of the propeller. As he worked, he sang an ancient melody to Lola. It was a tune taught to him by the elders, a tradition passed through the generations. The plane vibrated and hummed her own song to Jake. He stepped back and admired the full length of Lola, and mused about his special relationship with the aircraft.

Most people wouldn't understand how a plane could be alive, feel emotions, and connect with other life forms. Magicians understand. Some Folk, schooled by their magical partners, acknowledge the existence of these entities, but the majority of people view these partnerships as crazy infatuations that guarantee a one-way ticket to a padded room and mind-altering medications.

Those in tune with nature's spirits—wizards, witches, and alchemists of many other names—have strong relationships with their familiars, including swords, animals, and besoms to name a few.

The most unusual familiar Jake had heard of was a supernatural trash can that had partnered with a sorcerer in Fresno. That magician named his spirit companion Tippy. The entity was a small metal trash can, about two feet high with a flat, tight-fitting lid. The magical bin was adept at consuming violent souls. His skill for thoroughly eliminating nasty spirits was renowned in the magical world.

Jake heard amazing tales about this supernatural duo and had hoped to meet them one day. That opportunity finally arrived when Jake flew Lola to California to attend HEXMIX—an annual magical mixer, popular with magicians hunting for new spells and sexual partners.

"Nice to see you again, Mr. Pierson," the petite clerk said cheerfully as Jake checked into the host hotel. "I've texted you the names and times for your arranged encounters this weekend."

Jake scrolled through the messages on his phone. "Yep. I got 'em. Thanks."

"If you have any problems, don't hesitate to contact us. We guarantee our matches." The clerk played with her blonde hair as she peered at Jake. "We want to make sure you're completely satisfied." She winked an exaggerated wink that jerked the corner of her mouth into a sneer.

Jake stared at the clerk and then surveyed the room to either side. "Um, thanks?"

He strode toward the elevators, stopped, and glanced back toward the front desk. The clerk forced another crooked wink. *This is going to be an interesting weekend,* he thought as he punched the button and waited for the doors to open.

HEXMIX. 100% SATISFACTION

Jake read the poster affixed to the wall and mused about his arranged dates.

Despite his bravado and tough demeanor, Jake was nervous around women, especially strong magicians. The casual encounters boosted his ego and spared him the heartache of a failed romance.

Bethany.

More than twenty years earlier, he vowed he'd never give his heart to another.

Growing up with five sisters—all powerful witches—Jake had the advantage of learning the nuances of female interactions from his siblings. At seventeen, Jake was introduced to his first and last love, Bethany, by his older sister, Sasha.

A fair-skinned beauty from northern Alaska, Bethany ensnared Jake's heart during a picnic in the Mat-Su Valley. An elemental specialist, Bethany was fond of hikes through the pristine land which provided intimate access to her precious spirits like gnomes, trolls, undines, faeries, sylphs, and dragons.

The elemental world fascinated Jake who learned how to properly greet the spirits and offer the treats they preferred. He would lie in the grass observing Bethany as she entered her meditative trance. Once she penetrated the magical veil dividing the spiritual and physical worlds, Bethany conversed and played with the spirits that came forth. The positive flow of energy during these exchanges stirred emotions deep inside Jake, and he often watched with tears rolling down his cheeks or a wide grin on his lips.

Jake and Bethany were a perfect match. Bethany was born into the house of earth and Jake was a son of air; nobody was surprised when they became engaged three years later. The happy couple excitedly planned their wedding, which would be held in their beloved valley, in the shadow of Denali.

Nobody expected the Yfel Brethren.

Aningan had blossomed into a peaceful town due to Aaron's deal with the elders decades earlier. Still, families continued to cloak their where-abouts with magical spells and crystal gridding so the Yfel wouldn't locate them. Areas beyond the city limits were still unsafe for magicians to travel unless they had taken supernatural precautions to remain undetected from the Brethren.

Bethany and her parents had traveled to Fairbanks along with other families where they represented Aningan at the annual peace gathering. It was there, on the last day of the festival when the Yfel attacked groups of magicians exiting the protective bubble surrounding the complex.

Their attack was swift. Like the deadly stroke of a scythe, they spared no one—men, women and children.

There had been survivors of the tragedy. The Yfel hadn't wasted time with the Folk, whom they considered unworthy because they didn't pos-sess powers. The surviving nonmagical relatives returned to Aningan and described in grisly detail what they witnessed: the bloody arrival of the Yfel led by Stygian who had personally assigned individuals to specific soldiers, the battle cries of magicians valiantly defending their families, and the screams as children were beheaded in front of their parents.

A survivor returned to Aningan and collapsed on the dirt street. In anguish, the young man tore at his hair and cried unintelligible words to the sky. Jake knew this boy. He was a nonmagical cousin of Bethany's.

"Marcus?" Jake asked as he carefully approached the teenager and ten-derly placed a hand on the young man's shoulder. "Marcus, where are the others?"

"Gone. All gone," he sobbed as he continued pulling large patches of hair from his head.

Jake knelt beside him. Cradling the boy's face, he gently turned it so he could peer into the teenager's bloodshot eyes. "Marcus, who violated your household? Which soldier attacked your family?"

Marcus appeared younger than his fifteen years as he sniffed back tears and wiped the snot from under his nose. He searched Jake's eyes for answers. "They're all gone, Jake."

Jake swallowed the lump that had formed in his throat and asked again. "Marcus, help me. Who did this to your family?"

The boy stared at the ground and replied in a hushed whisper, "Everild."

The remembrance surprised Jake and he wondered why, after all these years, it decided to rear its ugly images once again, especially at an event that always brought him so much joy. Jake purposely buried that portion of his past. Now, on the verge of enjoying HEXMIX, the memory returned and poked at his brain.

"Bethany." He whispered her name before he realized it. Tears welled in his eyes, and he clenched his fists, forcing the sorrow away. "Everild took Bethany from me." The proclamation shocked him. He had no intension of saying it, but it tumbled out anyway. It was the first time he acknowledged the tragedy. Saying the words aloud released the pain he had smothered long ago.

The alarm on his watch jolted him from his reverie. He had fifteen minutes before he would meet his first arranged date of the weekend.

His spirits soared. He always anticipated the thrill and excitement from these encounters. And, just like that, Bethany was forgotten and Mistress Z was on his mind.

Jake's intuition heightened as he strolled into the hotel bar to find his date. Per the mutual message they both received from the event organizers,

Jake would wear a white carnation in his buttonhole, and his date would wear a wristlet of hemlock. He found the carnation to be very cliché, but whatever, he'd wear a bunny suit as long as he got laid.

He scanned the dimly lit room for Mistress Z. The bar bulged with HEXMIX revelers, and Jake's inner voice shouted at him. Something wasn't right, but when you're standing in the same space with over one-hundred other magicians, the energy tends to crash over you like an avalanche.

"Hello, stranger," purred a dark-haired woman with glowing yellow eyes. He quickly scanned her wrists. No hemlock.

"Not interested," he responded flatly. Dismissing her with a wave of his hand, he plowed forward into the mob, checking the wrists of every girl he passed.

No luck.

Mistress Z was either late or was purposely avoiding him. Suddenly, a chill drilled down his spine—a familiar feeling of being stalked, like that terrifying moment before the tiger pounces on its prey. Jake whirled around, expecting to see Mistress Z, but encountered a bug-eyed wizard holding two beer mugs.

"Hello," the magician hailed. Jake studied him as the man passed. What an odd coincidence that he also had bright yellow eyes. The rotund man pushed into the crowd and soon disappeared. Jake's instinct screamed, *Be wary!*

Reaching the bar, Jake recognized Ian, the bartender, and signaled him for his usual whiskey. "I'll be right over, Mr. Pierson," Ian said as he worked on three drinks at the same time.

Someone tugged the back pocket on Jake's jeans. Hoping to catch a pickpocket in the act, Jake clamped his hand over his pocket and spun around. Nobody. His wallet was safely secured by its chain.

"Here's your drink, Jake."

Pulling two bills out of his wallet, Jake turned around, "You can keep the—" Jake stopped, his eyes riveted to the hand lingering on the glass. A spray of hemlock encircled the wrist. He looked up expecting to see Ian, but locked eyes with a sensuous purple-haired woman wearing an emerald-green dress. Her golden eyes swam in a luscious dark-skinned face.

She slowly licked her dark red lips and whispered, "What's your pleasure, Jake? By the way, nice carnation." Her mouth twisted into a sneer as she threw her head back and cackled—a loud, screeching laugh reminiscent of a riotous murder of crows.

"Fucking shapeshifter!" Jake grabbed his drink and angrily stormed into the crowd. He'd been warned about rogue shapeshifters infiltrating the mixers. They were intent on thievery and mayhem. "Fucking waste of money and time," he growled as he headed for the door.

"What's wrong, Jake?" the woman called out to him. "Aren't I your type? Or do you prefer witches with swords?"

Jake stopped and gritted his teeth. He gulped the whiskey and slammed the glass on a nearby table. Then he turned, narrowing his eyes on the shifter who casually strolled toward him, mocking him.

"Can your witch do this?" Mistress Z stretched her arms upward as she gyrated, performing a bizarre belly dance. Her body undulated and enlarged like a humanoid amoeba. Jake scanned the crowd. Nobody watched her. It was as though her unusual display was seen only by him, invisible to the throng of magicians partying around the hellish spirit.

He clenched his fists, channeling the energy from his anger into his arms. As he prepared to attack the shifter, a calm voice stopped him.

"She's not worth it."

Jake glanced sideways. A disheveled man in rumpled clothes sat nearby, carefully observing the coiling changeling. He placidly spoke again. "She's not worth it. She intends to bring chaos to this space. Your anger will only intensify that energy. Let me handle this." The magician stared into Jake's eyes and winked.

Toting a small metal trash can in his left hand, the wizard jumped off his stool and positioned himself between the spirit and Jake. Mistress Z leered at him and hissed at his rude interruption. Maintaining his gaze with the sinister shifter, he carefully placed the dust bin on the floor about four feet from the woman and carefully lifted the lid. He then stepped backward and calmly uttered, "Tippy, please clean up this mess."

Initially, nothing happened. Mistress Z sneered at the magician who smiled politely. "Your metal bin is broken, wizard," the shifter mocked as she moved closer. She menaced the man with her hands, her fingers having morphed into long, black needles.

A series of rapid pops emanated from the can reminding Jake of a small cap pistol he had as a child. Intrigued, the changeling moved closer to the bin.

Whoosh.

A shower of sparks preceded a dazzling display of multi-colored fireworks that sputtered upward from the metal can. Mistress Z inched closer, bedazzled by the lights and sparkles. "What strange beast is this?" she inquired, peering into Tippy's metal mouth.

An intense bright light filled the room as a beam of energy shot outward, engulfing the shapeshifter. And, just as quickly, the energy returned to the can, sucking Mistress Z into Tippy's belly.

The magician replaced the metal lid and ensured it was secure. "There, that's done," he said, wiping his hands on his pants. "How about a drink?"

Jake gawked at him. Not only had he gotten to see the infamous familiar in action, but the entire show impressed the shit out of him. "That was amazing!" Jake acknowledged. "I'd heard about Tippy, but to actually see him in action was worth the money I lost on that sham date!" Jake shoved out his hand. "Hi, I'm Jake Pierson. I'd be honored to buy you a drink."

The wizard smiled and shook his hand. "Hi Jake. Call me Frankie. And, you already know Tippy." The man gestured toward the can which slightly vibrated on the floor in acknowledgment.

Frankie grabbed Tippy by a side handle and strode to the bar where he found three available seats. The magician grabbed the seat in the middle, placed the metal can on the right one, and hailed the bartender, "Ian, a round of beer, please."

"Sure thing, Frankie," the bartender replied. Soon, he delivered three mugs. "Here you go. Do you want this on your tab?"

"No, this round is on me, Ian," Jake interjected.

"Great, Mr. Pierson. Enjoy."

Frankie slid a mug in front of Tippy, removed his lid and poured the contents into the opening before replacing the top. Then he grabbed his mug and turned to Jake. "Here's to new friends." Jake nodded and clanked his mug with the magician's. Frankie gulped his beer in seconds and held up three fingers to Ian who prepared another round.

Jake was awestruck about Tippy. "Mind if I ask you a personal question, Frankie?"

The bartender slid another three mugs in front of the men. Frankie poured one into Tippy and then sipped his own beer. Finally, he responded. "You want to know why I give Tippy beers, right?"

Jake choked on his drink. "Um, yeah. How did you know?"

"Everyone asks." Frankie chuckled as he patted Tippy's lid. "It's not every day you see someone intentionally pouring a beer into a trash can. He's very efficient when consuming things. He doesn't make a mess." The magician sighed. "I wonder if all sorcerers are asked about their familiars the same way people poke their nose into my relationship with Tippy."

"I apologize for prying." Jake glanced around the room, trying to think of something else to discuss.

"It's okay. You seem genuine. At least you haven't asked to have your photo taken with him."

"That's happened?"

"More often than I care to track. Mind if I change the subject? Do you have a familiar?"

Jake eyed Frankie, calculating his intentions of asking the question. He reckoned if Frankie was willing to freely talk about his companion, then it's only fair he should talk about Lola. "Lola is a bush plane. She's at the airstrip."

"Fascinating." Frankie stroked the white stubble on his chin for a moment before asking, "What's her specialty?"

"She flies on her own. She navigates by following the magnetic ley lines. She's saved my skin more than once when all the instruments have failed." Jake stopped talking. He'd just met this magician and was already sharing more information than what many of his family members knew. He was surprised how comfortable he felt around Frankie and not because of the alcohol he'd consumed. Frankie had an approachable personality. He was calm, grounded, and seemed void of an agenda. He was a cool guy.

Jake watched a hoard of magicians reflected in the mirror over the bar. The revelers gyrated to electronic music while bright lights swept their bodies with color bursts of red, blue, and green. The crowd was louder and bawdier than earlier that day.

Glancing at his drinking companions, Jake chuckled and shook his head. He originally arrived with the intentions of having sex with a beautiful woman and now found himself hanging out with a pudgy man and his metal trash can. Fate could be cruel at times, but she could also be magnanimous when least expected. He turned to Frankie and asked, "Did you strike out with your date as well?"

Frankie chuckled, a giggle several octaves higher than his normal voice, which reminded Jake of a horse's neigh. "Yeah. She took one look at Tippy and bolted. In hindsight, I should have left him at home, but he loves to come into the big city."

Jake and Frankie burst out laughing. Frankie's high-pitched whinny caused Jake to laugh even harder. The new friends spent the rest of the night talking and drinking. Frankie even allowed Jake to pour a beer or two into Tippy's mouth.

Consumed by drowsiness, Jake collapsed against Lola's wheel. His head slammed her fuselage as he slid downward. Lola vibrated to her partner who knelt on the tarmac rubbing his forehead. Moments passed as Jake closed his eyes, allowing the recent memories of HEXMIX, Tippy, Frankie, and Bethany to flutter through his brain like the frames of an old movie.

"Bethany," he whispered. The painful events returned, strong and demanding, refusing to be pushed away and forgotten.

"Everild," he uttered. A giant wave of reality washed over Jake and he shuddered, realizing the connections between his past and present.

"Hilly."

Another door of awareness flew open, exposing the somber truth. Everild consumed Bethany's soul. All the spirits he consumed escaped into Hilly upon his death. Bethany's soul resided within Hilly.

Chapter 10

Kai Arrives in Alaska

"Here we are!" Sammy yelled. The nawiht gripped the steering wheel with both hands, and pulled himself vertical as he mashed the brakes with both feet. Old Val squealed to a violent stop by the curb, coughing black smoke. Hilly hunched in the passenger seat, both feet firmly planted on the glovebox. She called the posture her crash position because of Sammy's aggressive driving. Regardless, there were no seatbelts to keep her from catapulting through the windshield.

"Sammy, when are you going to get this seatbelt fixed?" Hilly fussed as she moved her feet to the floorboard and pushed herself up. "And, what about this door? It takes both of us to get the damn thing open."

Sammy trotted around to her side and tugged on the handle while Hilly shoved from inside. After multiple attempts (and enough cursing from Hilly), the door creaked open with a piercing metal-on-metal screech.

"I think Old Val needs a ton of oil, Sammy." Hilly complained.

"Yeah. She could do with a spa day." Sammy giggled. "I can see Old Val sitting on the rack while mechanics oil, lube, and buff her into shape." Hilly wasn't laughing. Sammy coughed and continued, "I'll stay here with Val. It's best not to turn off the engine. Took too long to get her started this morning." Sammy lightly patted the car's rear bumper. A shower of rust debris fell onto the pavement.

Hilly shook her head. It was useless to preach to Sammy about the benefits of another car, one that was a tad more reliable. "Okay. You shouldn't have to wait long."

Leaving Sammy in a no loading zone, Hilly trotted to the receiving area of Ted Stevens Anchorage International Airport and checked her watch. Right on time. She paced along the barricades of the pickup area, furtively glancing at the glass doors whenever they slid open.

Kai was late.

Where the hell is he? she thought. She checked her phone and confirmed the flight arrived on time. Her brother was MIA. She'd give him ten more minutes before she barged through the doors and searched for him.

Five minutes later, she heard a familiar voice singing a Broadway tune. The automatic doors opened and there was Kai accompanied by two burly security officers. Each standing well over six feet, they linked arms with Kai and held him aloft between them as they walked toward Hilly. She roared with laughter. Kai's feet were twisting in the air, inches above the ground.

Kai grinned at his escorts, his head rolled as he entertained them with "Some Enchanted Evening." Kai was soused from too many in-flight vodka tonics. With all inhibitions smothered by the alcohol, Kai entertained the officers with off-key songs from *South Pacific,* his favorite production. When he reached the words "You may see a stranger," he leered at his companions and then winked at each one.

"I'll take this obnoxious cargo off your hands, officers," Hilly said as she approached the trio.

One of the officers flipped the piece of paper pinned to Kai's collar and re-read the contents. "Are you Hilly Kemp?"

"Alas, that is me," she said as she produced her identification. The officer studied her ID card and scrutinized her face before responding.

"He's your problem now. Can you manage him?"

The two men hoisted Kai toward Hilly who grabbed her brother in a bear hug. His head fell forward onto her shoulder. "I love you, Hilly. I really, really do," Kai mumbled as he nuzzled his sister's neck.

The officer frowned as he pushed Kai's tote toward Hilly. "Are you sure you can manage him? He's quite a handful." He glanced back at his partner who stifled a laugh.

"I've got him. Thank you for putting up with my brother. The only way he can fly is via Vodka Airlines." The officers didn't laugh at her joke. Hilly shifted Kai so he was standing beside her. He gently swayed while waving his hand through the air in time to a tune only he could hear. "Let's go, Kai."

Kai tilted. He hadn't found his drunk legs and almost crumpled to the ground before Hilly snatched him around the waist. He dangled like a broken marionette against her hip. "Work with me, Kai," she barked as she hefted him up and steadied him on his own two feet.

Kai crouched low and held his hands out to the side for balance. Wobbling back and forth without assistance, he smiled triumphantly at the officers. "Ta-da!"

"Let's go, you nut job!" Hilly hooked her hand under Kai's upper arm and slowly led him away while she pulled the tote behind her. Kai duck-walked beside her, taking one exaggerated step after another.

"Looks like a circus trainer leading her pet monkey," the officer joked with his companion. They continued chuckling as they watched their afternoon cabaret amble away.

"Come on, Kai, help me a little," Hilly complained. As Kai lurched with each step, she tightened her grip around his arm. They were almost to Old Val when it suddenly occurred to her that, lately, the only men who said they loved her were both inebriated and had to be led around as if she was their caretaker.

"I'll help you, Miss Hilly!" Sammy yelled as he trotted toward her as fast as his little bandy legs would allow. "Is this your brother?" he asked while grabbing Kai around the waist.

Kai grinned at the little nawiht and patted his head. "Hello there, little fella. What's your name?"

"Sammy! What's yours?"

"I'm Keeper of the Keys. Nope. That's not it. I'm Kai. Yes. I'm Kai Kemp." He stopped to shake Sammy's hand.

"Come on, Kai. No time for formalities," Hilly barked. "We need to get you to the hotel. Sammy, open the door to the backseat." Sammy obeyed and returned to Kai's side. Together, Hilly and Sammy manhandled Kai onto the backseat as he began singing "There is Nothin' Like a Dame. "He threw his arms wide for emphasis.

"He sure is a happy fellow," Sammy said as he scurried to the back of Old Val and unhooked the wire holding the trunk closed. He tossed Kai's luggage into its gaping maw. "We're good to go, Miss Hilly! How are you doing with your brother?"

"Just a few more...seconds...and I'll...be done," Hilly grunted. Kai giggled and rolled around on the backseat like an unruly toddler while Hilly tried to maneuver him into a sitting position.

"I love you, Hilly. Really, I do," he proclaimed as he tried to plant a sloppy kiss on her cheek. She swatted his hands away and wrenched the seat belt across his body, pushing on his stomach while she stretched the belt toward the latch.

"Ow!" he howled. "You're pinching me."

"Kai, you're acting like a big baby!"

Kai looked lovingly at his sister through droopy, glazed eyes. His mouth flew open and a loud belch warbled for several seconds. "Oopsie. Sorry."

A pungent wave of alcohol mixed with stale tacos punched Hilly in the face. She furiously fanned the fumes away. "Good grief, Kai. What crawled inside you and died!" Hilly shook her head.

Kai's head gently nodded onto his chest as the foggy veil of alcohol descended. His eyes closed, the forced sleep of those who overindulge.

Hilly sighed. She gazed at her slumbering brother, happy to have him back in her life, but saddened by his current state.

Kai's head jerked up and he screamed, "I know something you don't know!"

Hilly jumped back and banged her head on the edge of the window. "Shit!" she growled, rubbing her head and scowling at her brother. "Honestly, Kai, I don't care. Let's get you into town and sobered up."

Hilly slammed the door and whirled toward the front of the car. Sammy patiently waited for her to get in before he backed up several paces, drew in a deep breath, and ran for the door, hands outstretched. Using his full body weight, he hurled himself at the rusty metal. *BAM.*

"Whoo hoo! It shut on the first try." Sammy raised his fists in celebration. The door may be flat against the car, but the metal angled out near the lock. It was as close to being closed as possible. They were relatively sure it wouldn't fly open on a severe curve and were confident it would stay in place driving the half mile to the hangar where Jake and Lola awaited them. Hilly rolled her eyes and assumed her crash posture: back against the seat, feet firmly planted on the glovebox.

"Thanks, Sammy. Let's get this drunken cargo home."

He trotted to the driver's side and leapt onto his driving pillow: a moldy, velvet sofa cushion that supported the little nawiht so he could peer over the steering wheel. "Here we go." he announced, punching the gas pedal with his boot.

Kai launched into a loud rendition of "Bali Ha'i" as Sammy peeled out of the parking lot. "Here am I, your special island! Come to me, come to me! Bali Ha'i, Bali Ha'i, Bali Ha'i!" Kai giggled. "Get it? I've arrived on *your* special island."

"Drive faster, Sammy," Hilly groaned. Sammy did as he was told and flew down the rutted asphalt toward the Pierson Express Flights hangar.

Jake adjusted his mirrored sunglasses and watched the thin trail of black haze in the distance. Old Val was returning, belching smoke like a chain smoker.

Minutes later, Sammy screeched to a halt near the hangar. He threw the car into park and bailed out of the driver's side. He scampered around to Hilly's door. Familiar with the routine, Jake joined them, and the two men tugged several times before a tortured screech announced the door had finally yielded to their efforts.

"Sammy, you really need to get this fixed," Jake advised as he extended his hand toward Hilly who smiled at his chivalrous behavior.

"Why, thank you, kind sir," she drawled in her best Southern accent.

Kai launched into another song, throwing his head back against the seat and bellowing the words into the air as if he was the only soul alive.

Jake peered through the window. "Something wrong with your brother?"

"This is what happens when you're afraid of flying," she said, jerking her thumb toward Kai.

"Isn't he gifted with flight? He's from a family that honors the element of air, right?"

"Yes, yes, all true. My brother can fly higher than anybody in the family, even me. But he's deathly afraid of planes. I'm not sure how he'd handle the cramped space in Lola if he wasn't already so hammered."

Jake chuckled. "You have an interesting family, Hilly. Very interesting." Jake opened the door and fumbled with Kai's seatbelt.

Kai stopped singing and gazed at the tanned man hovering over him. "Well, hello there. And what might be your name?" Jake met Kai's gaze, and Kai gasped. "What big, beautiful blue eyes you have, stranger."

Jake smirked as he unlatched the seatbelt, grabbed Kai around the chest, and gently pulled him out.

Kai swung his arms around Jake's neck. "Wow, the people here in Alaska are friendly."

With one final pull, Jake wrestled Kai out of the backseat and steadied him on the pavement. He placed his hands on Kai's hips as he wavered back and forth.

"Jake, call me Jake."

A flirtatious smile spread across Kai's face. "Hello handsome Jake. Just what are your intentions?"

"Kai!" Hilly admonished. "You're married. Stop flirting."

Kai stumbled forward. Jake snatched him around the waist preventing him from tumbling onto the ground. Kai wrapped his arms around his neck and pulled him close.

"Take me, handsome Jake. I'm all yours!" Kai flashed his brilliant smile and then passed out against Jake's body.

Jake glared at Hilly. "Hilly, you owe me."

Hilly sniggered and helped Jake with her brother. They dragged Kai toward Lola and the toes of his expensive leather shoes scuffed along the tarmac.

"Sammy, open the door!" Jake barked. "Hold him, Hilly. I'll jump in and hoist him up." Jake scrambled into the back seat and leaned toward Hilly. "Okay, hand me Sleeping Beauty." Hilly giggled as Jake hooked his arms under Kai's armpits, and Hilly grabbed his legs shoving him into the cargo area. After careful maneuvering and pushing gear aside, Jake finally positioned Kai upright into the seat. "Sammy, hand me his luggage." The nawiht lofted the tote up to Jake who wedged it beside Kai, and gently laid his head on the top. "There. Nice and snug. He won't go anywhere."

"Where am I going to sit?" Sammy whined.

"Up front with me."

"What about Miss Hilly? Might be a weight issue."

Jake shot a quick glance at Hilly. "She'll meet us in Aningan. She's got different transportation today." He winked at Hilly, who smiled warmly back at him.

"Sounds great. We'll see you in town, Miss Hilly. I'll watch out for your brother, but it looks like he's sleeping and won't wake up. But if he does, I'll make sure—" Hilly and Jake held up their hands to silence the rambling man. Sammy nodded. "Talking too much again."

"Stay with Lola and Kai, Sammy. I'll be back in a few minutes." Jake placed his hand on the small of Hilly's back as he accompanied her to the hangar. Once inside and away from Sammy's excellent hearing, he asked, "Are you sure you don't want to fly back with your brother? I could leave Sammy here."

"I'm sure. I'll meet you at your office." She glanced at the plane. "I hope Kai wakes up by then. He really is a sweet guy when he doesn't have to fly on a plane."

"I'm sure he is. By the way, what's his poison?"

"What do you mean?"

"What does he drink to keep the fear away?"

"Vodka tonic."

"I'll have Sammy run out and get some. I don't keep that crap in my house." He squeezed Hilly's shoulder. "Be careful when you open the portal and don't materialize inside some rock or something."

"Watch that Alaska Triangle on your way home. I wouldn't want you crashing into a mountain. My brother is precious to me. And so are you."

Before Jake could respond, she threw her arms around his neck and placed a kiss on his cheek. Then she walked toward the hangar office.

Jake watched her stroll to the hangar. Amorous thoughts zipped through his mind. Hilly was a great friend and a superb warrior, but she possessed a quality that made Jake's heart race. As infuriating as she could be at times, Jake realized he was falling in love, and that bothered him. Hilly was transforming into a being who would have no place in his world, but whenever she was near him or whenever she touched him an immense electrical charge set his cells afire and he lusted for her.

Hilly had claimed his heart like his lost love, Bethany had. Both women were strong shamans. With Bethany's soul now residing within Hilly, Jake found the concept of both women sharing one body intriguing and alluring.

One day, I will make her mine, he mused

Chapter 11

Fen Arrives

JEFF TWISTED THE REPORT in his hands. His thoughts raced to Kai, then Hilly and then back to the printout. Something was wrong. He chewed his lower lip as he studied the details of the email that arrived late last night, confirming Kai had landed safely in Anchorage. Allowing for the forty-five minutes for the short flight from Anchorage to Aningan, Jeff anticipated a call from Kai within the hour. The hour stretched to two hours. Jeff paced the floor, imagining Kai was hurt or stranded in the Alaskan wilderness with his sister and a bush pilot he'd never met. But the call never came. And Kai had promised.

Where are you, Kai? he thought

Years ago, Jeff and Kai agreed on a management plan in case Kai went MIA on one of his trips. Kai's airport adventures were legendary—jumping onto the baggage carousel and becoming lost in the bowels of the airport; singing show tunes in the lounge until patrons complained to security; and one instance when he absconded with a pilot's cap and attempted to board a plane posing as the captain. Jeff called in many favors to ensure Kai didn't go to prison on that particular skirmish.

So, the men had agreed on a plan they hoped would prevent Kai from going astray. Jeff paid an additional fee for the airlines to manage his husband during the flight. He stared down at the crumpled report in his fist. It contained specific details about Kai's behavior on the plane and after his arrival to Anchorage, including the two security officers escorting Kai through the terminal.

Kai's antics were not unexpected, but Jeff was disappointed. For several months, Kai had worked with a therapist who specialized in people with aerophobia. Jeff hoped Kai would be able to test the new methods, more deep breathing and no alcohol, during his travel to Alaska. Kai had promised he would try his best, but Jeff knew it was a lot to ask from somebody on their first attempt.

The Sedona morning sun rose higher in the sky. It was an ideal time to call Hotel Aningan and ask for Hilly. A layer of anger coated his thoughts. If he discovered Kai had arrived safely but had neglected to call him, Jeff would be furious. Kai was the guilty one, but Hilly would not be forgiven for her complicity. She promised that she would take care of Kai and would ensure he called home. Jeff considered his options if Hilly answered the phone—be angry or have a little fun—and, in his opinion, a little angry prank on his sister-in-law would make him feel tremendously better. He grinned like an impish child as he punched the hotel number into his phone.

Jeff's call woke Hilly. But she hadn't really slept. She had tried to snooze on the stiff loveseat but couldn't get comfortable. Her lanky frame hung over the arms and bent her neck at an odd angle. Resigned to sleeping on the floor, she threw cushions down and snuggled as best she could, nodding off for mere minutes at a time.

Squawking ducks filled the room. Jolted from a light snooze, Hilly scanned the room and looked for the birds. She realized it was only the ringtone on her cellphone. She answered in a tired, hoarse voice, "Hello?"

"Where's my husband!" Jeff screamed.

"Jeff, I *promise* Kai is fine. He's sleeping in this morning. You know how flying wears him out." Hilly paused and remembered her promise. "I'm so sorry I didn't call you, but by the time we got to the hotel, it was so late." The words had barely escaped her lips when she realized her explanation was lame. She winced as she realized those words were the *last* thing Jeff wanted to hear.

Desperate for a distraction, Hilly glanced out the hotel window and allowed her thoughts to drift away as Jeff fired angry questions at her like an automatic pistol. Across the street, Flanagan's Irish Pub opened its doors for the early crowd. The Tundra Trio Plus Todd fired up their instruments by playing random melodies until the notes and chords meshed together for an impromptu rendition of "Come On Eileen." Hilly watched the patrons come and go while wishing she was with them far away from Jeff's interrogation.

"He's hung over again, isn't he? I bet he was singing show tunes. Which one was it this time? *Grease? Auntie Mame?*"

Hilly bit her lip, mentally editing her words. Kai slept on the bathroom rug most of the night, curled in a fetal position, cradled between the side of the tub and the toilet where he wedged his head, finding relief in the porcelain's coolness. Liquefied tacos made frequent appearances until just after midnight when Kai surrendered, proclaiming he couldn't possibly have any more food left in his stomach. Hilly shepherded him to the king-sized bed, holding his hand like a mother with a sick toddler, and guided him into the welcoming pile of pillows she'd bunched against the headboard. Kai lay on his side, one hand on his gurgling stomach and the other hooked around an ice bucket in case of a vomiting emergency. Kai stared up at his sister as she swaddled his head with a wet face towel. She gazed into his pale face and thought, *Can a grown man look more pitiful?*

Jeff demanded the truth, but Kai was her brother. She couldn't betray family. *A little editing of the details never hurt anyone*, Hilly thought.

"He sang tunes from *South Pacific*. He has a great voice," she answered.

"Liar! His voice sucks, and you know it. A rusty gate has better pitch than my husband! He sang tunes from *South Pacific*? That makes sense. He did fly over the Pacific, and he tends to sing by association, especially when he's had too much to drink."

Jeff's voice softened. "Be honest, Hilly. What was his condition when he arrived? I'll know if you're lying to me."

Hilly rolled her eyes. Jeff knew her too well which was odd. Of all her nonmagical friends, Jeff was simpatico. He understood the way she thought and sensed all her emotions. "He was slightly drunk when he arrived."

"Slightly?"

Hilly fidgeted, uncomfortable at the thought of betraying her brother. She twirled a lock of hair calculating her next remark. "It's not like I made him breathe into a breathalyzer, but he recognized me without any problem."

"I see. So, he walked out of the airport on his own volition?"

"Not exactly. But he did walk to the service car."

"Hilly! Just stop," Jeff snapped. "If you keep dancing around the same bushes I'm beating, we'll never get anywhere."

Hilly watched a man and woman leave the pub, strolling arm-in-arm down the middle of the dirt street. Her thoughts drifted to Curtis. She missed him terribly and wished he was with her in Aningan. Happy thoughts overshadowed Jeff's voice, which had become a distant noise, a gradual whisper as she lowered the phone to the windowsill. Memories unfolded from the Renaissance Faire where she first encountered Curtis, where they shared their first kiss and made love for the first time. She smiled at the sweet memories as she followed the couple to the corner where they gently kissed.

"Hilly!" Jeff screamed, jolting her back to reality.

Hilly snatched the phone, inadvertently slamming it against her ear. She winced from the pinch of the metal against her earring. "I'm here, Jeff. I'm sorry. I'm cruising on zero sleep. I must have dozed off."

"Hilly, just tell me the truth about Kai."

A low snore emanated from Kai's bedroom, and Hilly gazed in his direction. Too tired to resist any longer, she knew she'd have to tell Jeff everything. "Two security officers delivered him to me."

"Go on."

"They carried Kai out of the airport while he entertained them with 'Some Enchanted Evening.'" Hilly moved the phone to the other side of her head and rubbed her soar ear lobe.

"I see. And then?"

"Kai walked to the service car, and we took him to the plane for the trip to Aningan."

"He walked on his own?"

Recalling the officer's comment about a circus trainer leading a monkey, she offered, "I helped him a little..." She paused, mulling over her response, and then blurted out her words in one long breath. "Okay, I helped him a lot. And he was such a brat in the backseat fighting me as I wrestled to get the seatbelt around his body. Your husband is a BIG BABY!" Hilly breathed deeply and hung her head waiting for Jeff to yell back at her.

Silence.

"Jeff, are you still there?"

Silence.

And, then she heard it. Rolls of laughter punctuated by periodic snorts.

A few moments passed before Jeff picked up the phone. Breathless and still chortling, he replied, "Hilly, my dear sweet sister-in-law, welcome to my world. Kai can be the biggest toddler when he wants to be. Let me guess...he's still in bed, sleeping off a queen-sized hangover and left you to catch a nap on the couch?"

"Sums it up, nicely. I would have stayed in bed with him if he hadn't been vomiting taco mush."

Jeff roared with delight, recalling the many times he had carried his incapacitated husband home after an exhausting gallery opening. The routine was familiar—hand Kai a vomit bowl, wrap his head with ice, and wish for the best. "Yeah, he's been on a taco kick lately. It's his new comfort food." Jeff paused and his tone grew serious. "Hilly, tell Kai I love him. And don't forget your promise to me: that you'll have him back to me in one week. Right?"

Hilly sighed. The immense love in Jeff's voice touched her. For a very brief moment, a pang of jealousy swept over her.

Kai has Jeff. I should have Curtis with me. The thought surprised her and she immediately wondered if Everild's spirit was plucking at her brain.

"Hilly?"

"Don't worry, Jeff. The minute Kai wakes up, I'll give him a huge hug and a messy kiss on his forehead courtesy of his awesome husband."

"And your promise?"

"I *promise* he'll be back in your arms in a week."

Jeff whispered, "Hilly, take care of my guy."

"Nothing will happen to Kai, Jeff. Not with me around." Hilly hung up the phone and gazed at the bedroom. Kai was in dreamland, snoring happily. But even though the words easily fell out of her mouth, Hilly doubted her promise. Her little voice tugged at her, poking at her brain with warnings of caution. She frowned. Kai was only here to unlock the Sentinel Boulder and then fly back home. Simple.

But if it was so easy, why do I feel so worried?

Just before two o'clock, Kai strolled into the living room wearing a white Hotel Aningan bathrobe. He vigorously rubbed his wet hair with a towel and called out, "Hello? Is anyone here?" He scanned the suite and cried out again, "Hello? Anyone?"

Two mugs sat alone on the dining table. Red lipstick smudged the edges and the cold remnants of black coffee stained the inside. The coffee maker suddenly burped a squishy, popping sound. It was half-full. Kai sniffed the contents and smiled. It was freshly perked, no more than thirty minutes old. He threw his towel on the counter and poured a cup, savoring the first coffee of the day. He allowed the fluid to roll inside his mouth, caressing every tastebud, before swallowing it in one gulp.

"Ahhhhh." He sighed. "Now, that's a great cup of coffee."

The lilting lyrics of "The Wild Rover" floated up from Flanagan's. Kai crept to the window, edging the curtains aside with his elbow. He sipped his coffee and studied the town. It was his first view of Aningan. People rushed along the dusty street which, despite the late hour, was void of automobiles. Another tune, the fast-paced "Streams of Whiskey," burrowed into Kai's musical ear. On impulse, his finger began tapping the windowsill as he watched a small crowd of men dance a jig on the boardwalk outside Flanagan's.

Looks like a great place to check out later, he thought. He made a mental note to ask Hilly about the bar across the street.

The door burst open. Kai twirled around to face the intruders; his hands thrust forward in a defensive posture. Unfortunately, the belt on his robe loosened, allowing the clothing to fly away and expose his body.

Hilly entered first. She gawked at her naked brother. Her mouth moved soundlessly as she tried to find the words to respond. Then she snorted a sharp grunt that she quickly suppressed by clamping her hand over her mouth. She stared at her brother, dumbfounded into silence.

After several moments, she finally chirped, "Good afternoon, Kai. I see you just got out of a cold shower." Hilly collapsed onto a nearby chair, holding her sides, tears streaming down her face as hysterical laughter filled the room.

Kai followed her gaze and finally noticed the source of her giggling. He yanked the belt ends together, secured the robe, and replied, "Nice to see you too, sis."

"Good to see you, too, Kai." The second female voice startled Kai, and he gaped at the door as Fen poked her head into the room. She waved at her bewildered brother who clutched his bathrobe in a death grip.

"Fen, is that really you?"

"If it's not, we'd better find out who stole my body." Fen shot a side glance at Hilly who rolled on the floor, gasping for breath between laughter. "You okay, Hilly?"

"I can't wait to tell Jeff about this little show, emphasis on 'little.'" Hilly convulsed at her humor, slamming the chair with her hand. "This is too funny!"

Fen shook her head. "Our little sister thinks she's the big comedienne today." She rushed to Kai and engulfed him in a hug that almost drained the breath from him. Kai gently lifted her from the ground and showered her with kisses on her face.

"Goodness! I've missed you, Fen."

"Likewise. It seems longer than six months when we saw each other at The Nine Muses." Kai gently pushed Fen back and studied her. Pure white hair, streaked with dark gray strands, replaced her light-blonde locks. Kai arched his eyebrows in wonderment.

"Like my new hairdo?" Fen teased. "I think it suits me. My hairdresser told me shock caused it. I wonder what could have happened to traumatize me?" Fen tapped her index finger on her chin and grinned at Kai. "Could it have been the battle on the beach against a dragon? Could it have been losing Prasad? Could it have been Hilly returning from the dead?"

Hilly joined Fen. "Life as we knew it no longer exists!"

Kai changed the subject from the bad memories. "You both look fantastic!" He gathered them into his arms clinging to them as happy childhood memories raced through his mind. He breathed in their faint scents of sandalwood and patchouli, familiar aromas from an earlier time when life wasn't so complicated and full of magic.

"You look remarkably healthy, Kai," Fen snickered. She immediately covered her mouth suppressing the giggles that bubbled up in short breaths. Her shoulders jerked up and down, as she stifled her chuckles.

A gradual shade of red spread across Kai's cheeks like a sunburn as he realized Fen had seen his impromptu peep show. He laughed aloud—a forced, unnatural chuckle—and the women soon joined him.

Kai blurted, "Okay, okay, we all know about the elephant in the room. This is a detail you can omit from your daily discussion with my husband, Hilly." Hilly's eyes widened. Kai frowned at her. "I heard you talking to him earlier, reporting on my airport antics."

Hilly feigned innocence. "Me? Why would I do that?" She dramatically batted her eyes and held her hands under her chin like a guiltless, angelic child.

Kai steeled his gaze on her, his lips stretched thin. "Hilly."

"How could you hear me? You were snoring really loud."

"It's a gift. I woke up when Jeff called. Maybe it was a psychic pinch between my shoulder blades or because your ringer sounds like a flock of quacking ducks, but I heard you mumbling nonsense about my arrival. I fell back asleep for a moment, and then woke up when you said, 'I promise.'"

"Since you were too incapacitated to call your husband when you arrived last night, he was worried." Hilly narrowed her eyes at Kai. "He's concerned about your drinking and the aftereffects."

"You know I need it to boost my courage on those mechanical birds."

"It's not just the flights anymore, Kai. You reach for your vodka whenever you have a stressful situation...like gallery openings."

"Or, like going to The Nine Muses," Fen added as she crept close to her brother. She gently encircled his waist with her arms and laid her head on his shoulder. Her psychic senses alerted her to his rising anger, and she instinctively engulfed him with her positive, healing energy.

"Yeah, yeah," Kai sputtered. "Fen, you're squeezing me to death." He tried to pry her away but only managed to flap his hands like a distressed chicken. "Help! I'm being snuggled to death!"

Fen released him.

"There, all better," she announced as she ambled to the window.

"Hey, my headache is gone. And my dry mouth. And my brain fog. What did you do, Fen?"

"Let's just say that I'm continuing an old healing tradition handed down by some special people." A faint smile drifted across her lips while sadness filled her eyes.

"You mean you've acquired the same healing gifts as Darrius and Prasad?"

Fen turned away, hiding the tears that welled. The mere mention of Prasad's name squeezed her heart, drained her energy, and made her feel utterly alone. Only six months had passed since he died so Hilly could live and continue her quest. Prasad had had no other choice.

Several painful moments passed before Fen faced Kai again and smiled—a weak demonstration that she was trying to cope with her love's death. "Indeed, I have! One of the fabulous gifts I received. It grows stronger every day."

After the Revelations restored their memories of their magical gifts, Fen and Kai formed a natural psychic bond when Stygian tried to control Hilly. That union left psychic markers on their hearts, allowing them to sense each other's emotions. Kai felt her anguish as she talked about Prasad and instinctively gathered her into his arms, holding her close and kissing the top of her head. "I've missed you, Fen. You're like the good half of our shared minds."

"Hey, let me have some of that love," Hilly pouted. Kai and Fen parted, allowing Hilly to fold into their embrace. For a brief moment, three of the four Kemp siblings were united in love and bliss.

"I know something you don't know," Kai teased.

Eyeing their brother suspiciously, the women stepped away. Hilly grinned and playfully punched him in the arm. "Oh, we're going to play that childish game, are we?"

"I need to tell both of you something, but you must promise not to tell a soul." Lowering his face inches from Hilly's, he emphasized, "And, you can *not* tell Jeff."

The sisters exchanged worried glances and sat down, expecting tragic news. Hilly demanded, "Go ahead. Tell us your pressing news."

Dramatically gathering the robe around his body, he straightened his back and cleared his throat. In his most authoritative voice he announced, "Mount Shasta visited me on the flight here."

After delivering the pronouncement he quieted. Fen and Hilly exchanged bewildered glances before looking back to their brother. Simultaneously drawing in a deep breath—an unplanned synchronized movement—they exploded into uncontrolled laughter.

Fen roared. "Kai, what was in your vodka?" She gripped Hilly who chuckled so hard she almost tumbled from the loveseat.

Kai frowned. He stood with his fists nudged onto his hips like a stern mother addressing two misbehaving teenagers. "I'm not kidding. It had nothing to do with the vodka. Shasta visited me in the cockpit."

Fen fell onto the floor in a convulsion of laughter. She held her sides and screamed, "Stop, I'm going to pee myself!"

Hilly taunted Kai. "A mountain dislodged herself from the land and joined you in the cockpit of the aircraft. Do you realize how crazy that sounds?" She snorted and fell onto the floor with Fen.

Infuriated, Kai retaliated. "I'm the crazy one? What about you traveling to the core of Denali and meeting a spirit made of quartz? And, magically, you teleport back to the snowy slopes again as though you walked through a door? If I'm crazy, you're insane."

The chuckling stopped and awkward silence filled the room. Hilly had been exposed. She sat up and glared at Kai, a shadow of anger spreading across her face. Her mouth opened and closed, but no words came out. Slowly, she turned toward Fen who had crawled up to the loveseat and stared at Hilly with an accusatory gaze full of clarity and betrayal.

A word slithered out of Fen's mouth. Though the actual word was one syllable, Fen drew it out into three, "Wha..aa..at?"

"Fen...I...c-can...explain," Hilly stuttered.

Fen held up her hand and silenced Hilly. She narrowed her eyes at Kai, and then glared at her sister. "What Kai said is true?" Hilly hesitated, stalling so she could think of something to say. "Answer me, Hilly. Did you do all that?" Fen pressed.

Hilly hung her head. She blew a long, audible sigh. She scowled at Kai who cowered like a puppy who had peed on the carpet.

"The short answer is yes. The longer answer will demand dinner and wine." Hilly avoided Fen's gaze, jumped up, and called room service. "Thirty minutes? Great. And add two bottles of cabernet, please. Thank you." She drew in a long breath and then exhaled.

Hilly studied Fen and Kai who perched on the edge of the loveseat with their arms crossed. Blank expressions masked their faces but two pairs of accusing eyes drilled disappointment into her soul. A sudden chill crawled up her spine and a wave of goosebumps spread down her arms. Static electricity fired throughout the room causing the lights to spasm on and off, blinking faster and faster as moments passed. Everyone noticed the phenomenon and shifted their gaze to all points around the room.

The energy in the hotel room became palpable, augmented by the anger the siblings felt toward Hilly. The sensation bounced off the walls and furniture as if hundreds of ping pong balls were suddenly in motion. An intense thrumming filled the air like a thousand honeybees were vibrating their bodies simultaneously.

Then a peaceful calm descended.

Hilly spoke. Her voice was tender and apologetic. "I'm deeply sorry Fen. I should have told you about Denali, but I wanted to do it in private. You know, face-to-face instead of over the phone or in emails."

Fen cleared her throat. "How did Kai find out?"

Kai groaned and hung his head. Fen had cleverly unraveled their ruse, bit by bit; and he yearned to dash into the bedroom and lock the door.

Hilly gazed at the ceiling, considering her options—lying to her sister, telling a half truth, or just divulging the full story. There was only one honest thing she could do. "I give up. I told Kai, but for a *very* good reason. He was in misery. He was having tortuous dreams about me and envisioning bloody battles through my eyes. Based on his accurate depictions, I realized he was psychically connected to me, fighting my attackers, and sensing my pain. The visions were destroying his marriage. The two of you share a spiritual bond, but Kai and I discovered that the link between the two of us is also powerful." Hilly knelt on the floor and gently placed a hand on both Kai and Fen's knees. "So, you see, I had to calm Kai's fears and tell him what occurred on Denali. I wanted to have a private moment to tell you."

Fen looked at her siblings, assessing their emotions, probing for their true intentions. "You were going to tell me at dinner tonight, weren't you?" she asked.

"That was my plan before this goofball opened up his mouth."

Fen looked out the window, lost in her own thoughts. Hilly and Kai exchanged worried glances.

Hilly telepathically messaged Kai, *What do you think she'll do? She's so quiet. Is she mad at us?*

Fen slowly turned, her face calm and emotionless. Then one corner of her mouth jerked upward in a twisted grin and her eyes sparkled with mischief. "I forgot to mention that I can now read minds as well."

Chapter 12

The Reunion

"To family reunions," Kai toasted.

The three siblings clinked glasses, and then Hilly dove into the tray of pulled-pork sliders. Room service had also delivered a shrimp ring, fruit, bread and butter, and an assortment of cheeses.

Fen scrutinized Hilly's actions as she spooned fruit onto a plate. "Meat? You're eating meat now?"

Hilly paused mid-bite and peered at her sister. She gulped the mouthful of food and replied, "Weird, isn't it? Every since The Nine Muses, I've craved meat...the messier, the better." She shoved another slider into her mouth.

"That's an interesting development," Kai observed. He drank sparkling water while his sisters enjoyed their wine. He had no intention of drinking alcohol today. The acrid burn of vodka-laced food seared the back of his throat, and his stomach ached from the all-night hurl fest. Instead, he planned to nap and hydrate in preparation for his Alaskan adventures. Today was too important.

Today, Kai needed to rest and recover for tomorrow's journey to the Mat-Su Valley, and to examine the Sentinel Boulder. His thoughts danced with excitement.

Despite his monster hangover, he was antsy to set out on his journey. This assignment was his first official mission as Keeper of the Keys, a title bestowed on him at The Nine Muses.

When Darrius had presented Kai with his family artifact—a small ebony box inscribed with magical, silver sigils—a bolt of white light stabbed through Kai's body. Kai froze, momentarily paralyzed, as the supernatural stream of energy imparted instant knowledge of the mystical keys he would apply throughout the world.

As he recalled that memory, nervous excitement launched butterflies in his stomach. To be invited to unlock the Sentinel Boulder was an adventure akin to discovering Santa Claus really did exist. For the six months since leaving The Nine Muses he had not used his gifts nor attempted any magic. Now, sitting with his sisters who happily shared their psychic experiences, he realized how important family was to his own personal growth as a sorcerer.

The frenetic explosion of energy created during their earlier encounter had dissipated. A peaceful calm swirled in the suite as if a tranquil ray of sunshine had bathed the space with positive light. As if influenced by this soothing shift in energy, Hilly opened up about her recent visitations with the mystical mountain, Denali, and her separation from Curtis. However, she refused to disclose that the Yfel leader, Everild, and thousands of magical souls inhabited her body.

Fen listened attentively. "I can't believe what you've already endured. A battle with Stygian, a fight to the death with his soldiers, and separating from your husband, all in a span of six months."

"It seems only like a matter of weeks," Hilly responded in a solemn tone. Despite her lack of sleep, her vigor returned. She had finished eating and lounged in the chair, one leg dangling over the arm as she sipped her wine, content to watch her brother and sister chat about nothing in particular.

"Time for some fun!" Kai shouted as he strode to the middle of the room. "Let me introduce you to Sedona's infamous art critic, Beatrice

Brandy." Standing on his tip toes, he held his water glass to the side with his pinkie elegantly elevated. Then he sashayed around the suite, slurring, "Theesh painting issh nothing but trassh!"

Hilly and Fen held each other as they laughed and cried. They loved Kai's impersonations and begged for more. Shoving his cellphone into his mouth, Kai pretended to be his lovable pup, Oscar, and acted out the dog's attack on his ringing phone. "Grrrrr," he growled as he swung his head. The cellphone slipped from his mouth and thudded to the carpet, breaking the theatric spell. "Hilly, you owe me a new phone!" Kai demanded playfully.

"Me? What did I do? You shouldn't leave your phone where the puppy can grab it."

"Guys, I need to tell you about this new group of folks I found," Fen interjected. She jumped to her feet and clapped her hands in excitement.

Kai and Hilly arched their eyebrows, shocked by their sister's unusual behavior. Usually quiet and reserved, Fen's boisterous interruption snatched their attention.

"I found this lovely group of people who study symbols. They study runes, hieroglyphics, sigils, etc." Fen paused and studied her siblings' reactions. Their eyes shifted from Fen to each other. "You're looking at me like I'm crazy person," Fen wailed.

"You're not crazy, but *you* are a Fen we've never seen before," Hilly admitted. "You're usually so quiet. Frankly, I'm delighted."

"Tell us more about this group, Fenny," Kai added as he joined her. He lightly patted her arm, encouraging her to divulge more information.

"After the incident at The Nine Muses, I returned to Georgia stunned and a little broken. It took a while to process my innate powers, my magical family legacy, and losing Prasad. I needed time to myself so I could figure things out. I took a vacation to a cabin in the woods outside of Blairsville. One day, while I was hiking, I stumbled upon an odd group of five people scrutinizing a rather large rock. At first glance, I took them to be birders because of the jumble of bags hanging from their shoulders and around their necks. Then I noticed their blue latex gloves, and considered they may be scientists of some sort. For a brief moment, I even considered they may be working a crime scene because of their quiet and focused manners.

"As I neared, a woman hailed me and asked for my opinion regarding a symbol. The elements had cloaked its original shape, filling it with debris and moss, causing a disagreement within the group on what it may represent. I didn't hesitate. I was *very* curious when she mentioned symbols. So, I joined them. An hour passed as though it was only five minutes, such was the camaraderie and brilliant discussions we shared.

"After exchanging contact information, I returned to the cabin with a renewed sense of purpose. It was then, in the stillness of the night, as I stared into the flames of the fire I'd built that I knew my encounter was not random. The coincidences were too many: choosing to go to Blairsville, a place I've never visited, selecting that particular hiking trail, and choosing the spur that led me directly to the group instead of following the other pathway toward the waterfall. I knew in my heart it was an orchestrated meeting arranged by Prasad's spirit. It was his perfect way of introducing me to like-minded people and to keep me focused on my journey."

Hilly leaned toward Fen and hugged her, giving her a reassuring squeeze. "That sounds exactly like something Prasad would do. He always had his subtle ways." Fen hung her head as her thoughts drifted to a happier time six months earlier. "Were you able to help them with the rock carvings?"

"Not exactly," Fen chuckled. "My interpretation added a sixth option to the confusion. But that initial gathering led to additional meetings where I encountered more members interested in symbols and languages. Random encounter?" She flashed a warm, endearing grin. "I think not." Her eyes softened, and her face exuded serenity as though she had found the key to happiness.

Silent moments passed. Then it was Fen who shattered the quiet. "But my story is nothing compared to the crazy kinetic energy flying around this room earlier!"

"Yeah, what the heck was that?" Kai asked. "Was that some kind of ramped up magical energy?"

"That was a first for me, and I've been around a lot of otherworldly beings." Hilly admitted. "I wonder if a unique energy generates when the three of us are together, especially when we're emotionally charged up?"

Kai added, "Or, it is possible that the natural flow of electricity in our bodies may be more powerful if all four Kemps reunite?" Kai popped a shrimp into his mouth and sat back.

Fen and Hilly stared in wonderment, contemplating the possibility that if their other brother, Chance, had joined them, then the situation might have created a more powerful paranormal experience.

"Perhaps we stumbled upon another aspect of our ever-evolving pow-ers," Fen said. "Let's attempt a little experiment to see if we can recreate it." Fen arose and strolled to a nearby floor lamp. The old halogen-style light was constructed of brass and topped with a colorful, stained-glass shade. Fen unplugged the electrical cord and moved the lamp into the middle of the room.

"Won't it need to be plugged in to test our theory?" Kai asked.

"Not if we can generate our own electrical energy," Fen responded. She gestured for Kai and Hilly to join her to form a circle around the lamp. Fen continued, "Now, hold hands." One-by-one, they gripped each other's hand. "Okay. Now focus your powers."

"What do you mean 'focus your powers'? I haven't knowingly used them in six months," Kai remarked.

Fen smirked at her brother. "Okay, smarty pants, what I mean is try to summon all your psychic gifts onto the lamp. Earlier, we ramped up the room's energy by being angry with each other. Imagine what might be achieved if we focus our thoughts on one simple item."

Hilly arched an eyebrow. "If this works, this is going to be amazing!"

"Take a deep breath, and when you release it, focus your powers," Fen directed.

In one synchronized movement, they all drew in a long breath and then slowly exhaled, lips pursed in quiet whispers. They waited, their eyes fixated on the light.

Nothing happened, not even a flicker.

A minute passed and still nothing occurred. Kai grimaced from exertion. Hilly and Fen remained calm, trance-like, gazing forward but not focused on each other or anything in particular.

After several minutes, the light sparked, surprising the trio with a loud snap. A faint scent of ozone drifted through the room. They glanced at one another, excitement sparkling in their eyes.

"Focus," Fen reminded.

Slowly, the bulb glowed. A soft, white light formed a halo around the lamp, growing in intensity as the siblings concentrated their powers. An odd humming began. It was a low murmur at first, but the sound continued to rise, reaching louder frequencies as the bulb became brighter and brighter. Soon, the entire room was illuminated by the bulb, an intense brightness as though the sun had settled into the middle of the hotel suite, its rays blinding everyone. The humming grew to a thunderous thrumming like a thousand honeybees filled the room.

The siblings gawked, wide-eyed, at the shimmering spectacle in the middle of their circle.

CRACK.

The lampshade burst. Multi-colored shards of glass shot upward toward the ceiling. Unlike most explosions, the debris did not spray outward toward the Kemps. Instead, broken glass soared into the ceiling, as though a concentrated force directed its movement away from inflicting harm on anyone in the circle. They gazed upward, fascinated by the multitude of tiny, dangling jewels.

No one spoke.

Hilly finally broke the silence. "Oh my god! That was incredible!"

Visibly trembling, Fen sat down and poured another glass of wine. "That...that was really fascinating." She slurped loudly, drinking the pour in one gulp, and then refilled her glass.

"Steady sis," Kai said as he placed his hand on hers. "Are you okay? You're shaking."

"Do you realize what we've done?" Fen spoke in a low, serious tone, "We combined our powers and directed energy. But we went too far and destroyed the lamp instead of allowing it to glow and provide light. Like any power, we need to wield ours carefully. We have no idea what we can do."

Hilly shoved the brass lamp against the wall and stared at the bejeweled ceiling. She joined Kai and Fen at the table and poured another glass of wine. "This damage will be hard to explain to the management," she joked.

The siblings sat in silence, drinking and thinking.

"Well," Fen began, abruptly changing the subject, "I was so excited when you contacted me about this Sentinel Boulder of yours. I was hoping to view the symbols beforehand, but the photos you texted were blurred and unrecognizable as though someone tossed water across the screen."

Hilly laughed, glad to shift the topic away from the bizarre energy experiment. "I thought it was my phone at first. I snapped a shot of the engravings, enlarged the image, and it blurred out of focus. I checked the settings and shot another, and another, and another, all with fuzzy results." As she spoke, Hilly scrolled through the images on her phone, sliding from one blurry photo to another.

"That is bizarre," Fen agreed. "I wonder if it has anything to do with the magic that surrounds the stone. What if the ancient Cererians, or whoever created the boulder, cloaked it with a protection spell that prevented the markings being seen unless they were viewed in person? A type of identity protection so only those destined to understand the meaning of the boulder—the Keeper of the Keys and the interpreter, AKA me—would need to be present. It's like a secure identity verification."

"That's an interesting thought," Kai remarked, "What makes you think you also need me to unlock the boulder? If you're able to interpret the markings, wouldn't that be enough?"

"I'm not really sure. This is all new to me," Fen admitted.

Hilly added, "I'm learning more each day, so I don't yet have all the answers. Jake mentioned the legend of his people speaks of star visitors using the location for special rituals and that the markings represent a code that will open another dimension. But a special key is needed. Hence the reason I thought of you, Keeper of the Keys."

"I think we're all learning our roles," Fen said. Kai and Hilly nodded in agreement. "I arrived at The Nine Muses angry and insecure. When I received my Revelation, the memories raced into my head as though a hole had been punched into a cement dam, first allowing a trickle of simple powers like telepathy, and, eventually, the hole expanded, releasing a torrent of supernatural abilities flooding into my mind."

Hilly eyed her sister with envy. Her experience had not been the same. Her powers cascaded into her life like an avalanche of boulders, ice, and snow, heaped upon her by Denali and nature's spirits. The last six months passed by in a matter of seconds for her. She knew, as did Darrius and Benedict, that this was just the beginning of her transformation. She felt isolated and different—the monstrous black sheep of a magical family. But she mustered a smile and a happy tone for the sake of her siblings. "It sounds like you've coped with your new abilities rather well."

"I have. If I hadn't connected with my powers, I wouldn't have been able to resolve my grief over losing Prasad." Fen glanced briefly at the table. She lovingly absorbed the iridescent colors emanating from a sweet-smelling flower set in a small container. She gestured to the flower. "By possessing his essence in the granon, the Cererian flower of love and union, my heart has healed and my resolve has strengthened."

Kai sat back, listening to his sisters' animated conversations. He decided it was finally time to relate his tale. "Ladies, ladies, we still have a little matter that needs to be discussed." He paused for dramatic tension. "Or have you forgotten about my visit from the spirit of Shasta?"

With one bottle consumed, and the second bottle half empty, Hilly grinned at Fen as she poured wine into their glasses and announced, "Better make it a big one since I reckon Kai has a lot to say." Both women laughed as they clinked their glasses.

Kai studied his sisters. He needed to discuss the interaction with the specter he encountered on the plane. He doubted Jeff would fully understand the intervention of a spirit, much less the soul of a great mountain. Only his sisters (and his brother, Chance) would really understand the magical occurrences that are now commonplace in their lives. "Where do I begin?"

"At the beginning," the women chorused.

"It's a long story, so I'll make it short," Kai giggled.

"No, you won't," Hilly countered. "Don't delude yourself, Kai. You've never been short with anything." The sisters clinked their glasses, sipped, and chuckled.

Kai ignored his sisters' antics. He arose with purpose, allowing the tension to build as he prepared the story in his mind. His sisters observed his every move and whispered to each other. He stood away from the table and flicked his arms to the side several times, testing the space around him in case pantomime might be required to illustrate some of the details. Clearing his throat, he began, "In the beginning..."

The next five minutes passed quickly as Kai provided an abbreviated account of the luminescent spirit, Shasta, who announced she was his earth mother and punched him in the chest with a lightning bolt that snaked from her hand. At this point in the story, he slid the bathrobe off his shoulder and exposed his chest. The women gasped, pointing to the odd, red welt on his left breast.

"Big deal, you have a new tattoo," Hilly smirked

Fen jumped to her feet and joined her brother. She was mesmerized by the unique symbol on his chest. She recognized it. It was a marking she'd studied in her father's alchemy book. She licked her lips with excitement and here eyes darted to Kai's. "Do you mind if I touch it?"

"If only I can get Jeff to say those words to me more often," Kai giggled.

Fen had transitioned to her serious persona and ignored her brother's childish behavior. She lifted her hand toward the marking, her fingertips twitching in anticipation of touching the magical symbol. Lightly, she traced the brand, noting that it was cleanly embossed into Kai's skin. Her fingers skimmed the larger diamond and then the smaller one inside it. Hovering her finger over the middle of the brand like an artist applying the last stroke to a painting, she dabbed the raised dot in the middle of the two diamonds. "It's as though someone stamped this on you with great force."

"I just told you. Shasta punched me with a lightning bolt finger," Kai exclaimed.

Still intensely studying the marking, Fen spoke in a reverent whisper, "This symbol is known worldwide as the Shaman's Eye. It's also known as the Eye of a Medicine Man. It gives the bearer the gift of physical and spiritual sight." She challenged Kai, "You claim a supernatural force branded you?"

"Claim your ass. I speak the truth." Kai stamped his foot for emphasis.

"What else did the spirit say?" Fen asked.

"Shasta said I would walk the shaman's path and return to my natural world. I didn't really understand what she was saying because I don't recall being on Mount Shasta before."

"You were born on Shasta, weren't you?" Fen asked as she gently closed Kai's robe and rejoined Hilly at the table.

"Well, yeah, but this spirit said I frolicked on the mountain as a child. I don't remember any of that. All, I know is that I'm supposed to find out more when I walk the shaman's path to Mount Shasta."

Hilly grew quiet as she listened to Kai's words. She now worried about keeping her word to Jeff that she have Kai back in his arms safe and sound in a week. An uneasy feeling crept into her soul. A sense of foreboding squeezed her heart as if the future raced toward the present with un-fathomable speed; she was merely the reluctant observer, witnessing the psychic collision that would change their lives.

She watched Kai. Like a child discovering a new toy, he excitedly dis-cussed his encounter with the magical spirit, Shasta, and eagerly planned the details for embarking on the shaman's path. He had unfolded a cloth napkin, grabbed a pen from the desk, and fired off a list of to-dos in prepa-ration for the trip. How could she deny Kai from living his preordained destiny? If Kai had tried to prevent her from seeing Denali, she would have fought him. She listened as he passionately explained how he planned to walk the Siskiyou Trail, an ancient shaman path from Oregon to Califor-nia. He had so many questions, and was desperate for the answers, which could not arrive fast enough.

As she recalled her own emotions when she embarked on her spiritual journey, she felt elated for her brother and for all the adventures that lay ahead in the future. Her heart ached from the pain she would cause Jeff when Kai would not return home as planned.

She was losing Kai. Not that she feared her brother would die, but because he was marching toward his moment of enlightenment. He was following his quest: a journey the Cererian Prophecy outlined and a future he couldn't control. The same situation would eventually occur with Fen and Chance as they submitted to the unavoidable lure of their preordained journeys.

Yet, Hilly wondered, what if? What if she and her siblings chose to take a stand against the demands of the prophecy that ran tirelessly in the background like a computer operating system. What if they combined their enhanced powers to make their own decisions, halting the manipulation of an ancient, alien prediction? She watched Fen and Kai and mused on their innocence, their unknowing of the challenges yet to befall them.

Past, present, and future revealed their existence as unique and separate realities, but Hilly also perceived them as constantly expanding and contracting, colliding together and then separating like the breath of life itself.

Chapter 13

Fen Meets Jake

JAKE PEERED UP AT Hotel Aningan. His eyes drifted over the aging architecture of the old hotel he'd known since he was a little boy. Each visit to the ancient building was like reuniting with an old friend, an acquaintance that wore the progressive signs of deterioration at each encounter.

A relic from the late 1890s, the building began life as an old, doublewide canvas tent pitched by an entrepreneurial trio of brothers chasing the gold rush migration into Alaska. As the miners toiled (and sometimes died) on the treacherous slopes, scouring the landscape for bits of glittering gold, the brothers prospected for a different prize—the hard-earned money and gold the miners carried in their pockets.

Their plan was simple, basic you might say, as they cleverly developed their establishment to meet the basic needs of every miner: food and a place to sleep. They often joked that they should carve their slogan—Survive Another Night to Dig Another Day—onto an oak plank and hang it by a knotted rope between two pine trees near the entrance to their modest business.

The oldest brother proudly called the enterprise an 'inn', noting that his claim was not too far from the truth since they did offer room and food. For the sum of two dollars a night, customers received an old canvas cot, one wool blanket, and breakfast and dinner (not guaranteed to be hot). To maximize their profits, the brothers stuffed the tent with two rows of cots, each bed abutting the next. This tight arrangement forced occupants to clamber over the foot of the bed whenever they needed to enter or leave. The businessmen even claimed they had indoor toilets, which were nothing more than two metal buckets placed near the back of the tent.

Exhausted from the fourteen-hour days mining the elusive ore, the laborers eagerly paid to eat, usually a watery gruel with occasional bits of stringy meat. and collapse onto a cot. The close proximity to their neighbors didn't matter since many of them already worked side-by-side in the field and were already accustomed to each other's stink—a fetid concoction of sweat, grime, and stale human odor.

So began the humble beginnings of Hotel Aningan, a dingy structure born of avarice. It evolved into a four-story hotel thriving on the dreams of others for the right price.

Like a rat in a maze searching for his cheese, Jake's eyes traced the rusted, metal downspouts snaking along the side of the building until he reached the corner window on the fourth floor—the room sheltering Hilly and her siblings. He sensed her presence and grinned. He mentally messaged, *Hilly, we're here.*

Jake and Sammy awaited the Kemps inside Sammy's old station wagon, Stella. The vintage car belched smoke as it idled in the hotel alley in a space prominently punctuated by a metal NO PARKING sign pock-marked by numerous bullet holes. Not too many souls ventured down the dark, foreboding lane, guaranteeing privacy and discretion while collecting their passengers.

"Jake, I can't afford any more tickets," Sammy moaned as his eyes darted up and down the alley, scanning for signs of the local constable.

Jake fixated on the corner window and dismissed Sammy's complaint. "Seriously? At this hour? They'll leave us alone. The drunks at Flanagan's will keep them busy for a long time."

The tattered refrains of an old Irish tune drifted through the alley accompanied by a low synchronous thumping reverberating off the brick walls, a sign that patrons had assembled on the floor and were now dancing a high-energy jig. Jake smirked, recalling his last visit to Flanagan's when Hilly eventually dragged him away from his celebratory party and took him home only to take advantage of his drunkenness and paint him in lipstick and mascara.

Hilly telepathically responded, *Hey there. We'll be down in a flash. I'm so excited to have you to meet Fen. You met Kai yesterday, but I'm not sure he remembers the encounter.*

There are so many moments from that meeting I would like to forget. Jake added, *Just kidding. Your brother seemed really nice.*

Ten minutes later Hilly, Fen, and Kai exited the hotel's side entrance and scanned the alley for Stella. The station wagon was parked behind a commercial garbage container, and Sammy realized the Kemps couldn't easily see her.

"Here we are!" he squealed, slamming his hand onto the steering wheel, smacking the horn. Stella managed a strangled squawk reminiscent of a dying goose. Meanwhile, Sammy waved furiously out the window, trying to snatch their attention.

Jake cringed, annoyed at Sammy's overzealous antics. The nawiht was a handy companion but his constant exuberance gnawed away at Jake's sanity.

Hilly waved, acknowledging she'd seen and heard Sammy.

Jake watched the trio stroll to the car, arm-in-arm like one big happy family. He assessed Fen and Kai by sensing their powers and measuring their energy. Unconsciously evaluating others materialized when he became a shaman. He couldn't switch this ability off any easier than commanding his heart to stop. He carefully watched the Kemps approach. He intuited that Fen and Kai harbored great power but he also sensed their trepidation about the trip to the Sentinel Boulder.

His attention shifted to Hilly, drawn to her carefree manner as she walked and chatted with her siblings. Intense joy emanated from her, and in his heightened state of awareness, he could see her aura—indigo and vivid blue blending together and then separating as the hues swirled around her body. This was a drastic change from times before when her energy field glowed bright red. He recalled the warning from Darrius: *We must all monitor her for signs that she is not coping with her transformation.* Although the different aura color seemed minor, he'd notify Darrius anyway in case the change was an indication of a larger problem. In the meantime, he'd maintain a watchful eye.

Jake and Sammy exited Stella. Jake remained beside the car while Sammy trotted toward the group. "Miss Hilly, it's so good to see you again. This must be your brother and sister." He stopped them in the middle of the alley and pushed his hand toward Fen. "Hi, Miss Fen, I'm Sammy." Fen forced a smile as she glanced at Hilly for assurances that the odd little man was harmless.

Hilly intervened, "Sammy, calm down." She tugged on his sleeve, forcing him to take several steps back from Fen. "Wait until I've introduced you before you start shoving your hand into people's faces." Hilly smiled warmly at the nawiht, putting his doubts at ease. "Sammy, this is my sister, Fen, and this is my brother, Kai."

Hilly had barely uttered Kai before Sammy rushed forward, "Hiya! I'm Sammy. It's so nice to meet you two. Miss Hilly has told me so much about you, and I can't wait to drive you out to the cabin and the Sentinel Boulder, and—"

"Sammy!" Hilly shouted as she held her hand up to stop the nawiht's rambling. Sammy stopped talking, but his mouth remained open mid-word.

Fen and Kai exchanged bewildered glances. Hilly had warned them about Sammy, but no amount of explanation could accurately describe an encounter with the nawiht.

Jake leaned against Stella with his arms folded across his chest. He grinned a warm, wide smile. Hilly led her siblings toward him, eager to get away from Sammy's babbling. "And, this is my friend, Jake Pierson."

Kai spoke first. "Ah, yes. I believe I owe you some apologies for my frequent flirting yesterday. You see, I wasn't feeling quite right—"

Jake interrupted, "No apologies are needed. Hilly explained about your fear of flying." Kai extended his hand, but Jake didn't move. His instinct screamed a warning, and Jake's eyes clouded with concern.

Awkward seconds passed as Jake's intuition and logic battled for control of his decision. His instincts warned of danger, but he reasoned that Kai was harmless, the lovable brother of Hilly. Jake dismissed his gut feeling and unfolded his arms to accept Kai's handshake.

The trap was sprung. Kai yanked Jake toward him, engulfed him in a bear hug, and planted a quick peck on his cheek. Then Kai quickly pushed him back and grinned like a mischievous child who knew he'd done something naughty.

"You're every ounce the gentleman Hilly described. Thank you for not taking advantage of me in the backseat yesterday." Kai winked at Jake and laughed. "See, I didn't forget everything, handsome Jake."

Hilly and Fen chuckled. Kai had previously advised them of his little scheme. Now, the embarrassed bush pilot stared at the ground, blushing a deep crimson, gathering his thoughts. He glared at the laughing trio as he realized practical jokes ran in the Kemp family—first Hilly and now Kai. He looked deep into Fen's eyes and shuddered to think what she might spring on him.

"You got me," Jake declared. His tense eyes relaxed as he forced a grin to his lips.

Hilly ran to him and encircled his waist, squeezing him hard. "I should have warned you the entire family can be brutal with our pranks. I couldn't resist watching you squirm in Kai's embrace. Thanks for being a good sport about all of this nonsense." She kissed his cheek. A faint scent of sandalwood tickled his nostrils.

Holding Jake's hand, Hilly announced to her siblings, "Jake is a shaman and was recently appointed elder of his community. He manages the town of Aningan along with Benedict, a Cererian you've not met yet. Kai you'll love this, he is also a member of the family that honors the element of air, just like you. Only, he doesn't mind flying in planes." Kai scrunched his face and stuck at his tongue. "Very mature, Kai."

Jake clenched his teeth as he listened to Hilly tout his accomplishments. Although he was proud of what he had achieved, he found it awkward to hear others boast about him. Success was easier to manage in the intimacy of his mind and not in the glare of a public spotlight. He managed to squeeze out a grin while Hilly gushed about him.

Fen stepped forward and studied Jake's face, spending a few moments absorbing his energy. Jake felt Fen probing his mind and attempting to peek into his thoughts. He abruptly blocked access. The action released an invisible ripple of energy back toward Fen as though Jake had waved his hand in the air, pushing her psychic power away. "I see you're a mind reader like your sister," Jake commented. The corner of his mouth bowed up in a devilish smile.

"I need more practice with my ability," Fen admitted. Her voice quavered with embarrassment. "I meant no harm., It's just one of those natural functions that spontaneously turn on when I'm around others." The apples of her cheeks glowed a soft pink as she extended her hand to Jake. "I'm so glad to meet you."

Jake took her hand and was immediately stunned by the warmth flowing from her palm. A strong tingling sensation penetrated his body and caused him to relax as though he had suddenly plunged into an aromatherapy bath.

Fen saw a flicker of uncertainty in Jake's eyes and added, "I'm also a healer. If you're experiencing any odd feelings, it's only because your body was in desperate need and accepted what I could provide." She released Jake's hand.

What a fascinating family of magical souls, Jake mused. Hilly exhibited new abilities almost every day—some innate while most developed during her ongoing transformation. Kai and Fen possessed unique psychic powers and there was the fourth Kemp, Chance—Keeper of the Records—a kindred spirit.

Jake considered the strength of the family's combined powers. He'd never met a group of magicians so adept in multiple disciplines of sorcery and the supernatural.

Chapter 14

The Power of Two

THE MAT-SU VALLEY UNFOLDED before the travelers. Her energy swarmed over them as they reached her forested outer edges. Nonmagical Folk might feel a twinge of vertigo upon entering her sacred space, but the senses of Jake and the Kemps rocketed into overdrive infused by intoxicating floral scents, a kaleidoscope of vivid hues, and sounds ranging from the flutter of hummingbird wings to the baritone bellow of a bull elk. The resulting natural high was a sought-after effect for those entering the valley.

Sammy drove along the banks of a brook which lazily followed the landscape gouged by ancient glaciers. The aqua waters flowed peacefully through the valley, gently following the curves of the land before veering away and trailing into the distance in search of the sea. Flocks of birds—geese, swans and ducks—scattered, squawking at Stella's rude interruption. Disgruntled musk oxen lumbered off the road just before the old station wagon flew by them. They watched the car pass and huffed at the mechanical bison kicking a cloud of dust into the air. Looming in the distance, the towering summit of Denali pushed into the pale blue sky, her broad shoulders wrapped in a white shawl of brilliant snow.

Stella raced along the dirt road. She lurched off hidden rocks and plunged into deep ruts. Sammy knew only one speed—fast. He urged the car forward, indifferent to obstacles, as he hummed a tune while tapping his stubby fingers on the steering wheel.

Beside him, Jake snoozed, completely unaffected by the car's jarring motions. Jake had prepared for the wild ride. He wedged his body into the front seat and planted his boots firmly on the dashboard while his elbows thrust out, one against the door and the other against the console. Tightly packed in this position, he barely wiggled as Stella bounced down the road.

The mood in the backseat was not so serene. Kai and Fen stared forward, paralyzed in fear and still in shock from Sammy's earlier incident where he nearly missed the cut off from the main road. Sammy had slammed the brakes and pulled the steering wheel to the left, forcing Stella to balance on to two wheels while making the turn onto the rustic road. The terrorized siblings gripped the headrests in front of them, tearing into the fabric so hard, their knuckles turned white. Wide-eyed, they gawked at the road in front of them, their mouths agape as fear strangled their screams.

Not all the energy in the backseat was chaotic. All too familiar with her friend's driving, Hilly planned a peaceful solution. As soon as they left Aningan, she whispered ancient words and drifted into a deep trance. Sitting calmly between her siblings with her eyes closed, she rested her hands on her knees and whispered her mantra. Moments later, her spirit took flight, astral traveling to the peaks of Denali. There she sat in the snow and meditated, communing with nature's spirits and with her earth mother.

Despite the jostling within the vehicle, Hilly barely moved. Her body hovered in the air suspended on a cushion of magic, lightly swaying with the movement of the car. Beneath the scarf around her throat, the blue opal vibrated. The spiritual connection with Denali was strong and even though her soul stood atop the mountain, a stream of energy led back to the gemstone on a delicate strand of enchantment.

Sammy slammed the brakes. Stella swerved, fishtailing to a stop while her wheels kicked gravel in all directions. Finally at rest, the car released a low grinding groan as the chassis settled into place.

Jake and Hilly bolted awake.

"We're here!" Sammy yelled as he turned off the motor and jumped out.

Fen and Kai still gripped the seats in front of them. They stared mutely through the windshield.

Hilly waved a hand in front of their faces. "Are you okay?" she asked as she peered first at Kai and then to Fen.

No response.

Jake whirled around in his seat, coming eye-to-eye with Kai who appeared catatonic. His face had transformed into a white mask with all the blood drained. Fen wore a similar look. "Uh-oh, Hilly. Sammy's scared them into silence."

"What...what...what the hell was that?" Fen stuttered. Having regained her ability to speak, Fen released her fury. "Hilly Kemp, how dare you put us in this death trap. My god, I've seen monkeys drive better than Sammy. He could have killed us all and I would have been FURIOUS if that had happened."

As Fen ranted, Jake and Hilly exchanged knowing glances. Sammy's antics never failed to produce outbursts from newcomers. The nawiht had never been involved in an accident except for the incident where he slid off the road during an ice storm. But he was by himself then. In all the years he'd been driving folks back and forth to Aningan, he'd never hurt anyone. He may have scared them into another dimension, but he had never harmed a soul.

The aftereffects of a ride with Sammy were unpredictable but amusing. The siblings' faces twisted into a blend of rage and horror, but Hilly and Jake couldn't contain themselves and chuckled. Fen's face glowed an angry tomato red while Kai, who'd finally recovered from his brief departure with reality, sneered at both of them.

Kai extracted his fingers from the headrest and hissed, "I'd be careful with laughing about our situation, dear sister. You're not out of the car yet, and we have ways of dealing with inconsiderate siblings." Kai glanced at Fen and mentally messaged her, cloaking his thoughts from Hilly. Fen nodded in agreement, and her lips curved into an evil grin.

The air shifted inside the car as though a massive fist had punched into a large bowl of water forcing strong ripples racing in all directions. Jake recognized the signs of powerful magic being conjured and reached for the door handle to escape. He pushed against the door, hoping to flee before Fen and Kai unleashed the full spell. "Sammy, get over here and help me get this door open."

The nawiht scampered to Jake's side and yanked while Jake kicked with his boots. Finally, the door burst wide, complaining loudly with a metallic creak. Jake tumbled onto the ground but quickly scrambled to his feet and grabbed Sammy by the shoulder. Together they ran from the car, away from the supernatural storm brewing inside.

An eerie silence filled the cabin. Fen and Kai stared at Hilly through slitted eyes as they focused their magic at their sister. Their anger swirled around Hilly like the winds of a hurricane, tossing her side to side.

"Come on guys, no harm was done. We're all here in one piece," she reasoned.

With pursed lips, Fen and Kai blew their magic into the car, creating a wave of powerful energy that pushed outward, filling the car as if Stella was a huge balloon. The increased pressure caused Hilly's ears to pop and a dull ache pulsed behind her eyes. No longer convinced her siblings were playing, Hilly calculated her options—concoct her own magic or teleport from the car. *Teleporting is the fastest and safest option,* she thought.

"Nice try, Hilly. But we've sealed the vehicle," Kai warned her. "You won't be able to teleport. And we've disarmed you magic. Go ahead and try."

Kai and Fen held their arms wide and chanted an ancient mantra. Their voices merged, thrumming intense energy throughout the cabin. The atmosphere thickened. Hilly thrust her hands toward Kai, attempting to break his spell but an unseen force repulsed her magic.

"Give up, Hilly?" Kai taunted. "All you have to do is apologize."

Hilly covered her ears. Her eardrums ached from the escalating force inside the car. She searched her siblings' faces. Unaffected by their spell, they smirked and continued mouthing the ancient words. Hilly could hardly breathe, her lungs strained to inflate with each breath. In short gasps she pressed her siblings, "Don't...you...think...you're...over...-reacting?"

No response.

Her pride prevented her from admitting defeat. She saw Jake hovering outside Stella, and yelled into his brain, *Get me out of here!*

Jake shrugged and responded, *What do you think I can do? They're your siblings."*

An explosive pain pounded inside her skull. Hilly winced and glanced at her siblings, hoping they would pity her and cease their assault. Her stare was met with a cold, unflinching glare. Hilly relented, her bravado and stubbornness melting away. She screamed, "Okay! I'm sorry. I'm sorry I laughed at you."

Kai winked at Fen. Within seconds the pressure in the car returned to normal. "I'm satisfied. How about you, Fen?" Kai gloated.

"I'm good. That will teach Hilly to be disrespectful to her older siblings."

Hilly leaned forward and rubbed her forehead, easing the last remnants of the headache. She squinted through bloodshot eyes. "What did you guys just do?"

"Remember how we focused our power in the hotel? Well, Kai and I zeroed in on you like a laser beam. Worked great, don't you think?" Fen chuckled, relishing the rare moment to teach her sister a lesson.

Hilly dug her fingers into the tense muscles along her neck. "That's potent stuff. And you guys weren't impacted?"

"Not one whisker," Kai answered. He flashed a wide grin as he basked in his sister's humility.

Jake banged on the window. "Is everyone okay in there?"

Simultaneously, both rear doors popped open, the latches manipulated by Kai's mind. "Let's let our dear sister out," he announced.

Jake jumped backward with his arms raised in defense, concerned spell remnants would engulf him. Kai chuckled as he exited. "Don't worry, Jake, all the magic dissipated inside the car."

Hilly slowly followed her siblings. She was still wobbly from the pressurized effects, and she leaned onto Fen's arm for support.

Jake studied her. She appeared drained. "Are you okay?" he asked.

Hilly replied in a weak whisper. "How should I feel? Not only did I get beat up by my sister and brother, but they prevented me from performing magic."

"What? They stopped your power?" Jake eyed Kai and Fen. He was incredulous their conjuring could subdue Hilly's superior abilities.

Kai grinned impishly. "Yes. When it comes to magic, apparently two Kemps trump one."

Chapter 15

The Journey

THE MAT-SU VALLEY THRUMMED with an unusually strong energy. A chilled, blue force swept down from the icy glaciers, teasing the grasses to release their cottony seed heads into the breeze. The white puffs delicately danced on the energetic currents as they drifted through the valley.

Nature greeted the newcomers.

Fen and Kai gasped as they sensed the valley's purity and indomitable spirit. They twirled with their arms outstretched, eagerly collecting the energy in their fingertips while they dispensed a dose of their own magic back into the wilderness.

"Gorgeous country, isn't it?" Hilly beamed as she followed their gaze.

"Beyond words," Kai uttered. A deer bounded across his path, its black tail flicking toward the sky with each leap. "And there's an interesting energy..." he tilted his head and closed his eyes, searching for the proper words, "...it's throbbing like a light heartbeat. It's peaceful and calming like when a baby lies against its mother's chest and falls asleep to the rhythm of her life force."

"Exactly," Fen exclaimed. "The air is more than fresh, it's exhilarating, as though I can get high just from breathing." To prove her point, she drew in a deep breath. Her cheeks flushed with the sudden rush of oxygen and her eyes flashed various blue hues—from navy to aqua—before returning to her natural sky blue. "This land is enchanted."

Hilly was pleased her family enjoyed the beauty and magic of her home. The pulse of joy pounded in her chest as she watched her siblings dart among the flowers, crying out at the brilliance of colors, the oddity of shape, and the pureness of the vibrations. Hilly hadn't experienced this much happiness since their gathering at The Nine Muses.

Losing herself in the playful antics of her siblings, Hilly realized she had neglected Jake. She called out to him, "Jake, were you this excited when you saw the valley for the first time?"

Silence.

Hilly wheeled around and noticed he was no longer standing behind her. She spied a figure in the distance, almost a hundred yards away. She frowned, puzzled by Jake's sudden departure. She reached out to him telepathically, *Jake, why did you leave us?*

Moments earlier, Jake silently slipped away from Hilly, cloaking his aura so she wouldn't realize he was gone. He marched toward the Sentinel Boulder, relieved to leave the Kemps behind. Jake needed solitude to figure things out, to clear his mind which had become muddled with thoughts of the Kemp's unique magic and the disarming of Hilly's power. That action, alone, disturbed him the most and he struggled believing Hilly had a weakness. It was hard to believe that his warrior friend—kin to Stygian—could be brought to her knees so easily.

Hilly's message buzzed in Jake's mind like an annoying fly. He wanted to swat it away and ignore it, but Hilly was a good friend and deserved a response.

We have a job to do. Play with your family. You know the way to the lupine meadow. I'll wait for you there. He erected a wall to block further communication. He desired more time to think about the recent events.

He knew closing the door on his mind would upset Hilly, but right now, he didn't care.

The muscles in Jake's jaw bunched, and he flexed his fingers as he observed the Kemps. Despite being in the land of his ancestors—a spiritual place with happy memories—he felt utterly alone. He glanced back at the Kemps who chased each other in circles, holding hands and laughing, enjoying life like close siblings do. Minutes earlier, Fen and Kai combined forces to overpower Hilly and now, they played together as though there had never been any animosity. Squabbles are a thing of the past when you belong to a close-knit family.

A brief pang of jealousy nudged Jake. A feeling of lost love and isolation dove deep into his heart, opening old wounds. He clenched his teeth and pushed the emerging emotions back into the darkened chamber of his heart like he always did. He wished he had allowed Sammy to tag along, instead of ordering him to stay behind with Stella. He'd rather have his devoted sidekick babbling about nothing than to languish on the Kemps and their unusual powers and their cloying love for each other.

The last time he walked upon this land, Hilly was his eager student. A novice to magic, she was confident but innocent of the powers that swirled in her blood. She depended on Jake to guide and instruct her during her vision quest. She trusted him to maintain a watchful eye as she slipped through the veil to the spiritual realm.

I'm more than her protector, he thought.

"I'm a lot more." The sound of his voice startled him and he paused, fondly remembering his adventures with Hilly. He mused about how close they'd become since the battle on Denali. They were warriors, comrades in arms, but they were also close friends.

His emotions baffled him. He glanced once again at the Kemps. Kai and Fen seemed nice enough, but there was an unusual magical glow about them. Their brother, Chance, didn't possess this quality. Chance was like Jake—a practical, no-nonsense fellow. Aside from Darrius and

Benedict, Hilly was the most powerful magician he'd ever encountered, and her abilities grew stronger every day. This recent altercation was a strange development, one he was sure Darrius would want to be advised of. Perhaps Hilly wasn't the only one transforming. What if all of the Kemps continued to develop powers beyond their initial abilities?

Hilly watched Jake stroll into the distance. Angered by his terse reply, she attempted to probe his mind only to discover he had sealed access. Jake was in an unusual mood, one Hilly didn't understand.

She rejoined her siblings who hovered over a patch of multi-colored flowers whose petals glistened like spun glass. Kai noticed Jake had disappeared. "Where did Jake go?"

"He left for the Sentinel Boulder," Hilly responded impassively.

"What?" Fen asked. She instinctively surveyed the landscape for their friend. "Did we upset him?"

"Nope, he's in a mood," she responded in a flat, chilly voice. "When he's on a mission, it's all about punctuality and execution. There's no time to stop and admire nature." Hilly didn't mean to let her bitterness color her words and she grimaced from the tone.

"Men." Kai shook his head. "We'll have plenty of time to play and explore. Let's join Jake and get this job done." He hugged Hilly, sensing she needed a dose of love to lift her spirits.

"Kai's right. We've got plenty of time to sightsee after we're done with the Sentinel Boulder," Fen added. She hooked her arm through Hilly's and set out on the dirt track. A few paces away she stopped and scanned the tundra.

"You have no idea where you're going, do you?" Hilly asked, her eyes crinkling with mischief.

"I'm the new one here. Which way do we go?"

"This way." Hilly shouldered her backpack and led them across the meadow. The azure sky shimmered in the summer sun's warmth, yet a cool breeze drifted along the trees. Their leaves whispered hushed secrets as the travelers passed. Only the most skilled sorcerer (or daughter of Denali) would detect the gossip being shared among nature's spirits. Hilly guided her siblings along the path, eavesdropping as the elementals spoke of the strangers in their midst and of the spiritual beast that recently penetrated their realm from beyond the veil. Hilly was intrigued about the magical entity from another dimension, and her senses twitched with excitement.

The group walked quickly hoping to overtake Jake before he reached the Sentinel Boulder. Fen and Kai struggled keeping their minds on that task, lured away by the valley's beauty as each new vista offered even more exotic sights and sounds. Hilly glared whenever they strayed from the path and snapped, "Let's keep going."

Not far away, they encountered a figure crouching by a small, gurgling stream.

"It's Jake," Hilly said. They quickened their pace. As they neared, they noticed him studying tracks in the moist soil along the banks. "Hi Jake. Find something?"

"We have company," he replied indifferently. "They're fresh. I'd say a few hours old. Looks like a coyote, but the paws are much larger." His eyes remained riveted on the marks in the dirt as the Kemps huddled around him. Jake lightly traced the outline of one print. "There's an odd mark in this track, perhaps an injury or a deformity. I sense something spiritual about this creature."

Hilly perked up, thinking the magical entity from another realm may have crossed their path. "Which way did it go?" she asked. She squatted next to Jake, their shoulders lightly brushing together. A light scent of sandalwood wafted as Hilly leaned toward him. Jarred out of his focus,

Jake turned toward her and searched her face. Their stares lingered, neither one speaking. A tension slowly grew as emotions swept over their faces.

Kai mentally spoke to Fen, *It's like watching two surly badgers perform a courtship dance.*

Fen burst out laughing, breaking the awkward silence.

Jake cleared his throat and returned to the paw prints. "They follow this creek and then break off. Hard to tell exactly where they're going." He stood, wiped the dirt from his jeans, and grabbed his pack. "Let's get to the Sentinel Boulder." He marched off without awaiting a response.

"Hilly, is there something you want to tell us?" Kai asked, arching an eyebrow.

Fen encircled Hilly's waist, "What's going on between you and Jake?"

"Nothing," Hilly snarled. The tips of her ears flamed bright red, betraying her emotions. "We have a job to do." Swinging her pack onto her shoulder, she tromped after Jake, leaving her siblings behind.

"That was an interesting scene," Fen mused.

"Mm," Kai agreed. "The rest of our adventure promises to be quite entertaining." He playfully offered Fen his elbow. "Shall we journey to the Sentinel Boulder, dear sister?" Fen laughed and linked her arm with Kai's.

Fen reflected on how she could heal her relationship with Jake. After all, it was in her blood to heal the physical, so why not attempt to soothe the emotional as well? She concocted a plan and whispered it to Kai who nodded. She seized the chance to repair Jake's battered feelings when he loomed into sight twenty yards away.

Fen trotted after Jake. She brushed by Hilly with a breathless, "Helllllo!" as she loped toward Jake who tramped several paces ahead. Hilly watched Fen pass, suspicious of her actions and concerned what she may say or do.

"Jake...hold...up...Jake," Fen huffed as she ambled through the wildflowers, carefully avoiding stepping into one of the numerous animal holes peppering the path. She stopped and sucked in a deep breath, and then released the air in one explosive yell. "JAKE!"

Halting mid step, he whirled, sensing trouble. He found Fen doubled over, her hands on her thighs. She panted furiously but managed to flash a tender smile at Jake before resuming her labored breathing. Jake rushed to her side. "Fen, are you okay?"

"I wanted to talk with you."

Jake slackened his grip and turned to walk away. "I'm not in the mood."

"I'm so sorry we delayed your journey," Fen blurted. "It would mean a lot to me if you would walk with me to the Sentinel Boulder." Jake stopped. He hung his head, considering his options. He could be rude and walk away or acquiesce. "Please," Fen squeaked.

He extended his hand as a peace offering for his rudeness. "I'd be delighted," he cheerfully said, and he meant it.

"Fantastic." She grasped his hand and quickly linked her arm with his. They walked together in silence broken only by the occasional moments when Fen lightly stroked Jake's arm and mumbled unintelligible words.

A subtle shift occurred in Jake's mood. The chaotic thoughts in his mind retreated, replaced by a peaceful calm. A euphoria overwhelmed him, and he instinctively patted Fen's hand and smiled at her while the tension melted from his face.

Fen saw her chance to engage Jake. "Alaska is so beautiful. What was it like to grow up in such an enchanted land?"

Now at ease, Jake eagerly chatted about Aningan, his people, and what it felt like to be an elder in his community. He shared his thoughts on improving services to his town and protecting the scenic lands surrounding the area. Fen listened attentively and asked many questions, allowing Jake ample time to speak. Once in a while, she'd stroke his arm and mumble some words. Little did Jake know she had intuitively determined what was lacking in his life. Jake desperately needed someone who would listen, a person who sincerely cared what he thought. Fen's magic soothed the gruff warrior.

After Fen had rushed by, Hilly waited for Kai to catch up. Together they strolled through the meadow and chatted about the shift in Fen's personality. Shy and withdrawn at The Nine Muses, their sister arrived in Alaska outspoken and confident. They agreed her emerging psychic abilities probably played a major role in that transformation. Kai admitted it was Fen who proposed playing the prank on Hilly.

"Tell me, Kai, what was it like to be co-conspirator in tormenting me?" Hilly nudged her brother in the side.

"I wasn't sure we would be successful. We focused on your life force and the energy did our bidding. I must admit, the power is daunting. Consider what we could do as a family." The two walked in silence.

Cresting a small rise, they encountered Fen and Jake who had stopped on the trail. "Well, hello Kemp family," Fen chirped. "About time you caught up."

"Don't do us any favors," Kai teased. "Admit it, you missed me."

"Dispense with the drama," Fen replied.

"We're almost to the Sentinel Boulder," Jake interjected. He smiled at Fen before continuing, "Fen thought it would be appropriate for us to arrive as one group." He joined Hilly and smiled warmly, conveying an apology through his eyes. He gathered her hands into his and turned to the others. "This is reverent land that knows Hilly and I, but you two are strangers and should have a proper introduction."

The ground shook violently. A rolling vibration catapulted Kai into Fen, and she caught her brother in a strong hug, preventing him from falling.

The momentum sent the duo lurching around the moving landscape like a pair of puppets dancing at the behest of their master. Unaffected by the jolt, Hilly and Jake stood their ground, instinctively closing their eyes. They recognized the vibrational welcome of their old friend, the Sentinel Boulder.

Moments later, the quaking stopped.

"Was that an earthquake?" Fen probed as she clung to Kai's arm for balance.

"That was a physical greeting from the Sentinel Boulder," Jake explained. "He knows we're here. He seems quite anxious to meet you two."

"You can respond to him telepathically," Hilly urged. "Focus on the energy surrounding you. Find the energetic thread deployed to you by the Sentinel. You'll know it by its steady, high frequency, and luminescent glow."

"Yes!" Fen squealed, "I see it. The strand runs in front of us and stretches into the distance like a lifeline."

"There's an accompanying ripple of energy like a cresting wave crashing over the meadow," Kai added. "I sense we're not far away."

Hello my children. The unexpected male voice flowed through everyone's mind like the reassuring words from a parent—warm and welcoming. Although Hilly had visited the giant rock before, this was the first time it had shared a conversation with many people instead of a private discussion. She relished its familiar voice—a sweetness so pure, tears welled in her eyes. *I have waited a millennium for those who will unlock my gifts. I am honored to have you in my presence.*

Fen and Kai exchanged glances, incredulous that the powerful spirit would be honored to have *them* in his presence. *We are your servants. We have come in the hopes of understanding the meaning of your symbols,* Kai responded.

A low chuckle rolled through the ground. Was the Sentinel Boulder laughing at him? Kai's cheeks flushed and he lowered his eyes, unsure of his next step. Tenderly, Fen grasped his hand. "He's not laughing at you. I sense the Sentinel's heart is so full of joy at our arrival that he cannot contain his excitement."

Kai searched his sister's face for reassurance.

Come, my children. I long to meet you!

Holding hands, Kai and Fen bolted from the group. Trotting along the dirt path, they plowed through the wildflowers and leapt over small bushes, eager to come face-to-face with the ancient earth spirit that beckoned them from afar. With their free hands outstretched toward the energetic lifeline, they reached forward, anxious to touch the etheric force, which pulsed just out of reach. Tears of joy ran down their cheeks.

Hilly and Jake watched them depart. Their unashamed display of pure joy didn't surprise them. Only those attuned to the vibration of nature would understand the exhilaration that arises in the company of the elementals.

Watching the Kemps race for the Sentinel, Jake recalled his first encounter with the boulder. As a young boy, hiking the Mat-Su Valley with his grandfather, an ethereal force lured him away and pulled him toward the lupine meadow. Jake's grandfather did not stop him. Instead, he took comfort in the knowledge that those who are called by the spirits of nature are the blessed. Jake joined the long line of ancestors, including his grandfather, who were invited to visit the lupine meadow and join their auras with the ancient earth spirit: the Sentinel Boulder.

Filled with a tremendous sense of jubilation, Jake had skipped and ran, beckoned by a tune in his head until he lay exhausted at the base of the giant rock. His intuition, still pure at the age of eight and unspoiled by adult cynicism, recognized the reverent force within the Sentinel. Instinctively he moved to his knees and placed his palms upon the cold, granite surface. A tingling sensation like the flick of static electricity played with his fingers while a warmth spread up his arms and throughout his body. In response, he'd bowed his head.

The boulder spoke in a low masculine voice with the easy cadence of an instructor teaching his pupil. The words resonated in his mind.

Jake, today you join your ancestors in an honored tradition of being united with the spirits of nature. Go forth and protect these vital lands. To guide you on your journey, I reveal to you my secrets, the wondrous mysteries that originated over a thousand years ago.

A purple aura materialized and engulfed the Sentinel. The living energy undulated and stretched until it engulfed young Jake. Flashes of electricity fired within the violet bubble, showering Jake with miniature sparks.

His head snapped upward as though an unseen force controlled it. He clenched his jaw, and his eyes rolled back while his body convulsed. After several minutes, the aura dissipated and Jake collapsed onto the ground. The young boy, now full of the Sentinel's magic, drifted into a coma. The slumber lasted six months as his mind processed the Sentinel's vast information and so his body could heal from the hand of the ancients. Jake's chest had been transformed into a holy text. There were hundreds of symbols tattooed along each rib, each mark represented the words and names of the wise ones, the original souls that came to Earth thousands of years ago.

When he awoke, the elders of his tribe bestowed upon him the title of shaman. Since his grandfather, a wise and respected leader, was a witness to the miracle, the Elder Council did not hesitate to grant this honor. Jake's grandfather taught him to be humble in his newfound celebrity and that the gifts bestowed upon him by the boulder and by his people should be loved and protected, never flaunted, or inflated by ego or self-importance.

At the innocent age of eight, Jake opened his heart to the peace and understanding of the spiritual world. And his life changed forever.

Chapter 16

The Great Reveal

THE SWEET, FRESH SCENT of honey drifted from the lupine meadow. Lingering at the Sentinel Boulder, the fragrant thread skimmed over the surface, collecting energy from the guardian rock while sharing its flower essence—a natural exchange of elemental magic. Now infused with the boulder's energy, the warm fragrance snaked through the valley with aromatic tendrils, searching for the magicians known in the spiritual world as the Custodians.

Fen ducked, escaping her brother's half-hearted grasp. "My goodness, Fen, I'm out of breath from chasing you," Kai huffed.

Fen stopped a few yards away and taunted him. "Maybe if you exercised more instead of drinking..."

He lunged for her and shouted, "Maybe if you weren't such an easy mark!" He snagged her sleeve and yanked. Their bodies slammed together with such force that they fell to the ground giggling. Still entwined in each other's arms, the laughing siblings rolled around in the wildflowers, as tears streamed down their faces.

A sweet aroma gently flowed over them, caressing their heads and tickling their noses. Fen bolted into a sitting position and sniffed the air, again and again. "The lupines! I can smell their sweet scent," Fen exclaimed. "They must be near."

"Which means the Sentinel is too!" Kai shouted as he scrambled to his feet. Grabbing Fen's hand, he tugged her forward.

Hilly watched her sister and brother bound away. Their excitement reminded her of carefree children chasing butterflies in the garden. "My first meeting with the Sentinel was nothing like this," she hissed in a low whisper.

Jake followed Kai and Fen as they ran together toward the lupine meadow. Hilly faced Jake and scowled. She studied his face but saw nothing in his blank expression. "Did you hear me? Even now, I don't feel the ebullience that they're experiencing." She stared back at her siblings. "Why is it so different for them?"

Jake sighed. He sensed his friend was troubled by the boulder's interest in her siblings. "The Sentinel communicates with each person differently. As one of nature's guardians, it possesses the knowledge of the ancients and, it alone, determines how that information is shared. Do you recall the message the boulder shared with you on your vision quest?"

"Yes, but it wasn't until *you* invited me to touch the stone that I received his words of wisdom. With Fen and Kai, the Sentinel is rolling out the red carpet, personally inviting them into his lupine meadow." She gestured toward her siblings. "Look at them. It's like watching two kids running into the arms of their grandfather." Hilly dropped her head and sniffed back tears. She hated crying and squeezed her hands in frustration. "My encounter was more like an afterthought." Her voice carried the bite of self-pity.

Jake gently touched her shoulder. "Your sorrow is unwarranted. I dare say that if the Sentinel overheard you right now, he may scold you for your selfishness."

Hilly shoved Jake's hand off her shoulder. "Selfishness?" she yelled. "How dare you."

Jake's eyes softened. He drew in a cleansing breath and calmly replied, "No, Hilly, how dare you."

Hilly reeled from his words. They were delivered without malice, but she received them like daggers aimed at her heart. She turned away from Jake and glared at her siblings. Jake sensed the bitterness of jealousy rising inside her and opted for a different tactic to ease the tension. "Do you recall the prank you played on me?"

Hilly faced him and tilted her head. "What? Why would you bring that up now?

Jake smiled, the corners of his eyes crinkling, "Remember?"

"I remember." Hilly relaxed and a mischievous smile spread across her lips as she recalled her actions.

Jake placed both hands on Hilly's shoulders and pulled her closer. Seriousness shadowed his face as he spoke in a low, secretive tone. "Why didn't you ask about the symbols."

"Symbols?" Hilly frowned as she replayed the images of that night. The scenes quickly flashed through her mind until the flicker of remembrance enlarged her pupils with delight. "Oh, those symbols."

Jake stepped back and unbuttoned his shirt, exposing his chest. "Yeah, about my tattoos." A sudden breeze tugged his shirt completely open, exposing black markings across every rib. For a brief moment Hilly caught her breath as she stared at Jake's chest and his taut stomach muscles contracting with each movement. "These are a gift from the Sentinel Boulder." He slid a finger across one rib and then another. "I received these at the age of eight."

Hilly stepped closer. She reached to touch a symbol but stopped, afraid she may be desecrating holy ground. Jake nodded for her to proceed. She lightly brushed the tattoos on one rib. Goosebumps rippled across his skin.

"That tickles," he joked.

"What do they all mean?" The air swiftly pulsed with a great force. Shockwaves buffeted them, causing their ears to ache and momentarily halting their breaths as though they had suddenly been propelled to an extreme altitude. A few seconds passed before the energy returned to normal. Jake's friendly demeanor faded and he rebuttoned his shirt. Hilly watched him, puzzled by his abrupt mood change. "Did I say something wrong?"

Jake forced a weak smile. "You did nothing wrong. Sometimes the questions go unanswered for a reason. And, right now, I can't answer your question. I hope you can accept that."

Hilly bit her lower lip, pondering Jake's reply. She narrowed her eyes, examining his face and probing his mind, which he had closed to her thoughts. Jake winked at her. His playful response threw her off balance. Sure, she wanted to know what the symbols meant, but if Jake wasn't at liberty to share that information, she'd have to be patient, something that didn't come easy to her.

"Okay, have it your way," she admitted. Then she quickly added, "For now." She winked back at Jake and scampered off to join Fen and Kai.

Jake closed his eyes, opening his mind to the incoming message from a familiar being. *My son. Be cautious about what you share. There are entities that would kill for your knowledge. Only you know how to wield the power and shield the secrets. The sorceress has her own destiny which she must fulfill. Do not deviate from your sacred mission.*

I understand. Jake nodded and opened his eyes. Hilly had joined Kai and Fen in front of the Sentinel Boulder, and he watched them with renewed interest.

A gust of warm air swept by him, and he sensed the energy from many magical entities rushing toward the lupine meadow. The spiritual beings were curious about the Kemps and eager for the Custodians to unlock the first marker.

"Do not deviate from your mission." He smirked. His mission began when he was eight years old, after the Sentinel confided the ancient secrets of the world. As the Cererian Prophecy dictated, he had delivered the Kemps to the lupine meadow, and they had willingly appeared before the Sentinel Boulder. The future was unfolding as it was preordained a thousand years ago.

Jake marched toward the siblings. His presence was needed beside Hilly where he would act as witness to the great Reveal.

Jake guided Hilly to the protective perimeter located several yards from the Sentinel. The worn track encircling the rock was a foot wide and several inches deep. Generations of worshippers had walked along this path paying tribute and offering blessings to nature's spirits. "We need to wait outside the energy field while your brother and sister unlock the marker."

"What will happen?" Hilly was curious about the details of the ritual but was also concerned about the unknown. The Sentinel Boulder was a powerful spiritual entity and could easily destroy the entire lupine meadow, and all living beings within it, if it so desired.

Jake sensed Hilly's trepidation. "They'll be fine. This moment is a thousand years in the making. Emissaries from other spiritual populations are also in attendance to bear witness to the moment the Custodians perform the great Reveal."

Hilly scanned Jake's face. "Emissaries? Custodians? The great Reveal?"

"It sounds like a game show but to the ancients, Fen and Kai are the official Custodians, designated by the ancients and sanctified by the Sentinel. Their sacred mission—opening the marker—is the Reveal. If you channel your psychic abilities, you'll feel the spiritual ambassadors that stand alongside us in this circle."

Hilly closed her eyes and freed her mind, allowing her sensory powers to emerge. In her mind's eye, she saw many beings—some humanoid, a few mimicking elements of nature, and many appearing as balls of energy. "Wow, there are hundreds gathered around the Sentinel," she said in awe. "It's as if they've arrived to witness royalty."

"In a way they are." Jake held a finger to his lips. "Shh, they're starting."

Fen and Kai stood shoulder-to-shoulder, facing the Sentinel. They pressed their palms together in front of their chests and bowed low from the waist while raising the tips of their fingers to their forehead. The Sentinel sighed a greeting to them.

"Help me kneel," Fen implored as she grabbed Kai's outstretched arm. Slowly he lowered her to the dirt in front of the giant boulder, and then moved behind her so she could lean against his legs for support. Fen placed her palms on the rock and was startled to feel a warmth emitting from the rough angles of the surface. Slowly, a steady pulse reverberated throughout the granite.

Kai placed a hand on each of Fen's shoulders, connecting with his sister's energy. Instantly, he sensed the Sentinel's heartbeat streaming through Fen penetrating his skin, and uniting with his soul. "Oh my god," he gasped in a hoarse whisper.

The siblings maintained their linkage to the rock until the carvings on the sides of the boulder illuminated, glowing in a bright white light. The symbols throbbed as Fen lightly traced each one with her finger, unlocking its message by using the knowledge she acquired from her father's ancient alchemy tome. She recognized the elegant carvings as letters and symbols from the ancient Cererian language. Joy filled her heart as the meanings materialized in her mind. She smiled knowingly, receiving the wisdom born a thousand years ago:

> Within this granite, a spark lies hiding,
> Awaiting the one who will remove the barrier,
> Embracing the one who will ignite the flame,
> And breathe life into the element of fire.

Fen spoke softly, "I have received the message. As it is shared with me, I share it with you now." Fen continued speaking. Her mouth opened and closed, but as she relayed the ancient message, Jake and Hilly heard nothing. Leaning forward they strained to hear any sound but only heard a muted whisper delivered by the wind. They turned to Kai who nodded and smiled, his face full of emotion. Obviously, he was hearing the sacred words spoken by his sister.

"We're only a few yards away, why can't we hear Fen?" Hilly demanded.

Jake surveyed the spiritual ambassadors within the circle before concluding. "No one can hear the message except for Kai. The ancients are wise. they've designated Fen as the orator of the word, and Kai must be the assigned listener. To protect the sacred text, complicated checks and balances have been installed to prevent the holy words from falling into the wrong hands."

"What? You're saying we'll never know the message?"

"Let's see what happens."

Finally reaching the end of her delivery, Fen asked, "Did you hear all of that?"

"The Sentinel's message was intended only for you and Kai. Hilly and I heard nothing," Jake responded.

"It's a beautiful message," Kai exclaimed. "Let me see if I can repeat the words so you can hear them." For several moments Kai excitedly gestured with his hands as his mouth went through the motions. Yet, his words fell mute.

"Kai, I can't even hear you," Fen declared.

"What are you talking about?" Kai leaned to Fen's ear and shouted, "Can you hear me now?"

Fen swatted at Kai. "I'm deaf now," Fen cried.

"We can all hear you now," Jake added. "It appears the Sentinel's message is encrypted so only Fen can speak the words and only you can hear them."

The ground shook violently. A strong vibration rippled out from the Sentinel Boulder and then the reverberation sucked backward toward the stone with such force it was as though an invisible tidal wave had crashed over the circle. Fen lurched sideways but Kai caught her, steadying her as the rumblings continued for several minutes. Despite the assault, Fen maintained her contact with the granite, her instincts warning her that if she lifted her hands, the ritual would abruptly end, and their work would be incomplete.

In desperation she mentally messaged her siblings, *What's going on? Did we do something wrong? Is the Sentinel Boulder upset?*

Just as quickly as it started, the quaking ceased. An intense silence descended over the magical circle. Even the usual sounds of nature quieted. The total absence of sound carried a note of malevolence. Jake telepathically advised the Kemps, *Be calm. The best is yet to come.*

Hilly glanced at Jake, her brows furrowed. Fearful to break the silence, she mouthed, *How do you know?* Jake grinned and winked.

Fen's sudden cry startled everyone. "Look at the Sentinel. Something is happening."

Below her hands, the rock cracked horizontally, creating a fissure almost two feet wide. Shards of gray granite plummeted to the ground as the surface morphed, undulating as though it was alive. A large slab—two square feet—inched downward, groaning with each movement. After several moments, the block grinded to a halt, exposing a dark, obsidian recess with a notched cavity just under ten inches high.

Fen's eyes widened in fascination. Not only could she feel the tortuous strain of the action but could sense the Sentinel's pain in producing the anomaly that had formed in the middle of the boulder. She instinctively deployed her healing energy into the rock.

"There's a keyhole!" Kai exclaimed as he peered over Fen's head into the black chamber. "Looks like a job for the Keeper of the Keys."

Fen scowled. "Watch your tone. This is serious work."

"I am being serious. I'm at my best when there's a little levity to break the tension." Kai knelt beside her. "Now, which key is needed for this job, ethereal or physical?" Placing one hand on the rocky surface for support, he leaned forward, probing the hole with his finger. "Hmmm, a physical key, and I know just the one." From within the brown, leather bag slung around his shoulder, he withdrew an ebony box with ancient symbols painted in silver on all sides. Kai twisted the unusual box in his hands. "That's odd. There's no way to open this little bugger."

"Then how do you open it?" Fen asked as she watched her brother fiddle with the curious container.

Kai grinned at his sister. "That's the trick I have up my sleeve as Keeper of the Keys." Holding the relic in his left hand, the fingers of his right slid along the edges of the box in a clockwise motion as he solemnly recited an incantation. Kai closed his eyes as his words came faster and faster until a low thrumming filled the circle. After several moments, a soft click was heard and the tiny box cracked open, revealing four skeleton keys.

"Ta-da," Kai announced triumphantly.

"Wonderful work, maestro," Fen mocked. "Which key fits that hole? Or do you try all four?"

"You can't do that," Kai exclaimed. "I can only use one key. Trying more than one negates the magic and will seal the opening." He studied the keys in the box. All appeared to be the same size and dimensions with similar scuffs of rust and worn teeth. "The key will need to choose me, not the other way around." Drawing in a deep breath, Kai slowly exhaled to calm his mind. He hovered his right hand above the keys. After several moments, Kai smiled and nodded at Fen. "I've been chosen."

Taking care not to disturb the other keys, Kai gently pinched one between his thumb and forefinger as he lifted it from the case. Placing the box on the ground in front of the boulder, Kai leaned into the chamber and maneuvered the skeleton key into place. He glanced at Fen and quipped, "Fingers crossed this works." Fen frowned but remained quiet.

Kai turned the key to the right with a clunk.

Nothing happened.

He nervously looked at Fen for support.

"Don't remove your hand," Fen cautioned. "It's been a thousand years. Perhaps it's a little rusty." Kai flashed a smile at Fen's attempt of humor, but his stomach lurched with alarm.

Tense seconds passed as the Kemps knelt in front of the granite, eyes riveted on the key. "Maybe I should have turned it to the left," Kai mused aloud. But as he finished speaking, a strong thrumming rippled down the rock and vibrated through the ground underneath their knees. "What's happening?" he cried.

Kai and Fen stared as the skeleton key vanished from Kai's grip. It reappeared beside the three others in the ebony box on the ground. The case slammed shut and the visible seal disappeared. A sudden harsh, grinding noise snatched their attention. Before them, the layer of obsidian slowly dropped, squealing and groaning as it moved back and away from the front of the stone. After it completed its tortuous maneuver, a small selenite chamber, barely eight inches high, lay exposed.

The crystalline walls glistened in the sunshine, launching luminous colors of every hue into the air. The dazzling brilliance forced those in attendance to shield their eyes from the intense glare.

"Oh my," Fen exclaimed, "It's breathtaking."

"I've never seen anything as wonderful as this," Kai added.

A light melody drifted through the magical circle. Barely audible at first, a soft sound rose in pitch until a distinct musical humming was detected. Similar to a bee's thrumming, the tone contained occasional squeaks and chirps, reminiscent of an electrical charge.

"The Sentinel is singing a joyous song in recognition of the key," Fen proclaimed. "This melody has not been shared in a millennium."

Abruptly the humming ended as the song had reached its conclusion. A reverent silence descended over the assemblage. Peace and calm blanketed those withing the circle.

Hilly had watched her brother and sister perform the ritual and now felt embarrassed, and a little childish, for harboring jealously toward their special relationships with the Sentinel Boulder. She was in awe of their powers and of the high magic they conjured in collaboration with the great earth spirit.

But now, she grew concerned. The absence of all sound was disquieting. An intense sense of trepidation seeped from those assembled in the circle as though something much larger was anticipated. Hilly mentally messaged Jake, *It's so quiet. I can't shake the feeling that something will happen soon.*

Jake replied, *Be patient.*

A soundless refrain drifted through the air, circling Kai and Fen before swirling among those standing in the perimeter. The tender notes floated purposefully, searching for its intended listener. In the quiet of the circle, Hilly detected the faint notes of a lyrical song. Unsure of what she heard, she swiveled her head back and forth, attempting to identify the source.

Jake noticed her behavior and reached out, *Is everything okay?*

I hear a melody. Don't you?

Jake's eyes softened as he replied, *This one is just for you, my friend.*

The song grew louder and echoed in her head. It was a familiar nursery rhyme, a happy tune she often sang as a little girl while playing on the patio at The Nine Muses. At first, she mouthed the words, but soon, the lyrics tumbled out in a soft whisper. She closed her eyes reveling in the peaceful familiarity of the song. Tears trickled down her cheeks.

Kai and Fen observed their sister with curiosity.

Evidently, only Hilly could hear the melody, the tune to which she now swayed. *I think the Sentinel Boulder is directly sending her a message*, Kai shared mentally.

Jake responded, *It's another layer of security. This part of the ancient text is meant only for Hilly and nobody else.*

Establishing trust with Hilly through a song only she would know, the Sentinel beckoned her to perform her role in the ritual. She lifted her palms toward the boulder. As if in a trance, her mouth fell open and her body tingled. The earth spirit cautioned her, *This message is only for you, my child. Only you will understand the meaning. If you attempt to share the holy text, only static will issue from your mouth.*

She nodded. Hilly understood the importance of what she was about to receive. Satisfied with her response, the Sentinel shared his simple but powerful message:

> *I stand alone, one of four,*
> *United, the four will be one.*
> *The torch you carry provides the flame.*
> *The world awaits your fire!*

Sobbing, Hilly fell to her knees as a surge of emotions overwhelmed her. Her life finally had purpose. All she endured to this point—the murder of her birth family, her death and resurrection, waging battles, and developing her unique powers—occurred for a reason. These simple words taken directly from the Cererian Prophecy recognized Hilly as the heir to the Family of Fire, and it was by her hand that she would open the first of four markers that would re-establish worldwide peace.

Hilly carefully shifted her backpack to the ground. As she rifled through the contents, she mused about how it was a last-minute decision to bring her precious relic on the trip. Had the Sentinel planted the idea in her head to ensure his ritual was completed? If the boulder had intruded, his mind manipulation was akin to emotional assault: unexpected and unwarranted. Hilly had no proof. The occurrence may have been purely coincidental. For now, she'd continue without prejudice. She smiled, recognizing the item for which she searched.

Hilly cradled her family jewel, the one she received from Darrius during her Revelation at The Nine Muses. The iridescent crystal fit snugly in her hand. Five flawless sides created a point at the bottom and angled up to form a multi-faceted top. As Hilly presented it to the Sentinel Boulder, the jewel brightened as though a flame had been lit in its core. It hummed a greeting to the great earth spirit, and the boulder acknowledged the artifact with its own energetic song, a vibrato that began low and rose high until their songs merged into a beautiful melody.

You may approach and place your offering onto its seat of power, the Sentinel Boulder instructed.

Hilly nodded and took one step over the circle's protective boundary. She hesitated, concerned she might disrupt the circle's magic. But the crystal glowed even brighter, showering the area with illuminated diamonds. Encouraged by the jewel's response, she inched toward the boulder, holding the crystal at arm's length. Fen and Kai moved to the side, allowing their sister ample room to face the boulder.

Hilly gazed into the exposed chamber. The glittering selenite walls reminded her of the ice queen's home in the depths of Denali. She drew in a long breath and calmed her nerves. She gently maneuvered her jewel into the raised holder near the bottom of the recess.

As the crystal neared the receptacle, it was sucked from Hilly's grasp and pulled into the vessel with a loud whoosh. The consummation created a shockwave that burst outward from the rock, the ripples racing across the

Mat-Su Valley. Expanding upward and downward, vibrations reverberated all over the globe, delivering the Sentinel Boulder's telepathic message: *Fire has been restored, and the first marker is secure!*

The crystal's center glowed with a pale, yellow flame. A smile fluttered across Hilly's face. She felt giddy, yet humble, as she gazed upon the jewel—the power of her lost family, the Family of Fire. Mesmerized by the flickering flame, she hovered her palm in front of it. Though the fire burned bright, there was no heat, only coolness.

The obsidian slab growled. Hilly leapt back and fell. Her butt skidded along the dirt. Her eyes widened in alarm as the rock slowly crawled back in front of the selenite chamber, screeching along its tortuous path. The massive cracks, initially created when birthing the recess, magically healed as the shards of granite that had fallen to the ground rejoined the boulder and fused the wounds shut. The Sentinel sighed and released a subtle soundwave into the ether. The Guardian was whole once again.

The news about the first marker carried on rippling seismic waves, washed over the globe many times. The joyful words arrived on interdimensional vibrations audible only to magicians and nature's spirits. The nonmagical Folk might have felt a shiver but would hear nothing until their magical partners informed them of the great news.

The world rejoiced, daring to feel hope for the first time in a thousand years.

Chapter 17

Jake's Secret

A BLANKET OF STILLNESS descended upon the sacred circle. Witnesses to the ceremony dared not move or speak for fear of breaking the spell—sorcery achieved by the unlikely collaboration between an earth spirit and humans. Only by combining their unique powers could they manifest the high magic required to return the Crystal of Fire to its seat of power.

After one thousand years, the precious stone had finally returned home. Hidden deep within the impenetrable depths of the Sentinel Boulder, the powerful jewel would await the return of its sisters: the Crystal of Earth, the Crystal of Water and the Crystal of Air. Once those jewels are set upon their pedestals, humanity will once again live in complete harmony with all magical beings and nature's spirits.

Eager to share the ritual's details with their own worlds, the invisible spiritual ambassadors quickly departed, riding magical air currents that whisked them away to their dimensional realms. A sudden, chilled breeze was the only indication that the cloaked entities had left the circle.

Fen waited near the Sentinel, troubled by the boulder's monumental efforts during the ritual. She gently laid her hands upon the rough surface. An unexpected, warm vibration tingled up her arms, a sign that the Sentinel acknowledged her presence. Fen pressed her forehead to the granite in a way a child might pull her parent close for comfort. *Please accept my gift of healing,* she mentally conveyed.

I graciously accept your gift and I also wish to share one with you to honor your kindness, the Sentinel replied. With mutual respect and trust, Fen and the great earth spirit united their life forces. A stream of healing energy flowed from Fen's fingers into the boulder's granite body. In return, the Sentinel dispensed his symbol magic.

From this day forward, you will possess the gift of sight which allows you to decode the other markers hidden throughout the world.

Jake sidled up to Kai and Hilly as they observed Fen. He flashed a warm smile, crinkling the corners of his eyes. "The ritual was remarkable. Were you aware you could perform that kind of magic?"

"It's what we do," Kai remarked, feigning arrogance. He poked his nose in the air while dismissing Jake with a wave of his hand.

Hilly playfully punched him in the arm. "Come on, Kai. You have to admit you and Fen rocked it today." She added, "Pun intended." Kai groaned and lifted his eyes to the sky.

"You two are quite powerful," Jake agreed. His jaw muscles tightened as the words slithered from his pursed lips. He attempted to cloak his bitterness, but the Kemps' increasing powers troubled him. Their abilities grew at an alarming rate, and their magic was unlike anything he'd ever witnessed. After the ritual, it was apparent that the entire family followed a divine purpose, a path outlined by the ancients. While he was aware of the specific steps of the ceremony, the Cererian Prophecy had not prepared him for what the Kemps could achieve.

He calmed himself before turning to Hilly. "The quartz crystal you presented to the Sentinel was fascinating. How did it come into your possession?"

Hilly blushed. Talking about her loved ones, especially her birth family always made her anxious. She shifted her feet and stared at the ground mindlessly brushing the dirt from her pants. She stalled.

Noticing Hilly's uneasiness, Kai interjected, "The jewels of our family are personal, as you can imagine." Hilly beamed at Kai. He always knew how to save her from awkward situations. "They carry tremendous power. Hilly received hers while at The Nine Muses, after she was awakened to her memories and to her magic. It was salvaged from her family home before the Yfel Brethren could steal it." Kai paused and nodded toward Fen. "The rest of us—Fen, Chance and I—have the formidable task of locating our family crystals. They were hidden by our ancestors so the Yfel would not locate them and destroy them."

"Do you have clues on how to find these precious relics?" Jake pressed.

Kai barked a harsh laugh, immediately clasping a hand to his mouth in a vain attempt to muffle it after he realized Fen was still in deep meditation with the Sentinel. The resulting strangled cough caused her to stir but nothing more. Kai cleared his throat and whispered, "I have no fucking idea where to start. Our missions are to return to the land of our ancestors and search for the artifact."

"The world is vast. Where the hell do you begin?"

"At the beginning," Hilly chirped.

Kai frowned. "Thank you, Ms. Philosopher. That's absolutely no help at all."

"Yes, it is," she countered. "You just said it. The first place to start is to return to the land of your ancestors. You go back to the beginning. And, from there you retrace the steps of the family jewel."

Kai spread his arms wide like a circus ringmaster. "There we have it, ladies and gentlemen. It's an easy solution. I'll have my crystal by noon tomorrow."

Jake suppressed a laugh, but the remnants of a smile remained on his lips. Hilly glared at both of them. "You think I'm nuts?"

"Dear sister, your crystal is already in place. It's easy for you to dole out flimsy advice to those who don't know where to begin."

"Kai, you're infuriating." Hilly folded her arms and steeled her gaze on him. Kai glared back. Their faces twisted and contorted as they threw mental insults at each other.

Jake watched their drama as he shifted nervously. "Ahem," he interjected, "I have another question. What do they look like? How do you know what to look for?"

Kai broke the mental stand-off with Hilly. "Oh, that's easy. They all look like Hilly's crystal. The only difference is that they carry the flame of their elemental power."

"Tell me more," Jake urged, his voice rising with excitement.

"Mine is the Crystal of Air, it will emit a light blue flame. Fen's is the Crystal of Water and will glow in a deep purple hue, and Chance needs the Crystal of Earth, which will flicker with a green flame."

The idea of family jewels burning with magical elemental fire intrigued Jake. He recalled his grandfather's stories about his own ancestors and the star people who visited a millennium ago. Of all the legends, family crystals were never discussed.

"Kai, you're a member of the Family of Air as am I. Why is it that you're charged with finding this crystal? Why not someone else...like me?" Hilly squinted at her friend.

"Gee, I don't know. I'm just relaying what Darrius told us. We each have to discover our ancient roots and find the crystals. If you want that responsibility, Jake, I'd be happy to let you take it on. We'd have to get Darrius' approval first."

For a quick second Jake considered the offer. A challenging quest would be a perfect adventure, something that promised excitement in new lands and would test the limits of his magic. But he shook his head, "No, this is your mission. This is something you must achieve, and only you." He clamped a hand on Kai's shoulder. "I do appreciate the offer."

"Damn, I thought you might take this on, Jake," Kai teased. "I guess I'll go back to my original plan and go back to the beginning." He winked at Hilly.

"Ha! I knew you would see it my way," Hilly boasted.

"Hey, Hilly," Kai began, "Why did you bring the family jewel to the lupine meadow? How did you know you would need it? Or was that dumb luck?"

"I was packing for our trip and the thought entered my mind. I dismissed it at first, but it kept creeping back in. Trusting my intuition has always been the right move, so I removed the jewel from the safe and packed it carefully in my backpack." Hilly paused, gently biting her lip. "Of course, I worried something would happen to the jewel. That was an incredible burden to bear by myself. I wanted to tell someone, but my protective instincts told me to remain quiet."

"The Sentinel orchestrated the entire event. I wouldn't be surprised if he planted the seed in your mind. You're lucky that's all he planted," Jake said, his lips curved into a wry smile.

Hilly frowned. "I don't like entities manipulating my mind," she complained through clenched teeth. "If they can implant their thoughts into my brain, what else can they make me do?" The trio quieted. Their actions were dictated by the Cererian Prophecy—a fact they had come to accept. Hilly shuddered. "I feel like a game piece on a huge chessboard somewhere in the universe."

As a disciple to the ancient text, Jake was more concerned about *why* he would be manipulated, and less by whom. Although he was privy to many passages of the Prophecy, his vision was limited, especially when it concerned his own involvement. He assessed the recent series of events. If this tremendous power was assigned to them by the Cererian Prophecy, maybe his suspicions were true that the Kemps actually descended from the star people who visited Earth a millennium ago.

Kai snapped his fingers, jolting Hilly and Jake from their musings. "I just thought of something...something Darrius didn't mention. Not only do we need to find the family jewels, but we also have to locate the sacred receptacles in which the crystal will reside." Kai twisted his face in disgust. "How the hell am I supposed to do that?"

"Watch your mouth, Kai," Fen admonished as she stepped into the circle with the others. "Try to maintain a little decorum, at least until we leave the lupine meadow." She flashed an exaggerated smile to temper her comment. "But you ask a very good question. It's hard enough to locate the crystals, but how can we find the sacred guardians like the Sentinel Boulder? They could be scattered anywhere in the world."

"Maybe I can help," Jake offered. "You might say the Sentinel and I are good friends. I suggest I connect with the great spirit to see if he can share information on the other guardians."

Jake approached the large rock, pressed his hands together at heart center, and bowed to the earth spirit. He inhaled a deep, cleansing breath and slowly exhaled through pursed lips. After performing the breathing ritual three times, he closed his eyes and very slowly slipped into a meditative state.

His eyes remained shut as he approached the Sentinel. Jake walked forward with his arms outstretched until his palms connected with the rocky surface. Once joined, an intense vibration rocketed through his hands and up his arms until it snaked through his brain, coming to rest in his frontal lobe. His forehead gently pulsed as his energy merged with the Sentinel's.

What do you seek, my son? The Sentinel's voice was familiar and kind.

Father... Jake paused. Wasting his precious time with flimsy reasons would only anger him, resulting in admonishment, or worse, banishment. Doubt crept into Jake's mind. What if the Cererian Prophecy had purposely veiled the locations of the other guardians? Perhaps the Kemps were meant to endure hardships in order to locate the sacred receptacles. Asking this question could be risky or viewed as interference in matters that didn't concern him. But, if he could aide his friends through a simple request, he was willing to take that chance.

He continued. *Father, long ago you entrusted me with the word of the ancients. I am the custodian of their text and songs, yet I'm confused as to how I can better serve the Cererian Prophecy and its servants, the Kemps. If they are to complete their mission in restoring their family crystals into the sacred vessels, where do they begin? How do they locate the jewels and find the remaining guardians?*

Jake paused. A shudder raced up his spine. Did he say too much? Did he appear demanding? The Sentinel owed him nothing and could reply with silence, which would be harder to bear than words of denial.

Moments passed. Too much time. Visions of retribution raced through his mind with each silent minute. Jake worried he had pushed his privilege too far and asked for too much. He was resigned to defeat and prepared to walk away.

The Sentinel sighed—a low groan echoed up from the dirt as though the rock spoke from its soul residing ten feet below the surface. *My son, long ago I entrusted you with the sacred words and the secrets of the ancients. I chose you because of all the magical humans roaming the earth, your life force pulsed with a pure energy unlike any other person. I know you have struggled finding your way in the world, but I encourage patience right now. Your place in the hierarchy will soon be revealed.*

Hierarchy? This was the first time he had heard that reference, and it puzzled him.

Before he could ask a question, the Sentinel continued, *You are the preserver of the holy word. It is your mission to ensure the Cererian Prophecy is followed as it is preordained. This is an overwhelming responsibility for one individual. As such, the ancients were wise in selecting others who would assist you, and you can aide them, as you each follow your journeys.*

Jake trembled. Hearing the Sentinel acknowledge his importance in the magical community validated his existence, something he had desired for so long. He dared to ask another question: *Father, are the Kemps these souls you reference?*

The boulder shifted. Granite dust sprayed the ground.

Yes. Your future and those of the Kemps are woven together. Your lives are like the individual filaments that comprise a length of rope. Together you create a strong presence but divided your power unravels and eventually snaps.

Thank you, father. Right now, I want to assist the Kemps in locating the other guardians. Emboldened by being validated, Jake pressed for one more question.

To where should they travel, and for what should they search?

Several tense moments passed, but Jake didn't worry as before. He remained calm and patient.

The words I must speak can only be shared in the ether and not on the physical plain. Join me in the astral realm, and I will share this information with you face to face. Telepathy is easily invaded by tricksters even when we deploy our protection barriers.

Agreed, Father. Jake descended further into his meditative trance until his heart rate and breaths were imperceptible. His soul lifted into the ether, escaping the shell of his body, which slumped against the hard rock as though he had chosen to nap.

Jake's spirit drifted upward, feeling weightless with all his burdens remaining in the physical realm. He hovered almost fifteen feet above the great boulder. He scanned the landscape, looking for the Sentinel. A few yards away, hovered a human form—a light-skinned man with chiseled features and sandy brown hair. Dark, indigo eyes sat above a sharp nose that plunged down to a ginger mustache upon his upper lip.

Jake gasped. This person was familiar...*very* familiar.

The Sentinel appeared as a duplicate of Jake's grandfather as a younger man of thirty. He even wore similar clothes: faded denim jeans, a size too big, with the legs puddled over dark brown work boots. On top, he wore a red flannel shirt striped with thin black lines. They stared at each other. A shiver spiraled down Jake's spine. The uncanny likeness to his grandfather should have comforted him, but he couldn't avoid feeling a little creeped out by the image.

The Sentinel sensed his trepidation and chuckled.

A warm smile spread across the man's face. "Come to me, my son." The Sentinel held out a hand and ushered Jake to step closer.

Jake hesitated. The specter before him was familiar but didn't match the image Jake had concocted in his mind for a powerful earth spirit. "Is that you, Father?" he squeaked in a timid, childlike voice.

"Don't be afraid, Jake. You have fought Yfel soldiers, dragons, and beasts. Surely, you do not fear me. I don't possess a physical form, so I assumed this likeness of somebody familiar to you, someone you love."

The Sentinel lifted a hand and directed a stream of soft, white light toward Jake. The swift-moving current encompassed him, surrounding him in a shroud of energy. Jake's senses thickened, and the Sentinel's voice lowered to a garbled murmur as though they had plunged underwater. Jake's eyes blurred, causing the image standing before him to stretch and compress like a twisted reflection in a carnival mirror.

"Relax. Do not fight my energy. This is a battle you will never win. I've deployed an impenetrable layer around you, so we can talk freely." Jake's heart hammered, and he panted in halting breaths. His head swam with vertigo, and he feared passing out. But he had to push through his fear and regain control of his emotions, or he would lose the opportunity to help his friends.

Closing his eyes, he envisioned a peaceful scene: the cockpit of Lola. Whenever he was stressed, flying his plane over the waterways calmed his mind. The steady hum of Lola's engines and the mesmerizing effects of the deep blue waters in the Bering Straits were more effective in calming him than four shots of whiskey.

Jake purged his lungs of stale air and opened his eyes. The Sentinel stood several feet away, observing him with the kind eyes of his grandfather. Jake's eyes widened as he scanned the bright space they occupied. The vastness appeared as an illuminated room, but there were no walls, nor floor, nor ceiling. Just intense white light that glowed all around them. The brightness pulsed as if alive but did not hurt his eyes. There was an insatiable desire to relax and be at peace. Jake wondered if this was the vision seen by those who die and cross the veil.

"I see in your eyes that you struggle to determine where we are." The Sentinel smiled and threw his arms wide. "You are standing within my aura."

Jake followed the entity's movements. A mix of awe and extreme delight flashed through Jake's eyes. He glanced around then down and then upward, puzzled by the spectacle. "Am I really here?"

The Sentinel chuckled a deep, rich laugh. In his human form, the hearty laugh rang pleasant and echoed in the space. "It is really you. Your physical body is still anchored to the earthly plain, and your hands are still connected with my granite skin." The magical entity observed Jake as he took tentative steps forward, obviously concerned he may fall though the ambiguous floor. Examining the unusual room, a sensation of completeness rushed through his core. Was this nirvana? Tears moistened his eyes as he realized the extreme privilege that was extended to him, to stand with a sacred entity within its aura and to be this close to the Sentinel's soul.

"I have no words, Father. I am in complete amazement at your powers."

"Aw, there's that word again. I detect that is the root of your concern, isn't it, my son? The powers wielded by some, and not others." Jake flinched. Did the Sentinel overhear his earlier conversation with Kai regarding the Crystal of Air? Or had he sensed his insecurity about his abilities?

"I only wish to help my friends. I've grown close to the Kemps and worry about how they will complete their journeys. Now that the Crystal of Fire has been seated, it is important that we find the other jewels and restore them to their pedestals so the world can be at peace once again."

The Sentinel stroked his chin. A behavior Jake's grandfather did often when he brooded over something important. The entity mimicked his grandfather in appearance and mannerisms. These considerations caused Jake to be more at ease in the spirit's presence. The two evaluated each other. The Sentinel mused about Jake's intentions, and Jake pondered about his relationship with the entity. He always reminded Hilly to be patient, but now he wanted all the answers and wanted them now. After forty-eight years, he deserved to have more answers about his purpose.

The entity broke the silence. "There's something you should know, Jake."

He called me by my name. He's never done that before. Jake trembled, anticipating the rest of the message.

"Your lineage is marked by shamans and warriors stretching back a thousand years. Each child born into the Pierson clan arrived with a clear purpose and with the magical abilities to fly and command the beasts of the air. There have been dark days in the past, and I fear the skies will darken again in the near future."

Jake recalled when the Yfel invaded their town, ferreting out the magical populations and killing as many as they could while consuming their magic. He had lost his dear Bethany during one vicious raid. His mood turned dark, recalling the moment he lost the love of his life. The Sentinel's message carried ominous overtones, and Jake tensed.

The Sentinel sensed Jake's uneasiness and unexpectedly placed a hand on his shoulder. A shiver coursed through Jake's body, goosebumps pimpled on his arms, and the hair on the back of his neck popped to attention.

"Be at ease, Jake. The moment has arrived for you to understand more about your family. Your understanding is critical for you to move forward on your journey." The old man's eyes watered and Jake realized that the Sentinel struggled with the information he was about to share. He patted the entity's hand, reassuring him just as much as the old man was comforting him. When the Sentinel smiled, the brightness of the room intensified.

"When you were five, your mother succumbed to the great sickness that had decimated much of the Folk population. Even today, the cause has not been determined, but it was clear that magicians were safe from its effects."

Jake didn't remember much about his parents. Blurry mental images of a fair-haired woman with bright-blue eyes drifted through his brain. Her hair and clothes smelled pleasantly of sandalwood. Oddly, he couldn't remember his father at all. His grandparents raised him and his sisters. Those were the only details his child mind could bring forward from the past.

"Your father, Ryan, was a strong magician, but his power could not save his beloved wife. After her death, there was no time for mourning. You and your five sisters depended on your father for survival. Despite the help of other families enduring tragedies from the plague, your father's mental health faltered. Depression consumed him, and he grew bitter and outraged."

The old man moved away from Jake and sat down on an illuminated seat which melted into the bright walls of the room. He lifted a leg and crossed it over the other. A warm, generous smile filled his face and he continued, "Ryan needed help and decided that assistance would come in the form of the Yfel Brethren."

Jake dropped his head. He felt embarrassed that a family member would associate with evil Cererians. "What else?" Jake croaked in a husky tone. A hitch in his breath betrayed his emotions.

The Sentinel admired Jake's fortitude and continued, "In exchange for extreme powers and abundance of food and riches, he betrayed the lives of his friends, the magicians for whom the Yfel thirsted. Your grandfather witnessed the pact with the Brethren and acted quickly.

"He warned the other magical families to flee and to cloak their whereabouts so the Yfel would not be able to track them. He spirited you and your sisters away, hiding you within the protection of the lupine meadow. He implored Denali to hide his family, and she rewarded his devotion by layering your bodies with a fine coating of cloaking snow. To protect you and your sisters from the trauma, your grandfather performed mesmerizing magic so you would think your mother and father had *both* died in the plague."

The truth pulled old memories to the front of Jake's brain. Snatches of images flickered by of a robust man who allowed Jake to travel with him in his aircraft; a happy family man who dressed as Santa every Christmas; a compassionate man who cared for his wife as she withered away from consumption. His father represented all the qualities Jake had adopted for himself—trustworthy, committed, determined, and loving. But desperation and a hunger for power twisted his father into a man of betrayal. Somewhere on this planet, Ryan Pierson ran with the Yfel, indulging his thirst for magic and power.

Jake's hands clenched into fists, and his fingers turned white. The truth angered him, but the revelation renewed his determination to help his friends. He was not like his father. No, he would continue following the sacred path his grandfather paved decades ago.

"Do you, too, thirst for the power of others as your father did so long ago? Do you desire to be more than what you are?" The question punched Jake in the gut. He wasn't entirely sure how to answer. Recently, he had been jealous of the Kemp's increasing powers. He had questioned his purpose and his role in the magical community. Answering this question was complicated, so he posed one of his own.

"I had heard that the firewalkers were all killed. Is that true?"

The Sentinel tilted his head. "The firewalkers were the strongest magicians in the clans, so they stayed to fight, hoping they would easily defeat the Yfel." The old man's eyes darkened. "They were not prepared for the powers Stygian and his followers had amassed through the slaughter of magicians before them. Feasting on the dead's magic strengthened their own abilities. The firewalkers fell within thirty minutes while Ryan stood nearby, witnessing the savagery, an order from Stygian himself."

"The elders spoke of a baby escaping the massacre. Are their words true?" Jake pressed.

The old man's eyes crinkled; a faint smile returned to his lips. "A female child was the only survivor. She was spirited away by Prasad, a gentle Cererian."

Jake fidgeted, fighting the impulse to ask the question that lingered on his lips. But he had to know. "Father, is Hilly the firewalker child who was saved that day?"

The old man stood and stretched his hands high, bending first right and then left, working out the kinks of sitting too long. He took several steps toward Jake and peered into his eyes. His brows tilted, and his lips thinned as he considered his response. When he spoke, it was in a firm, gentle tone, "Jake, I cannot say yes to your question. I have shared with you all that you were intended to receive."

Jake grimaced. His first reaction was frustration. He tired of half-truths and riddles from the spiritual entities he encountered. The men didn't speak for several minutes. The Sentinel allowed Jake ample time to process the words he shared, and those he didn't. Jake knew the Cererian Prophecy forbade the Sentinel from sharing more with him. But it seemed his simple question could be answered. He bit his lower lip and considered rephrasing and posing the question again.

As if the great spirit sensed his every thought, he spoke, "Now that I've shared all that I intend on your past, I believe you wanted to find out about the future—not for yourself, but for your friends, the Kemps."

Jake sighed. The old man's words felt like a heavy door being slammed in his face. He narrowed his eyes at the old man who returned his stare with bright, youthful eyes which belied the age of the spiritual entity. Jake weighed his options, but now was not the time to push his luck. Now was the time to help his friends and get the answers he needed. "Yes, Father, my friends have a most difficult task to locate not just their family jewels, but they must also locate their sacred guardians.

"Darrius provided clues for finding the crystals but gave no indication on how to locate the sacred receptacles. Is that something you can share with me?" Jake held his breath, hoping he had not asked for too much. After the Sentinel had abruptly ended the conversation about Hilly, he worried he may have compromised receiving additional information.

"You're a good friend," the old man began. "I admire your courage at making the request on behalf of the Kemps. They are very powerful magicians, and your place among them is warranted. The locations I share with you, are *only* for you. So secretive are their homes that if others learned of their whereabouts, it could endanger them and impact the future of the world. If I share this information with you, you must be prepared to accompany the Kemps on their quests, for only you will be able to lead each individual to their sacred guardian. This is a huge undertaking, and you should consider the consequences if you consent."

The Sentinel had been kind in providing information about his family. He had always been available when needed and validated Jake's very existence in the community of magicians. Jake grinned.

The old man squinted, confused by his reaction. "Did I say something amusing?"

"No, Father, the situation is comical. Earlier today, Kai offered to let me undertake his quest. I wanted to, badly, so I could experience new lands and utilize my powers. I refused because it was his journey to make."

"I see," the old man said, stroking his chin.

"But now, you're giving me that same opportunity to join him on his quest. So, you see, I'll still be a part of their journeys while embarking on my own."

The old man nodded. "Yes, yes, I see. I'm extremely proud of your decision. You are a great friend to the Kemps and an extraordinary warrior. They will benefit greatly from your companionship." The old man stepped closer and the brightness intensified as he stopped inches from Jake. "Now, I will share the locations of the remaining guardians. Remember what I tell you and never speak to another about these locations. Do you swear it?"

Jake's pride swelled. The old man's words landed on his heart as though his own grandfather had uttered them. He was proud of his heritage, but the truth about his father was a stain on the family, a blemish that must be removed. He had to prove the Piersons were an honorable family.

Like a warrior preparing for battle, Jake squared his shoulders and straightened his back before replying, "Yes, Father, I swear."

Chapter 18

The Black Beast Returns

"KAI, YOU CAN'T BE serious. Jeff will kill both of us!" Hilly paced in front of the hangar at Pierson Express Flights stopping just briefly to glare at her brother before stomping off in the opposite direction.

"Did you think I was going to travel all this way and not visit Mount Shasta? That would be inconsiderate. After all, Shasta's spirit visited me on the plane and invited me." Kai's face softened, the corners of his mouth drawing downward in a mock pout. "What kind of son would I be if I didn't visit my earth mother?"

"Did you know yesterday?" Hilly whirled and glared at him with her hands on her hips.

Kai's lips thinned, and he glanced away, avoiding her gaze.

"Kai? Did you know yesterday after the ceremony at the Sentinel?"

Kai held his hands up in surrender. "I decided the same day Shasta visited me."

"Argh!" Hilly huffed and stormed away.

"But, Hilly..." Kai's voice trailed off as he chased after her.

Escaping the drama, Fen and Jake distanced themselves and walked further out onto the tarmac. "When those two get together it's like lighting a match and throwing it into a bag of fireworks." Jake grinned at the mental image, imagining who would win that particular contest. "Come on, Fen, let me introduce you to someone special." Jake lightly touched Fen's arm and guided her to the gleaming single-engine plane affectionately known as Lola.

"Oh my, her energy is staggering." Fen raised her hands in front of her body and closed her eyes. The vision drifting through her mind materialized as a wave of yellow energy, streaming outward from the plane like rays of sunshine. Gesturing toward the aircraft, Fen asked, "Would Lola mind if I touched her?"

"Go ahead. I can tell she likes you." Jake recalled the moment when Hilly first met Lola and also requested to connect with the aircraft and unite their souls. Fen brushed her fingertips along the fuselage starting at the wing and tracing toward the propeller. Along the way, she'd stop, cock her head sideways as though listening to an inaudible message, and then she'd continue along the metal skin.

As she neared the cockpit, a low hum arose from the plane and the vibrations raced up her arms. "That tickles," she giggled.

"Lola really likes you," Jake beamed. "She can sense your magic, and your kindness." He gazed at Fen with gentle eyes. Fen blushed and turned away. She held her hand to her chest. Her heart galloped under her fingertips. She was unsure if her reaction was from the connection to Lola or from Jake's intense stare.

Fen chirped, "Such a beautiful spirit. I've never seen a familiar this size before. I'm more accustomed to smaller spirits that fit in one's hand like a cat or a broom."

Jake lightly stroked Lola's body. "She is beautiful. She has saved my life more than once. I don't know what I would do without her."

Hilly's voice abruptly pierced the air as she pushed between Jake and Fen. "Kai is driving me crazy!"

Fen winced, upset at the harsh intrusion shattering her intimate chat with Jake. She wheeled to face her sister and barked, "Hilly, if you're still fighting with Kai, please take your anger back to him. Jake and I were having a very pleasant conversation." Fen forced a weak smile at Jake.

"Don't listen to her!" Kai yelled as he strode up to the group, his arms flailing with each word. Fen pursed her lips. Jake sauntered to the other side of the aircraft, pretending to clean Lola's wings while he eavesdropped on their conversation.

Fen held up her hands. "Shh, please speak quietly. You're giving me a headache."

"Kai wants to go to Mount Shasta," Hilly whined.

"What's wrong with that?" Fen folded her hands in front of her, a calming technique she adopted from Darrius and Prasad.

"Well, he *can't* go because I promised Jeff he'd be back in a week!"

"You don't need to yell at me, Hilly. I'm standing right in front of you." Fen interlaced her fingers and touched her chin as she turned toward Kai. She continued in a steady, calm tone, "How long would it take for you to go to Mount Shasta and accomplish what you need to do?"

"Finally! A voice of reason," Kai taunted as he squinted at Hilly. "At the most two days."

"Come on, Kai, we all know you take double the time as everyone else. Bottom line, I promised Jeff, and so did you," Hilly said.

"That's not true!" Kai screamed inches from Hilly face. The siblings squared off, their hands clenched and ready for battle. Balls of emotional energy shot outward, and Fen dodged the invisible bullets as they whizzed past her head.

Fen maneuvered near the combatants and wriggled between them. She pushed a hand toward each sibling and enlarged the neutral zone. In a matter of seconds, both Kai and Hilly quieted. Their hands relaxed, the flurry of energetic missiles ceased, and their eyelids drooped as they entered a drowsy state.

Hidden from view, Jake watched from the other side of Lola. As Fen directed her energy at Kai and Hilly, he saw a light green glow drift from Fen's fingers as though she sprinkled a luminescent dust on her siblings.

Lowering her hands, Fen whispered, "Now that I have your attention, we will discuss this matter like adults, meaning we don't scream, we don't call each other names, and we work toward a peaceful solution. Agreed?"

Kai's mouth had fallen open and a viscous drop of drool formed in the corner. He slurred, "What did you do Fenny? Did you cast a spell?"

Hilly raked her hair with her fingers like a drunkard attempting to push the sleepiness away. "Yeah, Fen, what sorcery is this?"

"My name does mean Guardian of Peace. This is a little trick I learned after our Revelations at The Nine Muses. I can change the energy in a space by raising my hand and channeling my magic. Now, answer me, do you agree to the terms?"

Kai and Hilly obediently nodded in agreement, but one could argue they really didn't have any recourse but to accept their sister's wishes. Fen dropped her hands, breaking the magical stream feeding into her siblings. Slowly the fog lifted. But they had changed.

That moment spent in a forced stupor had altered their mood, changed their behavior, and removed their anger. Fen stepped away, allowing space between Kai and Hilly. The siblings stared at each other for several moments before Kai sobbed, "I'm sorry, Hilly. I didn't mean to yell at you, but it's important for me to go to Mount Shasta. There's this inexplicable urge to get there as soon as possible."

Hilly's eyes moistened as she listened to the emotion in her brother's voice. "Believe me, I understand what you're feeling. That's how I felt about going to Denali. I want you to go on your quest, but I feel bad about our promise to Jeff."

"Hon, we haven't broken any promise yet. I can go to Shasta and be back in plenty of time."

"Your definition of 'plenty of time' is screwed up. You only have two days." Hilly grimaced at her brother.

"We're wasting time standing around yammering." Kai hailed Jake, visible only by his boots jutting underneath the aircraft. "Jake, what's the fastest way to get to Mount Shasta?"

Jake hung his head and sighed. No sense in prolonging the inevitable. "I would suggest Lola since she's reliable and fast. But at her speed, you're looking at a ten-hour flight. So, I think your best bet is—"

Kai cut him off, "Ten hours! That's a hell of a long time to be in the air!"

Hilly snorted. "Kai, you need to live up to your family gift one day. How can you be a descendant of the Family of Air and still struggle getting on planes? You know you can literally fly, right?"

"One day, I'll face that fear, but today..." He grabbed Hilly around her waist and lifted her up. "Let's see how well you fly, Hilly." He twirled her around as she giggled uncontrollably. After several passes, he finally set her on the tarmac. Breathless, they clung to each other. "Man, I'm out of shape."

Jake cleared his throat. "What I was going to say was that your best bet is to travel through a portal. Hilly can get us to Shasta with a flick of her wrist."

"Now, you're speaking my language." Kai hugged Hilly. "I'm ready. Let's go now."

Jake held up his hand. "Not yet. Promise your sisters you'll be careful, and that you'll come back as promised."

Kai's lower lip drooped in an exaggerated pout as he turned to Fen and Hilly. "I promise."

"Promise what?" Jake pressed.

Kai's eyes shot up to the sky as he exhaled loudly and dramatically. "Good grief, I promise I'll be careful and will come back as promised." Grimacing at Jake, he pouted. "There, can we go now?"

Jake chuckled and laugh lines creased around his eyes. "Oh boy, Kai. I can see you're going to be a handful on this trip"

"You'll be the lucky one to find out," Kai flirted.

Fen and Hilly glanced at each other as they mentally messaged, *One problem at a time, one problem at a time.*

Jake turned to Fen, "Sammy will be here soon to take you to the airport." Jake peered into the distance, cupping his hand above his eyes. "I see blue smoke, I think he's on his way."

"Yippee," Fen lied, her eyes clouding with disappointment.

Jake added, "I look forward to catching up with you later, Fen."

"What do you mean you'll catch up with each other later?" Hilly faced them, her brows angled with deep concern.

Fen gently touched Hilly's arm. "Don't worry. Jake and I are sharing notes on the other guardians in the world. So I can make plans for travel."

"Oh." Hilly relaxed. "Of course, of course, I knew that. Wait, when are *you* traveling?"

"Why all these questions?" Jake asked. "We're not sure yet. The Sentinel Boulder shared the locations of the other three guardians with me, but, as an extra layer of security, I'm not able to tell others about their whereabouts. I can't even write the information down. You can see how frustrating it can be to forge a plan."

"I see," Hilly said. "So, only you, Fen, and Kai will go in search of the guardians?"

"Sometimes, Hilly, you're like a squeaky-clean window. I can see right through you. Of course, you're coming on the trip, and so is Chance. It will be a family affair," Jake soothed.

"Chance too? Cool. I'm looking forward to that."

"Hello, Hilly? Anybody?" Kai's voice warbled into the conversation. "Remember, we're on the clock, and we need to get to Shasta. Chop, chop. Let's get portaling, or whatever you do."

Hilly shook her head. "Kai you're exasperating. It's all about you. You, you, you." She trudged off to join her brother.

Fen watched her sister walk further away before speaking. "Jake, be careful of the promises you make to Hilly. Only those who are instrumental to the ritual are allowed to be in attendance."

"I know, Fen. I couldn't break her heart. She felt excluded. Besides, a lot can happen between now and then." Jake winked at Fen and grinned. His stunning white teeth sparkled in the sunlight. Jake's smile could melt a solid block of ice, reducing it to a mere puddle. Fen's stomach was that quivering pool at the moment. Butterflies fluttered as she gazed into Jake's eyes. An irresistible pull prevented her from glancing away. Her instincts screamed a warning.

Jake leaned closer, lightly brushing against Fen's arm. An unwelcome, eerie sensation raced along her skin. Jake's eyes flashed a vivid violet before returning to an icy blue. His eyes pulsed again. Vertigo ensnared Fen causing her world to tilt and twirl as she desperately tried to keep her balance.

She lost the battle. Her knees buckled.

Jake encircled her waist and gripped her hand. "Are you okay, Fen? You almost tumbled."

She drew in a lingering breath inhaling his scent as he leaned into her body.

Something wasn't right. Why did she feel so weak? Her voices screamed, demanding she escape and run away. She slumped into his arms, and her head fell onto his shoulder. "I'm fine, Jake. It's warmer than I anticipated. I need a little bit of a rest."

Jake guided her to a nearby bench. "Sure, Fen, anything you need. I'll sit with you until Sammy arrives." Fen struggled to lift her head.

The perfect smile returned to Jake's face. Fen's world tilted again as his eyes pulsed a third time. "Jake..." She couldn't finish her sentence. The words felt thick on her tongue. She squeezed her eyes hoping to break the connection with his gaze. Her world tilted back and forth as she descended into an inky void.

Unable to move, Fen tensed as a dark vision entered her mind.

A black beast—a winged dragon—flew toward her. It screeched, releasing a foul concoction of death and putridness. The fetid, warm breath washed over her, triggering an urge to vomit. She fought to shield her face from the assault, but her hands lay paralyzed by her side. Mute and immobilized, she watched the vile creature draw near as terror raced up from the depths of her soul.

Another screech pierced the air as the beast lunged for her, its teeth snapping at her neck.

Chapter 19

Ominous Warning

"FEN! WAKE UP!" HILLY screamed.

Fen lay unresponsive on the tarmac. Old Val's rusty bumper hovered inches from her throat.

"She's having a seizure!" Kai yelled as he gripped her arms. Jake and Hilly each held a leg as Fen thrashed beneath them. Her teeth and hands spasmed uncontrollably, clenching and relaxing repeatedly.

Worry edged into Jake's voice, "She walked right out in front of Sammy. One minute she was talking to me, and the next she marched directly into the path of Old Val."

"It wasn't my fault," Sammy babbled as he hopped around the group poking at Fen. "I didn't hit her." He jabbed her again like he was prodding a large log in a fire.

"Stop that!" Hilly yelled as she snatched Sammy's finger.

"Ow, Miss Hilly, that hurts!"

"Damn, Sammy. I'm sorry. I'm just worried about Fen."

Fen's eyes fluttered open. "Fen? Fenny? Are you okay?" Kai softly stroked her cheek. "Hi, baby girl, are you with us?"

Fen's eyes lolled in their sockets before rolling toward Kai who hovered inches from her face. She squeaked a hoarse whisper, "Kai? Where am I? I was with Jake..."

"It's okay, Fenny. Take it easy." Kai guided Fen to a sitting position. Though most of her muscles had relaxed, her fingers still twisted as though she grabbed something."

"The beast!" she screamed. Fen's eyes widened in terror as she pushed into Kai, clutching his arm. Wild-eyed, she scanned the faces around her until she found her sister. Fen yanked Hilly close, and her mouth twisted, but she said nothing as though the words were shards of glass tearing at her tongue.

With a final burst of energy, Fen finally spit it out, "Hilly, the dragon is back!"

A stillness descended over the group. An absence of sound so intense that a butterfly's wing beat would have sounded like cymbals clashing. Sammy realized the seriousness of the situation and quieted, his eyes darting from person to person.

Several tense moments passed before Fen spoke. "Kai, help me to my feet, please." Fen didn't relish being the center of attention nor was the uneven concrete under her body a comfortable place to remain for very long. As Kai steadied her from behind, Fen rose on unsure feet.

She tipped sideways, but Jake caught her arm and eased her back into Kai's embrace. She flinched from Jake's touch as though he had branded her with a searing iron. She huddled against Kai while glowering at Jake.

Fen's behavior was troubling. Deep wrinkles of concern etched into Jake's forehead. He looked to the others and shrugged. He had no explanation for Fen's reaction.

Hilly mentally messaged him, *What was that all about?*

I have no fucking idea. Jake peeked at Fen who recoiled into Kai's arms. *We were just talking. I don't know why she's so afraid of me now.*

Stay here while Kai and I take Fen to get some water.

Jake nodded. His eyes darkened with concern. *Honest. I didn't do anything.*

"Fen, let's go into the shade and get some water." Hilly gently took one elbow while Kai steadied the other one. Together the siblings ambled into the gaping maw of the old hangar. The temperature in the metal building dipped almost fifteen degrees, a welcome relief from the assault of the summer sun. Kai lowered Fen to a metal folding chair and massaged her shoulders, comforting her. Hilly trotted to the cooler in the office. She quickly returned with water. "Here you go, Fen. Sip this."

Fen dismissed her with a weak wave of her hand. "I need something stronger."

"What do you mean?"

"I need something that will give me an extra kick in the ass. I need some alcohol. Kai, I know you have one of those tiny vodka bottles in your pocket. Would you indulge me?" Fen peered at her brother through bloodshot eyes, her lips drawn down in a pathetic pout.

Kai shook his head. A corner of his mouth jerked upward in a mock sneer. "Fen, could you look more pitiful?" He retrieved the nips from inside his jacket and held it aloft. "If anyone is deserving of this sacrifice, it is you. Look, it's not even open yet." A sharp *snap* echoed in the cavernous hanger as he twisted the cap and dangled the bottle in front of her.

She grabbed at it and sucked the contents dry in a matter of seconds. Then swiped her hand across her mouth. "Aww, much better." Kai and Hilly gawked. Mild-mannered Fen. The Guardian of Peace, Fen. Who knew she could guzzle with the best of them?

"Damn, Fen, I'm impressed," Kai said, patting her back.

The sudden rush of alcohol teased Fen's senses. She leaned toward Kai, but inadvertently lurched headfirst into his stomach, barely missing his nether regions. "Okay, Fenny, I think you better sit back and let the buzz settle." Kai gently eased her back into the chair.

Fen's head lolled back and her sleepy eyes closed while a goofy smile danced across her face. Several moments passed. "Is she asleep?" Hilly asked. But as the words left her mouth, Fen's head jerked forward, surprising everyone.

Her eyes were still closed, but Fen spoke in a clear, articulate tone, "Little known fact about your sister. I used to drink vodka martinis with Lance at the end of the workday, and sometimes on the weekend!" She giggled.

Fen abruptly leaned back in the chair with a bemused grin frozen on her face.

Jake observed the Kemps from the tarmac. Something bothered him. Every hair on his body stiffened with alarm, and he knew from experience to never ignore his instincts.

His grandfather used to advise while they hunted in the Alaskan wilds, *When your fur is up, you can bet your ass you're being stalked by something wearing fur.*

Jake sensed a predator in their midst.

Despite the accusing glare Fen threw at him earlier, he needed to talk to her. He had to ask for more details about what happened. Why was she suddenly afraid of him?

The distinct clunkity clunk of Jake's boot heels echoed inside the building as he entered the hangar. Kai casually looked up, not surprised by his appearance, but Hilly frowned. She had wanted to sort things out with her sister, make things right before bringing Jake back into the mix. Before Hilly could stop Jake, Fen's eyes fluttered open.

"I thought I sensed trouble," she hissed. She narrowed her eyes. The muscles in her face tensed, and her jaw muscles bulged as though she gnawed on a grisly bone.

Jake held his hands up, palms facing Fen. He hoped to ease the tension by being submissive, by showing Fen he meant no harm. In a soft, soothing tone, he asked "What happened? You and I were talking by Lola, and your face suddenly went blank. Then you turned and walked away from me as though someone lured you away."

"Liar!" Fen lunged from the chair. Her index finger crooked in his face like a meat cleaver poised to halve his face in two. "I felt faint, and you helped me to a bench where you hypnotized me." Fen wheeled around to point at the bench. "It's over there..." Her words trailed off. There was no bench, only the hanger and Lola. Fen stumbled around the tarmac. "It's around here somewhere. It must be."

"Fen, there is no bench," Jake reasoned as he swept the area with his arms. He shot a glance toward Hilly. His brows furrowed. Something was really wrong.

"No, there *was* a bench and you walked me to it." Angry energy eked from Fen's pores as she confronted Jake. Mere inches separated them as she jabbed her finger into his chest with every word. "Your eyes pulsed different colors, and then my legs buckled—"

Fen stopped talking. She glanced at Hilly and Kai. Their faces wore masks of sadness and fear. She turned back to Jake, her finger still lingered on his shirt where she had poked him. He gazed at her with a peaceful calm.

Fen stared at the ground. She needed a new canvas on which to focus her attention. Was it all a dream? Did she imagine the last few moments of her life? She replayed the recent events in her mind, unaware that her fingers twitched by her side as if by staying in motion they could pull the answer from the air. She drew in a sharp breath and held it. She knew exactly what happened.

Fen slowly raised her head. Her eyes no longer flickered with the shadows of doubt. Now they glowed with the brightness of confidence. "It was a vision," she proclaimed. Months had passed since her last premonition, which had occurred at The Nine Muses. The circumstances were very similar in which her reality shifted and mutated into ugliness. As with her experience at the family estate, this recent snapshot of the future brought foreboding.

She whirled and grabbed Hilly's arms. Peering deeply into her sister's face she searched for that glimmer of knowledge and understanding she knew lay on the fringes of Hilly's psychic awareness. Hilly's eyes widened as the realization pushed forward. Simultaneously, the sisters drew in a long breath before yelling in unison, "Stygian!"

Sammy hopped from person to person, repeating, "Who's Stygian? What is Stygian?" Stunned silence met his questions as the Kemps and Jake processed the seriousness of the situation.

"What did you see Fen?" Hilly asked. Ugly memories returned when they uttered the Yfel leader's name—mental images of the bloody battle, Prasad's death, and banishing Stygian to his interdimensional cell.

Fen recalled the vision, pausing only to gather her strength and her emotions as she described each detail, ending with the moment the dragon lunged for her, its mouth agape with rows of pointed teeth covered in blood and sickening decaying matter. She cringed recalling the horrible screech produced by the beast.

"That must have been the moment Old Val screeched to a halt in front of you," Jake concluded.

Fen evaluated Jake's words, mulling them over as she looked at the ground. Then she turned to Hilly, "Do you think Stygian somehow jumped into my mind from his interdimensional cell? How is that possible?"

Hilly folded her fingers together while thoughtfully preparing her next words, "Jake wields incredibly strong magic. I believe a powerful sorcerer used Jake as a supernatural conduit through which he tranced you and delivered your vision. Jake, do you recall any sensations or odd feelings when you were with Fen?"

Jake dropped his head and relived the moments before Fen walked in front of Old Val. He shook his head. "Nope. First, we were talking about Lola, and then she's on the tarmac," he answered.

Sammy circled the group like an annoying mosquito. "What's going on? Who's Stygian? What vision? Will someone tell me something?"

Jake broke away from the Kemps. Drawing Sammy aside he whispered softly, "Sammy, it's important you make sure Fen gets on the plane for home. Don't drop her off outside. Walk her to the gate and wait until she boards the plane. Do you understand?"

Sammy cocked his head to the side. "Sure, Jake." He glanced toward the siblings. "Is someone in trouble?"

Jake followed Sammy's gaze. "I don't know, buddy. But I want to be prepared. Okay?"

A long shadow fell over the two men. "Jake, may I have a word?" Fen stood several feet away with her hands clasped in front of her.

Jake nodded at Sammy, "Go on, Sammy, go join Kai and Hilly. I'll talk to you soon." Jake approached Fen while averting his eyes. He was keenly aware that his gaze was the catalyst for her disturbing vision. "Do you need something, Fen?" He stared at the ground and shifted his feet.

Fen lightly touched his arm. Jake flinched, shocked by the unexpected contact. "Please look at me, Jake." Slowly, Jake lifted his eyes. For a few minutes the two silently looked at each other, scanning each other's faces, and respectively trying not to probe each other's mind. Fen was the first to break the silence, "I apologize for yelling at you. I don't know what happened, but I realize you had nothing to do with it."

Jake was not convinced. "Are you sure there are no remnants left from your vision that will cause you to mistrust me?"

Fen looked away. She bit her lower lip and turned to face him. She took a step closer so she could grip both his hands. Jake tensed.

"Please don't be afraid of me, Jake. I don't bite." She forced a smile to her lips, one corner jerking higher than the other, causing Jake to relax. "That's better." Fen squeezed his hands harder. "I trusted you one hundred percent before the vision. That feeling has not changed at all."

Fen paused, "What bothers me is how, or why, someone used *you* to feed me this vile vision."

Chapter 20

Axel

NATURE'S SPIRITS OBSERVED THE magicians from afar. Wispy sylphs hung in the azure sky, buzzing their discontent while drifting on the air currents. A huddle of gnomes peered out from an earthen hole near the corner of the hanger, frowning as they eavesdropped on the humans' conversation. A family of fairies nestled in the heads of nearby dandelions, clicking their disappointment. The spirits bickered among themselves, arguing the finer points of the Cererian Prophecy and the meaning of the black beast's appearance in Fen's vision.

Unable to interfere with the magicians, the supernatural souls listened to the humans with a keen interest. "How can the winged beast appear? Is he not caged in his interdimensional cell?" growled Andor, leader of the gnome tribe.

"The writings of the Prophecy predicted nothing of this incident. This is very troubling, indeed," hissed Santine, patriarch of his fairy family. "Someone has manipulated the Word. Someone has used dark magic to interfere."

"I fear chaos will consume our worlds," trilled Salina, priestess of the Sylphs.

The premonition forced upon Fen threatened pandemonium unless the magicians could thwart the intruder's efforts. Nature's spirits could do nothing except gnash their teeth and continue to observe. They mentally spread the word to the otherworldly beings around the globe: *Be prepared, the beast approaches!*

Sugar pines spilled up Shasta's slopes. The green, aromatic sea flowed for miles, parted occasionally by bus-sized angular boulders—projectiles from ancient volcanic explosions. An inconspicuous animal trail snaked through the trees and led to a blue pool of water fed by two converging waterfalls. It was here, deep in the middle of the forest, unspoiled by humans, that Hilly's portal opened.

When the trio emerged, they noticed the landscape shimmering as though everything had been bathed in luster dust.

"Interesting," Hilly observed. "I feel like we walked into the realm of the fairies. When I was a little girl, this is how I imagined their land would appear." Within seconds the glimmering effects dissipated as the portal closed.

Jake's senses were still alerting him to be cautious. While he was sure they had traveled through the portal alone, he felt like something otherworldly stalked them. He loosened the straps on the twin scabbards on his back in case he needed access to his battle daggers, Cadmar and Cathal.

Kai bumped into Jake who caught his arm and steadied him. "First time in a portal, Kai?"

"Mm," he mumbled. "I feel like I was rinsed and spun dry."

Hilly rubbed her chin, her eyes fixed on her brother. "Gee, Kai, you do look a little green. Perhaps sneaking that sip of vodka before entering the gateway was a bad idea." She playfully punched his arm.

"Funny, very funny. Perhaps if you knew how to work these portals with a little more finesse." A sudden blast of cold air cascaded down the slope, battering the soft pine needles into a flurry of hushed whispers. The gust washed over the magicians. "Argh!" Kai screamed. Clutching his chest, he dropped to the ground.

"What's wrong, Kai?" Hilly knelt over him as he rolled, groaning.

"We're not alone," Jake warned. In a flick of second, he held Cadmar and Cathal in each hand. His eyes narrowed to slits as he peered into the thick woods, trusting his intuition more than his eyesight. Circling slowly, he kept his back toward Hilly and Kai as he scrutinized the trees. Although he could see nothing, the hair on the back of his neck cautioned him that a predator was nearby. He menaced the unseen adversary with his battle daggers, twirling them and slicing the air. The blades sung with each pass.

"It hurts," Kai whimpered.

"Where, Kai? Your chest?" Hilly ripped his shirt open, fearful Kai was having a heart attack.

"My shirt! You've ruined a perfectly good shirt!" He jerked backward in pain as he yelled, "There...there!" Kai tapped the tattoo Shasta had branded onto his skin.

"Oh my god," Hilly uttered. Steam rose from the marking, which glowed orange-red as though molten metal had just been poured onto his chest, filling all the lines of the symbol. "Look at it, Jake. It's pulsing like it's alive."

Kai wailed, "Hilly, make the pain stop. Use your magic."

The witch and the warrior are not welcome on these slopes! The unexpected thought spoken in an unfamiliar voice startled everyone.

Hilly rose and brandished her sword, Raven. While Kai thrashed on the ground between them, Hilly and Jake stood back-to-back, prepared for an attack.

"Who are you?" Jake demanded. He mentally messaged Hilly, *There is something to our left. It keeps fading in and out like smoke.*

"Show yourself!" Hilly shouted.

A stronger gale swept over them, knocking Jake against Hilly. They buried their heads into one another, protecting their eyes from the dirt and debris swirling around them. The magicians were buffeted for several moments before the wind abated. Jake and Hilly regained their footing and resumed their protective stance over Kai who continued to writhe and cry out.

"Coward," Hilly provoked. "Show yourself!"

A long howl followed by a series of yips called out to them from the northern slope. Jake and Hilly whirled to face that direction. But as they turned, the yelps cried out in the opposite direction—south—and they spun to face the intruder.

Is there more than one? Hilly messaged.

A sudden howl, closer than the first, yowled from the east, and they turned to face whatever might be attacking.

I sense only one being, but they are very fast, which makes me think they possess magic, Jake responded.

Grrrrr.

The menacing growl pulled them to the west. Their eyes grew wide with alarm, and they gripped their weapons tighter. A large coyote faced them. His head stretched forward, his lips pulled back to show immense, pointed teeth. Red pupils swam in bright yellow irises. The animal growled again. Drool dripped down its jaws as it crept closer.

Jake messaged, *Hilly, I'll fly up and attack from the air if you keep its focus on you.*

Hilly nodded as she brought Raven in front of her, pointing the tip at the beast.

"STOP!" Kai cried out,

"What's wrong, Kai?" Hilly asked as she maintained her gaze on the coyote.

"I know what Jake...is going to do...and I want... you...to stop," Kai panted as he struggled to rise. He held his hand against the symbol on his chest which pulsed violently as though its eruption was imminent. "Please, lower your weapons."

Jake traded glances with Hilly before shaking his head. "Nope, I'm standing my ground." He pointed Cadmar at the coyote. "Maybe he's the one causing the pain." The beast growled deep and guttural as though he understood what the magician said.

Kai sucked in air. "Shasta did it." Kai staggered a step toward the creature. "This is how he knows who I am. Kai lurched toward the coyote again before falling to his knees a few feet in front of the beast.

"Kai don't get any closer," Hilly yelled. "You can't trust this animal. It possesses magic."

Kai slowly turned toward his sister, "So do we. Why should this animal trust us? Please, lower your weapons." Agony clouded Kai's reddened eyes, which implored his sister and friend to sheath their blades. "Trust me."

Hilly lightly touched Jake's arm. She nodded at his daggers. Meanwhile she slid Raven into its scabbard and swung it onto her back. Tight-lipped, Jake resisted the dangerous action. It left them completely exposed and vulnerable to attack. Kai noticed him hesitating and pleaded again, "Please Jake, for me."

"This is against all logic, Kai."

"When have you known me to be logical? Humor me."

Jake bit at his lower lip as various scenarios raced through his head, all of them ending badly. Exasperated, he thrust his daggers back in their sheaths and crossed his arms defiantly across his chest. "Know this, creature, I can withdraw these blades quicker than you can snap your jaws."

Kai rolled his eyes at Jake's display of superiority and commented, "Men!" He remained on his knees and his head drooped low. Slowly, he lifted his head and gazed at the coyote through dulled eyes. Mindful of the other two magicians, the beast observed Kai, sensing his intentions. Then it took a step closer.

Hilly gasped and the creature stopped and narrowed its eyes on the witch.

"Everyone, please be still," Kai begged. Addressing the coyote, he continued, "Please come closer. I won't harm you." Kai held his arms wide as if to embrace the wild animal.

The beast took another step closer.

It stretched forward, its nose twitching and sniffing the air, inhaling Kai's scent.

Closer.

The coyote's black nose bumped Kai, beginning at his head, along the pulse points in his throat, down to the marking on his chest. The minute the animal touched Shasta's brand, the pulsing and pain ceased. Satisfied, the creature sat down. Its long tongue unfurled like a red carpet and slipped to the side over a row of teeth as it smiled.

You have changed since playing on Shasta's slopes. Shasta's beacon—the shaman's eye she branded into your chest—is the only way I could locate you. But now that I'm close and can inhale your essence, I know you are the chosen one. I am known by many names, but you may call me Axel. Mother Shasta has sent me to guide you through the three tests and to deliver you into her arms. The animal paused and stretched before Kai, bowing his head between his front paws.

Kai politely dipped his head in return before responding, *I am Kai. The person on my right is Jake, and he is joined by my sister, Hilly.* Kai tapped the tattoo on his chest that now appeared as a red welt. *You recognized this brand. Can you tell me more about it?*

The animal cocked his head, *It is the mark of a shaman. The outer line represents the four corners of our universe—north, south, east and west. The inner line represents the spirit world, and the dot in the center represents your spiritual vision. Welcome home, shaman!*

Kai beamed. He finally received validation for what he'd been feeling for many months, that he was a shaman like Hilly and Jake. *You mentioned tests? What exactly are those?*

The animal grinned and yapped several times before responding, *Mother Shasta has many secrets, shaman. You have been away from her forests far too long. To prove you're worthy to penetrate the veil and embrace the mother, you must survive three tests. Each test is conducted by a member of her tribes. They will judge whether you are worthy or not to join them behind the veil.*

Kai rolled back onto his haunches and stood. With the pain removed, he felt instantly better. The coyote also stood on all four paws. Kai reached down to touch the creature. The beast watched his fingers approach within inches of his head before he bounded away barking and yelping. He ran several yards into the trees before whirling and slapping the ground with his fore paws. "Ah, it looks like we have a trickster in our midst. Just like me!" A happy grin filled Kai's face.

Jake and Hilly observed the exchange between the animal and Kai. Jake messaged Hilly, *The animal said Kai had previously been on this mountain. Did you know that?*

Kai was born in Mount Shasta. Perhaps the creature means that he was from the town.

The coyote mentioned Kai grew up on Shasta's slopes, and that he was the "chosen one." What does this all mean?

I guess we'll find out. Hilly's eyes twinkled with mischief. She loved a good adventure, and she felt one materializing. She watched her brother jumping around and playing tag with the coyote. "Kai, what did your friend mean when he said Jake and I didn't belong on these slopes?"

She addressed Kai, but the coyote suddenly romped toward her and replied, *I am here only for the shaman. You and the warrior can leave now that you've delivered him to me as was preordained by the Cererian Prophecy.*

Kai interrupted, *No. They stay with me. Or I won't endure your three tests nor meet Shasta.* He lied. He desperately wanted to meet Shasta and find the answers to the questions that nagged him in his dreams.

The coyote stared at Kai.

Finally, the animal sat back and grinned, his tongue unfurling out the side of his mouth. *Very well, shaman. They will accompany you as far as the veil if you make it that far. But only you can enter into the realm of Shasta.* Thrusting his snout toward the sky, the coyote howled and then bounded down the forest trail yipping and yapping.

Kai grinned at Hilly, "Well, I guess I have a journey before me. Care to join?" He offered his elbow, which Hilly gleefully accepted. The siblings trotted after the coyote.

Jake lingered near a print left by the animal. He hunched and studied the one pawprint that contained an abnormality like the one in the Mat-Su Valley. Jake traced the lines. As his fingertip followed the outline, the marking glowed a golden hue before vanishing.

Jake huffed. He was sure Axel and the animal that stalked them in Alaska were one and the same.

Jake surveyed the area around him. He sensed more life forces. They hid in the shadows and watched from a safe distance. He sensed no malice, only curiosity. He touched the ancient amulet around his neck, the one given to him by Darrius when he ascended to elder.

He called upon his ancestors to surround them with a layer of protection and then ran down the trail after Kai and Hilly.

Chapter 21

1st Test: Bravery

AXEL TROTTED THROUGH THE thick woods. Occasionally, he'd stop and gaze over his back to see if the shaman still followed. Kai would smile and nod to show he was still keen to follow, and the grinning coyote would yip in delight and romp along the trail with his tail held high.

Axel's black nose twitched constantly, inhaling the scents of the forest, seeking the telltale signs of prey. Catching a promising smell on the breeze, he suddenly leapt into a bush. The branches shook violently then grew oddly quiet before the coyote emerged licking his lips, freckles of blood covering his snout.

"Your guide is quite the hunter," Hilly noticed. The nonchalant savagery of the creature disturbed her. The quickness in which it dispatched the poor animal amazed her. The way Axel peered at her as though he could see right into her soul troubled her.

They passed the killing bush. The brown carcass of a rabbit lay on the ground. Kai grimaced. "It's a good thing he's on our side."

Jake followed several yards behind the siblings. His gaze swept the dark forest on either side. Except for the occasional rat-a-tat-tat as a woodpecker hammered a snag for food, the woodlands were quiet.

Eerily silent.

The magicians weren't the only ones hiking up Shasta's slopes. Although he couldn't see them, his intuition detected hundreds of souls following closely. Supernatural beings marched alongside the humans, moving through the trees as if they didn't exist.

As a young boy, Jake learned nature was full of preternatural entities. Many of them were cloaked behind magical veils so humans would never see them. But, as humankind destroyed more of the wilderness, the supernatural souls retreated further into the arms of their earth spirits. His grandfather taught him that the mountains of the world, like Denali, fiercely protected their slopes against civilization. Their peaks were the last strongholds for these magical populations. When humans ventured too close, they protected their children by deploying storms, mudslides, avalanches, and volcanic eruptions. Though these events were effective against the human onslaught they did not harm the spiritual entities living on the other side of the veil—the magical realm of the earth spirits.

The group reached a small clearing with several pathways leading in different directions like spokes on a wheel. Axel bolted into some nearby bushes. Squawking and screeching ensued as a covey of quail took to the air. The animal returned chomping the remains of one hapless bird. Hilly scrunched her nose in disgust as the proud coyote stared at her, licking its lips. "Where to now?" Kai asked as he scanned the trail options.

Your time has come, shaman. You have reached the first test.

The coyote thrust his head into the air and howled—an unnatural combination of beastly growl and human scream. The magicians clamped their hands over their ears and gawked at the creature. Axel flopped on the ground like a fish on land, his mouth agape. A strangled gurgle bubbled out of his jaws as the animal shook and shuddered. It opened its mouth for another howl but released a squeaky whine as his nose flattened against his skull. The toes on his front paws expanded into four fingers and a thumb, yet the claws remained, lengthening into four-inch nails. His back legs snapped and groaned as they straightened into long legs.

Within a minute, the red-coated coyote stood before them as a hunched, furry humanoid, glaring at them with intense red pupils swimming in bright yellow eyes. His jaws gaped open as the creature panted heavily, strings of thick drool streaming onto the ground.

I take this form to conduct the test, shaman, Axel heaved.

Horrified at the coyote's transformation, Kai responded, *That had to have been incredibly painful.*

Indeed, shaman. But it's nothing compared to what you will now endure. Swiftly the creature raised its arms. A gelatinous bubble materialized and engulfed Kai and Axel.

"It's a trap!" Hilly yelled as she pulled Raven from its sheath. Gripping Cadmar and Cathal, Jake sprinted to her side.

Keep your distance or the shaman will never see Shasta! Axel glared at the two magicians, daring them to make another move.

Glowering at the transparent bubble bobbing in front of her, Hilly bit her lip and glanced at Jake for support. *What do we do?*

His battle daggers swirled in the air, reading to strike. His eyes shifted from Hilly to the hideous creature menacing Kai. He was unsure of how to proceed.

The eight-foot oval membrane shimmered in the bright sunlight. The undulating orb completely covered Kai and Axel. The sides continued into the ground beneath their feet, creating an impenetrable cell. Kai faced his sister and friend. Resigned to his fate, he forced a smile and poked the slimy wall of his prison. A damp, sticky residue clung to his fingertip. *Jake...Hilly, I'll be fine. This is why I'm here. How bad can this be?*

Excellent, shaman. Are you ready to begin? Axel asked.

Kai turned toward the beast and replied, *Yes.*

To take your place beside the great earth spirit, Shasta, you must prove your bravery in the face of insurmountable odds. You must demonstrate you are a courageous warrior who can withstand pain without flinching or crying out. Do you accept these terms, shaman?

You don't have to do this, Kai. Say the word, and I'll open a portal, Hilly messaged her brother.

What word is that? Kai quipped.

The creature snapped, *Enough! Prepare yourself. The test will now begin. Remember, no flinching and no crying out or you will never see Shasta.*

Kai sucked in a deep breath. He stretched his head to the right and then to the left as he flexed his fingers, mentally preparing himself for what was to come. He turned to Axel and nodded his readiness. Without warning, the beast slashed Kai across the chest with its four-inch nails, carefully avoiding Shasta's brand. Shocked at the ferocity, Kai's eyes widened, but he clenched his teeth and squeezed his eyes against the agony, refusing to move or utter a sound.

Hilly charged the bubble and slashed the outer skin with Raven's blade. But the sword deflected off the surface, leaving no marks. Jake sprang into the air and landed on top of the membrane, plunging Cathal and Cadmar up to their hilts before the bubble yanked them from Jake's hands and violently propelled them into the trees.

Waves of pain rolled across Kai's chest. Torrents of blood pulsed from the gaping wounds. Gasping for breath, he tensed for the next assault. Axel circled him, snarling a sinister chuckle.

The creature attacked again, raking Kai's back, peeling his skin off along with his shirt. A scream raced up his throat, but Kai bit his lower lip to stop it. His front tooth sliced a deep cut, and the warm, pungent blood trickled down his chin.

Outside the bubble, Hilly and Jake raised their hands, casting spell after spell like a volley of bullets against the dome but every puncture sealed instantly. Hilly held her hands in front of her and channeled the element of fire. Blue flames licked inside her palms. When the fireball was a foot wide, she hurled it against the side of the blob. The flames landed against the dampness with a loud whoosh as the fire extinguished.

Hilly and Jake could only watch as Axel prepared for another strike.

Dizzy from blood loss, Kai clenched his fists and squeezed his eyes against the looming black out, wishing the nightmare would end. Visions of Jeff fluttered through his mind, prompting instant tears. Jeff's image released a surge of energy that fueled Kai with a new resolve. He would not be defeated just yet.

Axel whirled for his third and final assault. With the speed of tornadic winds, the beast pivoted around Kai, biting every inch of his legs and arms. His movements blurred as he chewed his way up Kai's body until he reached his throat. Hovering over the pulse point, Axel bared his teeth, yanked Kai's head to the side, and tore into the skin. A jet of blood spattered the inside of the dome.

Hilly shrieked.

Teetering on the edge of consciousness, Kai faced his assailant. He swallowed the scream caught in his throat. Instead, he released his emotions in a torrent of tears that dripped down his cheeks, mixing with the gore covering his face.

Axel grinned at the shaman.

Outside the bubble, Hilly and Jake ran around the perimeter punching and kicking, doing anything they could to get to Kai. When the attack ceased, the magicians also stopped. Kai gazed at them through dull eyes, his head tilted to the side, displaying the vicious gash in his throat. His fists clenched so hard blood oozed from where his fingernails dug into his palms.

The beast messaged, *Well done, shaman. Well done! You have successfully passed the first test. I am proud of your courage. Mother Shasta chose her champion wisely.*

Despite his wounds and immense pain, Kai joked, *That's all you've got, coyote man?* He flashed a weak smile.

I like you shaman. You have a great sense of humor like me. The beast nodded approvingly. *Now, let me heal your wounds.* The creature opened his massive jaws and blew a fine mist toward Kai. The pale blue droplets filled the entire bubble like a gentle snowfall and coated every inch of Kai's body. The cerulean flurry prevented Jake and Hilly from seeing anything.

Hilly messaged Kai, *Are you okay? Kai?*

Anxious moments passed. A loud hiss surprised the magicians and they jumped back, gazing up at the dome's crown where a hole appeared. The pale blue mist escaped into the air as the membrane slowly melted down the sides, erasing all evidence of the battle cell. Axel had reverted to his original form and sat on the ground, his tongue lolling over his teeth while his eyes sparkled with mischief.

Kai didn't move. His eyes were closed as though he had drifted to sleep—a peaceful and serene nap. His arms hung limply at his sides, his fingers flexing and contracting in an effort to awaken the muscles that had grown rigid during his ordeal. Jake and Hilly gawked at him.

"Where are your wounds?" Hilly anxiously asked as she examined him from head to toe. The shirt that was shredded during the attack appeared crisp and new, no imperfections whatsoever. She lightly touched his arm and Kai finally opened his eyes.

He blinked several times in the bright sunlight. He looked at Hilly, exhaustion clouding his eyes. "That was certainly different." He managed a grin before faltering, a little unsteady on his feet. She caught him and ushered Jake to help. The two walked Kai to a nearby rock where he willingly sat and gazed up at them with a dreamy, faraway look that reminded Hilly of her brother's misadventure with too much pot.

"I remember every detail. Crystal clear. The slashes and the bites. And the pain. My god the agony. But, right now, this is the best I've felt in a long time." Kai lifted his face toward the sun. The slight movement caused him to lurch backwards. Jake caught his arm before Kai fell off the rock.

The healing mist is also a relaxing potion. The shaman may need some sleep before we proceed on to the next test. It is quite some distance from here. The coyote looked up the slope and yipped. A soft whistle returned.

Jake and Hilly whirled. "What was that?" Jake asked.

The wind, warrior. Only the wind. I suggest you all rest before we continue on the path. The creature tilted his head and barked three times before bounding into the shrubs.

Hilly watched the coyote depart, anticipating his quick return with blood on his muzzle from another victorious hunt. But minutes stretched into hours, and still no coyote. Their guide had left them alone and that unnerved Hilly.

She examined the five different pathways spoking away in the small clearing. She strolled clockwise, pausing in front of each spur, using her psychic abilities to determine which trail would take them to the second test. She hoped to narrow her search on the right trail so she could explore and discover what lay ahead of them.

"Which one do you think leads to the next test?" she asked Jake. When he didn't respond, she turned. Her heart instantly melted. Kai snuggled against the warrior, his head on Jake's shoulder, a soft snore fluttered from his pursed lips.

Jake furrowed his brow. His brilliant blue eyes pleaded for help. Hilly shook her head as she observed, "I think Kai's got the right idea. We'll relax for a while. We can't go anywhere until Axel returns anyway. I'll hunt for Raven, Cadmar and Cathal. They couldn't have been thrown too far away."

Kai whimpered and stretched his arms wide, encircling Jake's waist. A satisfied smile spread across his face, and he pulled the warrior close. Nuzzling Jake's shoulder, he murmured, "I love you, Jeff," and fell into a deep slumber.

Chapter 22

Troy the Bigfoot

THE DREAM HAD RETURNED.

Kai strolled along a trail winding up a mountain slope. Although it was night, he was not afraid as he knew these woods and could walk the path blindfolded. The full moon's light draped a silver veil upon the trees and boulders, creating animated shadows that quivered as he passed.

A soft buzzing snatched his attention. The high-pitched trill fell to low tones before rising high once again. As he peered into the blackness, six glowing orbs advanced toward him. Each ball of light pulsed a kaleidoscope of reds, blues, and yellows. The orbs stopped a few yards away, hovering two feet from the ground. Moments passed before they moved forward, slowly maneuvering around Kai, encircling him in a ring of pulsating light. The air sizzled with magnetic energy, causing the hairs on his arms to stand at attention. Kai swayed to the dizzying effects of the soothing sounds and mesmerizing colors.

He was finally home.

When Kai awoke the next morning, he was curled in a fetal position beside the large boulder. Jake's jacket covered his upper body. Something pointy, yet soft, cushioned his head. He propped himself on his elbow for a better look and found a mat of soft pine boughs placed on the ground. He smiled at the thoughtfulness for his comfort. He sat up and leaned against the boulder. The morning sun bathed the clearing with a warm light that fell across his face. His eyelashes appeared on fire as the orange light glinted off each hair. He stretched and hailed Hilly, "Good morning, sunshine!"

"Morning, Kai!" Hilly took his hand and pulled him to his feet. "Did you get some sleep?" She dusted the dirt from his clothes and picked stray pine needles out of his hair.

Jake's jacket draped Kai's shoulders and he pinched the flaps together in front of his chest. "It's funny. But I felt I was sleeping with Jeff all night. I don't know if it's the scent of Jake's jacket, but I slept fantastic."

"Want some coffee?" Hilly wiggled a tin cup toward Kai.

Kai eyed the dark contents suspiciously. "How did you make coffee out here?"

"Magic, dear brother, magic," Hilly chirped as she rifled through her backpack and produced a cinnamon sugar donut. "And, I have your favorite treat."

"Wow, it doesn't get any better than this." Kai snatched the pastry from her hand. He devoured the donut in three wolf bites and licked the sugary cinnamon dust off his fingers before taking a big gulp of coffee.

Jake sat nearby with one hand wrapped around a coffee mug and the other hand holding his head. Kai studied his friend's demeanor. "Did you get any sleep, Jake? You look a little tired."

Hilly burst out laughing. "Oh, he got a little."

Jake glared at Hilly through bloodshot eyes. His thin lips and clenched jaw signaled he was in no mood for jokes. His gaze shifted between Hilly and Kai before he finally spoke. "I slept fine, Kai, once I entangled you out of my arms." He gulped the rest of his coffee and stood up. He rolled his eyes at the siblings and marched away.

"What's with him?" Kai asked.

Hilly slapped Kai's back. "You nuzzled Jake all night. Right over there on that rock." She pointed toward the boulder where Kai had dropped off to sleep hugging Jake. "He finally laid you on the ground when you kept sucking his neck." Hilly snorted, "It was so damn funny. He kept looking at me to do something, but all I wanted to do was take a video of the two of you." She pulled out her phone. "Unfortunately, the minute I tried to use my phone the battery drained. It's like someone or something didn't want any evidence." Hilly shook her cellphone and stared at the screen, but it remained black and unresponsive. "Anyway, Jake tired of your canoodling and placed you on the ground. You made a bit of a fuss, but when he draped his jacket over you, you shut up and started snoring again."

Kai grinned, envisioning a night of cuddling with Jake. "It's a shame I don't remember any of that." He gazed at Jake who stood several yards away contemplating his empty coffee cup. "Hilly, what did you do while I was lost in my dreams?"

"Jake and I explored the slopes while you slept."

"Did you find anything?"

"I don't have a straightforward answer. We both agree someone doesn't want us snooping around." Hilly hitched her thumb toward the pathways behind her. "We explored each and every one of those five trails. We followed each path only to find ourselves back in the clearing. We even deployed psychic markers so we wouldn't get lost but those mysteriously disappeared. Yep, somebody wants to keep us right here for the time being."

"I guess Shasta didn't want you wandering too far on her slopes." Kai slurped the remnants of his coffee and begged for more. Hilly obliged.

"What bothers me," Jake interjected as he joined the siblings, "is that Axel's paw prints are everywhere in the clearing, but nowhere on the trails. We were careful where we walked. Still, there was no trace of your coyote guide. Also, where is he now? We're prisoners in this place. I don't like having my wings clipped." Jake pushed his cup out to Hilly for more coffee. She smirked at him before dribbling the remains into his mug.

"I think Axel and Shasta are the same entity." Hilly studied her companions' reactions.

Kai's eyebrows arched. "Hmm, that is an interesting thought. But why take the form of coyote? Why not address us like Denali faced you?"

"Bullshit," Jake blurted. "This creature who calls himself Axel was in Alaska, following us as we journeyed to the Sentinel Boulder. I've never known Denali or any earth spirit to walk outside their territories. This coyote is only her spirit animal. That wily beast is not the embodiment of the great earth spirit, Shasta."

Right you are, warrior!

The trio whirled toward the source. Axel sat near a trail head, grinning a toothy smile.

Jake marched toward the animal and demanded, "Where have you been all night?"

Ignoring his question, Axel scampered away from Jake and ran to Kai. He looked up at him and wagged his tail. *I hope you had some restful sleep, shaman. We have a big day planned for you.*

"We? Who's we?" Kai knelt to peer into the coyote's eyes. Despite the brutality meted out by Axel during the first test, Kai felt a kinship with the beast as if they shared a common past—something he wanted to know more about.

Axel barked and trotted down a pathway for several yards before stopping. He looked over his shoulder at the magicians. *Come on, shaman, your second test awaits you.*

Kai didn't hesitate. He eagerly followed the coyote. Hilly grabbed his shoulder as he passed, stopping him in midstride. "Hold up, Kai." She then spoke to Axel, "Jake and I went down that trail several times last night. Each time, it brought us back here. Where are you taking us? Tell us or we won't follow." It was a bold move to threaten the magical entity, but Hilly felt it was time to test the limits of Shasta and her guide.

Axel huffed into the dirt and narrowed his eyes on Hilly. *This journey is not about you, witch. Nor is it about your warrior friend. These tests are for the shaman only. If you don't want to follow me, that is perfectly fine.* Axel turned and trotted down the path until he disappeared from view.

Kai took several tentative steps to follow, but Hilly pulled him back. "Don't go, Kai. This test could be even worse than the one you endured yesterday."

"If I don't follow Axel, I will never see Shasta. You had your chance to see Denali. I want the same opportunity. I want to find out who I am." Kai kissed Hilly on the forehead. He winked and quickly ran down the path shouting, "Axel, wait up!"

Hilly watched her brother leave. She felt the biting pang of a premonition, a realization that Kai would eventually leave her forever. She trembled at the vision.

Jake noticed her eyes clouding with concern. "What's going through your mind, Hilly?"

She looked at Jake with sorrowful eyes, the vibrant green dulling to a soft gray. "It's probably nothing, but I feel as though the day is approaching that Kai will leave me forever. Watching him run away was like observing him in a future event. One that I can't stop. One that I can't control."

Jake glanced down the trail and then back to Hilly. "Instead of watching him run away from you now, why don't you catch up to him and be with him for as long as you can? If you feel your premonition will come true, there is nothing you can do to change the outcome. But you can definitely change the way you spend the remaining time. Focus on that and enjoy the hell out of it."

Hilly considered Jake's words. A corner of her mouth lifted into a half grin as she convinced herself Jake was right. She loved it when he willingly stepped outside his warrior persona and acted like a good friend. She hugged him, her head leaning on his chest. She breathed in his scent and felt warm and secure. She pushed back. This time a full smile spread across her face. Her emerald-green eyes sparkled. The old Hilly had returned, "You're right, Jake. If my time is limited with Kai, why not make the most of it?" She grabbed his hand and dashed down the trail.

Jake allowed Hilly to tug him along. Her hand felt warm and snug. She trotted ahead like a little girl anxious for a new adventure. He loved that about her—her spontaneity, her willingness to plunge into deep waters without fear.

They followed the pathway for about two miles without catching sight of Axel or Kai. "I think we may have lost them," Hilly said, her voice full of disappointment.

"Axel mentioned the site for the second test was far away. Let's keep moving until we find them or we end up back at the clearing like we did last night." Jake assumed the lead. Still holding Hilly's hand, he led her under a group of low-lying branches. The forest was thick in this area. Sugar pines grew side by side with ash, spruce, and cottonwood. The sun blazed overhead, but the canopy filtered out the intense light. Only dim forest shadows remained.

When they emerged through the thicket, they found the pathway blocked by a massive tree that had fallen across the trail. The girth of the ancient pine towered over Jake and Hilly. Brambles snarled the areas on both sides of the behemoth. "Looks like we're going up and over," Jake observed.

He interlaced his fingers and bent low so Hilly could step into his hands. Then he pushed her up. She grabbed a spindly branch near the top and pulled herself into a sitting position atop the trunk. She offered her hand to Jake, but he launched into the air and jumped over the pine, landing safely on the other side.

"Why didn't I think of that?" Hilly laughed as she jumped to the ground with a thump. Once on the other side, they realized they were on the outskirts of another clearing surrounded by several trails leading in different directions.

Axel and Kai stood in the center of the clearing, chatting near a ten-foot tall, shaggy tree. "What type of tree do you suppose that is?" Hilly whispered as she slowly walked toward them.

The unkempt tree abruptly whirled and growled, "Who are you?"

Axel yipped in distress as he raced toward Hilly and Jake, *Stop, you have not been invited into the circle.*

Hilly gawked at the hairy, tree-like thing striding toward her. Each of his footfalls shook the ground. Jake drew alongside her and reached back to touch Cathal's hilt. Anxious that they may be attacked by the unusual creature running toward them, he prepared for the possibility.

Axel reached them first. *You are intruding. You did not inform me that you would follow. Your behavior is egregious. Go to the other side of the fallen tree NOW!*

Axel glanced back at the large beast approaching them. *Now! Go now!*

Jake grabbed Hilly around the waist and hoisted her into the air just as the shaggy monster reached the space they had been occupying. Hovering in the air, they peered into the creature's black eyes as he glared up at them. The beast lifted his arms—long, hairy appendages that seemed at least eight-foot long—and leapt upward toward Jake and Hilly, narrowly missing Jake's boot.

Go now! Axel implored.

Jake pulled Hilly away until they were safe on the other side of the fallen pine tree. "What the hell was that?"

Axel's voice startled them. *He is known by many names in the human world: Bigfoot, Yeti, Sasquatch.*

Jake and Hilly whirled to find Axel sitting a few feet behind them. Despite the perpetual smile on his jaws, his eyes drooped with disappointment. Hilly stepped toward the coyote. "Is Kai safe with that beast? You left him all alone."

Axel yipped several times. *Witch, have you not learned that Shasta's slopes are not the playground for Denali's children? Your brother faces his second test, and you dishonor him with your rude interruption.*

The coyote turned toward Jake. *And you, warrior, should know better than to threaten a magical creature. It detected your movement toward your weapon before you even knew you wanted to withdraw your dagger. Silly magicians. You are in Shasta's realm. Act accordingly.*

Hilly hung her head in shame. In her eagerness to join Kai, she thoroughly embarrassed him in front of the creature that would measure his worthiness to meet Shasta. "Did I destroy Kai's chance of participating in the next test?"

"It wasn't her fault," Jake defended. "I delayed our arrival. If you have to blame somebody, let it be me. But please don't let Kai suffer because of our misdeeds."

The coyote huffed. A cloud of dust rose from the ground. *Humans are exhausting.* Axel approached them. He barked loudly for emphasis. *Like the first test, you can bear witness to your brother's attempt, but you cannot interfere. Your transgression today was to walk into the magical field uninvited. Because of that, we must start over from the beginning.* Axel snuffed the dirt again. *Await my invitation before coming to the other side of the fallen tree. Agreed?*

Hilly and Jake nodded their heads. Axel faded away until nothing was left of him. Even his paw prints disappeared as though he was never there.

"Things are so different here on Shasta. I feel like a baby learning how to crawl and speak. I want Kai to succeed and discover his family roots, but there's a part of me that wants to whisk Kai away and end this trip."

Jake gathered her hands into his. "I can remember how adamant you were to get to Denali. Nothing could stand in your way, or if someone did, you simply pushed them aside. I reckon Kai feels that urge like you did. Just like Chance and Fen will someday. You won't be able to hold any of them back. They must discover who they are as it is written in the Cererian Prophecy." He managed a weak smile and gripped her hands harder. "Everything will be fine. Kai knows what he must do."

Witch and warrior, join us on the other side of the tree.

Axel's request was clipped and not his usual friendly banter. Without a warning, Jake scooped Hilly into his arms and flew into the sky, carrying her over the fallen tree. On the other side, he carefully placed her on the ground. As they looked up, they stared right into the furry midsection of the beast that had chased them earlier. Their eyes widened as they followed the brown, matted fur upward into the creature's dark eyes. They both shivered, not from fear but from the enormity of the creature's size and the intensity of its magic which enveloped him like a transparent cloak. It was a feeling neither had experienced before, and they were in awe.

The beast growled a greeting, "You are welcome into the circle, but you must never interfere. Is that understood?" The guttural syllables sounded like two rocks scraping together. It was apparent English was not the creature's natural language, but he made the attempt to communicate in their own words. He left them and joined Kai in the clearing.

Kai raised a hand and casually waved at Jake and Hilly as though old friends were getting together for a few beers. "Welcome to the party," he quipped.

Hilly waved and followed Axel to an area near the side of the circle. She opted not to respond lest her words ruin Kai's chance to succeed.

"Shaman, are you ready for your second test?" The furry creature asked.

Aware that each test would probably be worse than the previous one, Kai summoned his internal strength by diving deep into his psyche. He latched onto the elements of power that always sustained him—his husband, his magic, and his spirit. He drew in several deep breaths and faced the beast, "Let's get 'er done."

Drawing his long arm across his belly, the shaggy entity bowed deeply toward Kai. "You may call me Troy. Humans know me by many names, but the Modoc call me matah kagmi. I am the Protector of the Woods." The shaggy beast swung his arms wide, narrowly missing Kai's head as he gestured toward the surrounding forest. "My relatives live all over the world. Our sacred mission is to protect the trees from being ripped from the ground. Without our sentinels, our world would no longer exist. I, and all my kin, have adapted to the harshness of mountain life to protect the forested slopes." Troy smiled. Kai flinched at the massive pointy teeth filling the beast's mouth.

Following Troy's example, Kai bowed to the beast. "I am Kai."

Awkward silent moments passed.

"That's it?" Troy inquired. "Those are your accomplishments?" The beast shook his head, matted dreadlocks slapped the sides. He eyed the coyote. "I'm not impressed Axel. I don't know about continuing this test."

Axel howled his displeasure. *Shaman, explain who you are, and what you do. You are more than Kai.*

Kai grew anxious. He sensed the disappointment oozing from Troy and the impatience filling Axel's howls. Worry lines creased his forehead and he bit his lower lip in frustration. What was he supposed to say? Axel howled again.

Kai cleared his throat, "I am Kai. I am the adopted son of Ted and Freda Kemp. I am a magician born into the Family of Air, and I am known as the Keeper of the Keys." Kai stopped and considered his next statement. After all, he had just learned it from Axel yesterday. He squared his shoulders and continued, "I am a shaman for Shasta...I am her champion."

Troy nodded, "Much better. It's important that we know who we are and how we contribute to the world." He grabbed a nearby log and hoisted the four-foot-thick tree in front of his chest. He snapped it in two as though it was kindling wood, "Welcome to your test of strength."

Chapter 23

2nd Test: Strength

KAI GAWKED AT TROY's demonstration. "There's no way I can beat you in a contest of strength!" he protested.

"You give up easily," Troy taunted. He turned toward Axel. "You brought me a weak human. He is no shaman. He is no champion of Mother Shasta." The beast shook his head at Kai and turned to walk away.

Axel yipped. *Shaman, if you do not participate, you forfeit your chance to see Shasta. You will be banished from these slopes and can never return. Is this what you want?*

Hilly mentally implored her brother, cloaking her words from everyone else, *Kai, this is your only chance. Don't turn away. Ask about the terms of the contest.*

Kai nodded at Hilly's suggestion. "Wait, Troy. It's apparent you are much stronger than I. So, what is involved in your test of strength?"

"Humans are exhausting," Troy muttered. "You either want to take this test or not. I don't care, but don't waste my time." The giant sighed. A gust of hot, fetid breath washed over Kai. The shaman shuddered at the foul stench of decaying meat.

He discreetly fanned the air in front of his face. "I only want to clarify. You call it a test of strength. But there are so many ways to prove a person's power. For instance, will you and I wrestle? If so, that's no contest."

Troy chuckled. He gently patted Kai's head with his massive hand. "Silly shaman. You won't wrestle me. I can flatten you with my foot." The shaggy creature chuckled again and shook his head. "No, you will prove your worthiness by breaking a tree in half."

Kai shot a glance toward Hilly, his eyes wide with fear and disbelief. "You mean, I will need to break a tree in two like the one you just did?"

"Oh, no. You'll be breaking one of those." Troy pointed to an ancient forest of pine trees. Their trunks were eight feet thick like the one that had fallen across the trail. "Those should be easy for someone of your abilities." Troy laughed, and the rumbling chuckle echoed off the trees.

Axel joined in with a series of yips and twirled in circles.

"Enough stalling, shaman. Do you accept the terms of the contest?"

Kai rolled his eyes. He walked over to a nearby tree. Standing on his toes, he could barely reach the lowest limb that was full of an explosion of dark brown pinecones. Grasping the branch, he pulled down and then released it. The bough lazily shot upward and waggled a couple of times before settling back in place. Kai placed his hands on the trunk. This pine was full of tremendous energy. The vibrations poked at his palms like a flurry of pin pricks. He snatched his hands away and studied the tree by glancing at the top which disappeared into a thicket of green needles. He strolled back to his position in the clearing. "Yes, I accept your terms."

Hilly and Jake shared confused glances. Kai's hands were adept at creating masterful works of art from humble paint not at snapping eight-foot trunks in half. Despite their concern, they said nothing, mindful of what their interference may cost Kai.

"Excellent, let's begin." Troy led the way to a group of trees. He placed a large hand on the rough trunk and gazed upward. "This tree is over six hundred years old. She has survived blizzards, fires and numerous earthquakes." He pointed toward the bottom where a large hole revealed a tangle of roots and assorted rocks. "During one quake she nearly toppled over but notice how her neighbors kept her from falling." He gestured at the nearby pines whose branches intermingled with the branches of this tree. "She has been through a lot of misery. But she has also enjoyed many celebrations of life. She is the home to many species of birds and mammals. They live in her boughs and in the natural cavities of her trunk. Like her sisters and brothers surrounding her, she not only breathes life into the atmosphere but also provides shelter for many creatures of nature. This is the tree you will break in half."

Kai listened carefully as Troy spoke lovingly about the tree's history and the communities that lived within her branches. His mother had always taught him to respect nature. He recalled her words, *No harm to others lest you invite harm upon yourself.*

Troy observed Kai's hesitancy. "What's wrong?"

"There must be a better way to prove my strength. I'm not comfortable destroying this beautiful tree to prove how strong I am."

"Look Axel, the magician is impotent in the face of a challenge," Troy taunted, "Some champion he turned out to be."

Embarrassed by Troy's words, Kai blushed. He could easily break this tree by summoning the winds. As a child of the element of air, he could manipulate the currents and could focus the gales on this lone tree. If he must prove his worthiness, he could snap one tree in half and save the others. That would be okay. Just one tree. His mother's words vanished as he made his decision.

He turned to Troy, "Just to be clear, do you want this tree destroyed? I can break it without harming any of the others surrounding her. Is that what you want me to do?"

Troy huffed. "The shaman has a little fight in him after all. Show me what you have, magician."

Kai closed his eyes. He drew in three long breaths to steady his mind and his heart that hammered from the anxiety of making the painful decision. Slowly, he opened his eyes and focused on the trunk. He studied the bark's deep crevices and bumpy surface. He raised his hands—his right palm faced the tree while his left hand hung parallel to his hip, palm upward. Drawing upon his magic, the incantation flowed from his lips like hurried whispers as he called upon the element of air to assist him in his mission. Although many words were spoken, the sound produced was one continuous buzzing.

A flicker of lightning appeared above the tree followed by a deep roar of thunder. Dark clouds swirled above—a mixture of blacks, grays, and deep purples—growling as they churned clockwise above the tree's canopy. Kai increased the cadence of his spell. Gusts pushed through the branches which creaked in resistance. Pine needles ripped from their boughs, turning the air into a dark green flurry. A monstrous storm swirled around Shasta's snowy summit as vortices raced down her slopes. Kai focused the storm's intense energy and pushed hurricane force winds against the chosen pine tree.

Troy glanced toward the top of the tree.

Kai screamed into the maelstrom, focusing his hands and magic on the trunk about ten feet from the ground. A mental scream penetrated his brain. Startled, Kai dropped his hands, momentarily reducing the intensity of his spell. His eyes darted up and down the tree, searching for the entity that called out to him.

Troy noticed. "Is something amiss, shaman?"

"I thought I heard something...or someone." He raised his hands to continue the conjuring. This time, the combined voices of many—the birds, the squirrels and the magical entities who call the pine tree home—roared in his head, begging for mercy. A migraine erupted from the cacophony, and Kai gripped his head in pain. With his tongue silenced and his hands turned away, the magic ceased.

Once the spell halted the headache vanished and his mother's words returned—*No harm to others lest you invite harm upon yourself.*

Kai gasped. He realized he was destroying hundreds of lives to prove a point. He immediately reversed his incantation. The winds ceased, and the storm completely disappeared. Only light breezes remained. He faced Troy. "I will not continue. I cannot do it. Breaking this tree not only kills the tree but also destroys the home for hundreds of lives." Kai hung his head in defeat. "I'm sorry, but I will not break this tree in two."

Troy smiled. He placed a hand on Kai's shoulder, his long fingers reaching almost to the magician's waist. "A test of strength is not always about who is physically tougher, but who is strongest in their wisdom." Kai peered up at the shaggy beast.

Tears misted in Troy's eyes as he continued, "As you recall, I am the Protector of the Woods. Watching you wield your magic on my children was painful to watch. I could hear their cries for help. I could sense their pain. I was very close to intervening as I could feel the tree was almost ready to break."

Troy scooped Kai into his arms and twirled. "You have proven yourself worthy to be Shasta's champion. You have passed the second test." Kai gripped the beast's matted fur and held on. The spinning made him dizzy, and Troy's musky smell forced bile into his throat, but the creature's overwhelming joy was infectious.

"That's great news," Kai gasped. "But could you put me down? I'm a little dizzy."

Troy stopped twirling and gently placed Kai on the ground. He lurched sideways, and Troy caught him before he tumbled. "Maybe I should hold onto you while you get your bearings."

Axel howled into the sky. *Congratulations shaman! You have one more test to pass before you will meet Shasta.*

"Will we go there today?" Kai leaned against Troy for support. His eyes jerked to the side as though he still moved in circles.

No. Now you rest. Troy and I will leave you for the night. As you learned yesterday, there's no reason to follow us. You will never be allowed to go any further than this clearing. Axel stared at Jake and Hilly who blushed for being called out for their antics.

"When will you return?" Kai asked as Troy guided him to a nearby boulder and lifted him on top. Kai's legs dangled over the side. Troy patted him gently on his head and turned to leave.

That's for me to know and for you to discover tomorrow. Axel growled a long burgling chuckle. *Prepare yourself, shaman. Tomorrow is the day that the past, present, and future reunite. What you do in that moment decides the fate of the world.*

Axel and Troy vanished into thin air with no trace left of their visit. Jake scuffed the dirt where the magical duo once stood. "They have an interesting way of coming and going. I'm curious how they manage that kind of magic."

Hilly joined Jake. "At least we know we don't need to bother searching the trails." She rifled through her backpack. "Who's up for dinner?"

"I'm famished!" Kai proclaimed. "What do you have?"

"Anything your heart desires. I'm making it with magic, so if you can think it, I can conjure it!" Hilly laughed easily. After the stress of the day and almost ruining Kai's chances, the silliness was welcome.

"I'll have a vodka tonic on the rocks and a prime rib." Kai's eyebrows wiggled at Hilly, "I need to be prepared for the final test tomorrow."

Chapter 24

Aaron Escapes

DISTURBING NEWS ARRIVED AT midnight.

After Hilly's magical dinner, after Kai's multiple toasts to Shasta, and long after the friends sang familiar tunes into the night, Benedict mentally contacted Jake, *It's urgent that we talk.*

Full of drink and food, Hilly and Kai collapsed into each other's arms, huddled together in a peaceful slumber.

Jake opted to prowl the pathways, hopeful to discover areas beyond the clearing, despite Axel's caution that attempts would be futile. After each foray into the woods, he wasn't surprised to find himself back in the clearing. But he didn't mind. The exercise was good for his recent bout of insomnia.

Jake was restless. During dinner, his intuition poked at him, demanding to be heard. Something was amiss, but he didn't know what. Then he received the Cererian's message.

Benedict was succinct. *Find a private location so we can converse.*

Jake checked on his companions. Hilly snored softly into Kai's chest. Kai muttered and giggled between sleepy snores.

Jake walked into the thick woods and telepathically contacted Benedict. *I'm alone. What's the urgency?*

The Kemps are in danger, Benedict warned.

Morning arrived on a cheerful warm breeze.

"Have more pancakes, Kai," Hilly insisted as she piled two more flapjacks onto his plate.

He poked his fork at Jake who stared into space by a trailhead. "What's with him?"

"I'm not sure. He was standing there when I got up this morning." Hilly studied her friend, noting his stooped posture and the worry lines scrunched on his forehead. "He took the coffee from me but asked to be left alone."

Jake stared absently into the forest. His jaw muscles bulged and clenched like a dog worrying a bone. "Something is definitely bothering him," Kai observed. He cleared his throat and yelled, "Yo, Jake! Want some pancakes?"

No response.

"Something's grabbed his attention." Hilly stood up and stretched. "I'll check on him." She raised an eyebrow and grinned at Kai.

"Uh, oh. I've seen that look before," Kai giggled.

Jake needed to be nudged from whatever consumed his focus. Hilly approached him from behind like a stealthy ninja. Maintaining a wary eye on her friend, she tip-toed in the soft dirt, carefully avoiding leaves and branches that might make noise. As she crept forward, she collected several pine cones. She clutched each one in her hand, measuring its weight and effectiveness as a projectile, before transferring it into the crook of her arm. Her arsenal was complete.

Lost in thought, Jake stared at the ground. He raked his fingers through his hair, absently twirling his blond curls hugging his neck. He sighed and looked to the sky before peering into the woods at nothing in particular.

What an easy mark, Hilly thought. She touched the pinecones. Although lightweight, each cone was at least six inches long and fully armed with pointed umbos. They would be quite effective against a distracted magician.

She glanced back toward Kai who clamped a hand over his mouth, stifling a chuckle. Although she hadn't lobbed a single pinecone, the anticipation was too much for him to bear. She selected a cone and wiggled it at Kai. He eagerly nodded and snickered.

With only six feet between her and Jake, Hilly tossed the pinecone underhand. She swung her arm in a practice throw, careful not to make any noise. The center of Jake's back was the perfect bullseye. She narrowed her eyes on the target, lifted her arm high behind her, and followed through. The cone arched toward Jake's back and smacked between his shoulder blades. A perfect shot.

Jake shifted his feet and stretched but didn't turn around.

Hilly rearmed. This time she focused for the top of his head. After two practice swings to calculate the arc and release, she tossed the missile forward. The pinecone curved high into the air before plummeting on top of Jake's head. Momentarily, the cone snagged in his hair before lazily falling onto his shoulder and then dropping in front of him.

Hilly giggled and looked back at Kai who rolled on the ground laughing.

"If you throw a third one, I'll have to retaliate." Jake's response caused Hilly to giggle more.

"Maybe it will be worth it," she teased, swinging her arm that was clutching the third missile.

Jake faced her. His blue eyes dulled with weariness. The corners of his mouth drooped like a sad-faced clown. "Hilly, any other day, I'd be pitching these back at you. But please stop. I need to concentrate on a serious matter."

Jake's weighted words punched her hard, scattering all remnants of silliness. The pinecone tumbled from Hilly's fingers as she shifted into her serious persona, ready to take control and solve Jake's problem.

"What's wrong," she urged.

Kai noticed the shift in their energy and sidled up to his sister. "Jake, what happened?"

Jake peered at the siblings. The anxious looks on their faces tore at his heart. He couldn't delay the inevitable any longer. "I received word from Benedict last night." Jake sighed the burden of his knowledge.

"Is everything okay in Aningan? Did something happen to Sammy?" Hilly peppered Jake with questions. She knew Benedict could easily manage any issue that might arise. The Cererian wouldn't contact Jake unless something catastrophic had occurred.

Jake held up a hand. "Please let me say what I've got to say. This is not easy for me."

Instinctively, Hilly squeezed her brother's hand. Kai wrapped his arm around Hilly's waist and pulled her close. The siblings stood united as they searched their friend's grim face.

Jake continued. "Benedict contacted me last night after you two fell asleep. The conversation lasted almost five hours."

"Five hours!" Hilly yelled. "This is really serious." She pulled away from Kai and paced the clearing.

Jake was familiar with her reaction. This was Hilly's method for working out issues that troubled her. She'd stomp around, imagining various scenarios and then she would shuffle them into logical order before speaking.

After several minutes, she stopped. With a hand on her hip, she demanded, "What did Benedict tell you?

"Yeah, that is a long time, especially when you're chatting telepathically. My brain is fried." Jake massaged his temples. "After Benedict spoke with me, we determined Darrius needed to provide advice on the issue as well. Then the Cererian High Council weighed in on the matter." Jake rubbed his bloodshot eyes and sucked in a long breath that lasted so long Hilly feared he would never exhale.

Jake squared his shoulders and spit it out. "Early yesterday, Uncle Aaron escaped his prison cell on Ceres."

"What!" Hilly screamed, "How?"

"I can't release the details at this time." Jake dropped his head and walked away. He hated withholding information, but there was a time and a place. He couldn't reveal the truth. Not while Kai prepared for his third and final test. This was news that should be meted out as needed. How could he explain to the Kemp's that Fen's premonition about the black dragon was coming true. Aaron was that vile beast and Jake was the reason for his escape.

Hilly trotted after him. She lightly touched his shoulder but he flinched as though her fingertips were hot pokers. "Jake, look at me. Please."

Jake turned. She gripped his shoulders, her eyes pleading for more information. "Hilly, I've shared what I can. Darrius is managing the situation. I'm only following his direction."

"Do we know the perpetrators?"

Hilly's attempt to get to the root of the problem was endearing. He loved that about her.

"The Cererians are confirming the details," he lied. He was well aware of the scoundrels who helped Aaron escape. He may not have known all the names of the Yfel Brethren involved, but he was very familiar with the one human who orchestrated the crime—his father. A wave of nausea boiled up from his belly. Jake felt betrayed by his father. But he also saw himself as the betrayer to the Cererians.

He reached for Hilly and pulled her into his arms. He squeezed hard, wishing they were back in the Mat-Su Valley or hiking Denali's snowy slopes.

Hilly returned his embrace. For several moments they clung to each other without a word. Then she pushed back and peered into his eyes.

Jake fought back tears of frustration, but Hilly could tell he struggled with something that caused pain and conflict deep within. "You have to go back to Aningan, don't you?"

A twisted grin stretched on Jake's face. He wasn't surprised by Hilly's question. She was always several steps ahead of everyone else when it came to problem solving. He lightly stroked the soft skin of her cheek. Then he tousled her hair before kissing her forehead. "Yes. I'll be leaving immediately. I wish I could stay and witness Kai's final test, but I look forward to hearing about his adventures in person." Despite his efforts to appear strong and confident, his eyes revealed a dark foreboding.

"What's the plan? What's our next step? Is there any danger to the two of us?" Hilly joined Kai and wrapped her arm around his waist. "Has the Cererian High Council considered how we can avoid Aaron? Or are we left to our own devices?"

Jake snuffed at Hilly's sarcasm. "Hilly, Mount Shasta will protect both of you from Aaron's reach."

"How do you know this? Have you spoken with the earth spirit?" Hilly turned to her brother. "Kai, has Mother Shasta informed you of this agreement?"

Jake interjected, "Hilly, it's what I know. It's what the Cererians know. Please accept that answer as the truth."

"Not good enough. I did my job and locked Stygian away in his interdimensional cell. Explain to me how Cererians, who are far more advanced in their powers, could not keep Aaron contained."

"I understand your frustration. But I can promise that Aaron and his Yfel Brethren will not venture to Mount Shasta. You are safe on these slopes."

Hilly studied her friend. He gazed back at her with weary eyes but a determined smile. "Okay, Jake. I believe you."

"I have one more request."

"What's that?"

"Would you open a portal to Aningan so I can meet with Benedict and Darrius?"

Hilly laughed. "You're such a demanding bush pilot." She stepped away from Jake. Thrusting her hands into the sky she invoked the powers of earth, air, fire and water. The swirling maw of a gateway appeared before her. Jake strode to the entrance and glanced back at Hilly. A generous smile brightened his face as he fell backward into the darkness.

The portal closed with a soft hiss.

Chapter 25

3rd Test: Ancestral Song

AND THEN THERE WERE two.

Kai and Hilly twirled around, both of them startled by the voice in their brains. Axel sat in the shadows sneering at the siblings.

"You have an annoying way of popping up without warning," Hilly snipped.

Axel glared. His eyes flared a crimson red. *I see the warrior has left. Will the witch follow?*

"There was an emergency back home." Hilly crossed her arms and squinted at the coyote. "I'm not going anywhere."

My condolences on the unfortunate news.

Kai and Hilly traded anxious glances. "What unfortunate news?" Hilly probed.

The news about Aaron Aningan's escape has already traveled the world. Those who reside on the other side of the veil know such things because we are connected by magical energy. The Cererian Prophecy warned of this day.

"Are you concerned Aaron will come here?" Hilly asked.

Ha! Mother Shasta has not permitted a Cererian on these slopes in many years.

Hilly smirked. "Why would an earth spirit prevent Cererians from visiting?"

Axel howled and his long, warbled cry echoed off the rocky slopes. *Our history is protected and is never shared with outsiders. If the shaman passes the third test, he will learn Shasta's secrets. I warn you, shaman, if you cross the veil and learn our sacred stories, you can never share them with her.* Axel nudged his nose toward Hilly.

The mood had turned too serious for Kai. Careful not to let Axel see his expression, he peeked at his sister. He raised his eyebrows and crossed his eyes, hoping to make her laugh. Hilly looked downward and bit her lip, suppressing the giggle that perched in her throat. She didn't want to insult Axel and ruin Kai's chance to see Shasta.

The sun had dropped behind the mountain hours earlier. Afternoon shadows had elongated, creeping along the ground until they merged with the forest gloom. A chilled breeze swept through the clearing. Axel stood on his hind legs and followed the scents swirling in the air as if invisible fingers tickled his nose.

It's time to go. The third test awaits us.

"How far away is the location?" Kai asked. "It's getting dark."

The black of night is the perfect setting for your final test, shaman. Axel trotted down a dirt path and disappeared into the blackness.

Kai hesitated. "Hilly, I'm nervous about this final test."

She chuckled. "You've been mauled by an animal. Then you matched your wits against a bigfoot and passed with flying colors. What could be so bad about this test?"

"If I pass, I'll cross the veil and see Shasta. You won't be able to come with me. Axel made that point clear. What if she doesn't let me come back?"

"Kai, you're overthinking this. When I met with Denali, she shared her secrets and then released me. It will be the same with Shasta. I promise."

Shaman! I will not wait forever! Axel's warning pierced their brains like an icepick.

"We better get going," Kai said as he jogged down the trail.

"I'm right behind you!" Hilly shouted.

The Kemps ran into the night.

Darkness churned in the forest as evening rolled down the mountain slopes like an inky blanket. Shadows and shapes fused together forming an impenetrable blackness under a moonless sky.

Unable to see his hand in front of his face, Kai trusted his instincts as he hurried forward, slapping branches aside. "Look out, Hilly!" he shouted as he ducked under a low-hanging limb.

"Thanks," she puffed. Concerned they may be separated in the thickening gloom, Hilly followed closely. Her hand lingered on Kai's shoulder, maintaining constant contact as they plowed through the darkness together.

Kai slipped on leaf litter and stumbled over tree roots as he rushed along an ancient animal trail. The single-track path meandered haphazardly through the woods, passing several gurgling streams and sweet-smelling glades. The pathway narrowed and Kai hurdled into the thorny clutches of a wild bramble. Its spine-covered branches snagged his skin and clothes as he struggled to free himself. The more he thrashed, the tighter the briar held him.

"Help. I've been captured by a barbed beast."

Not able to see Kai's assailant, Hilly trusted her sense of touch. Her fingers crept along her brother's arm until she located the spiny fingers grasping his body. She pulled and bent the thin twigs until Kai was free of his prickly prison.

"My hands are on fire thanks to that wretched plant," she moaned.

"No doubt you have hundreds of tiny stinging hairs embedded in your palms. It will be impossible to get them all out," Kai sympathized. "But I really do appreciate your help."

"Yeah, I bet you do, big brother. Otherwise, it would be *your* hands throbbing." Hilly winced. "Shit, these little spines hurt."

"When we catch up to Axel, I'll take care of your hands." He took her wrist and gently tugged her forward. "Come on, Hilly, we've got to keep moving."

The route gradually edged upward. In the higher elevation, the air thinned and the siblings struggled to breathe. Kai marched forward with his head down, and his arms chugging back and forth while his elbows brushed along his ribs. "We've...got...to...be...close," he gasped.

"We've been...on this...trail for...over thirty...minutes," Hilly panted.

Welcome to the third test, shaman.

The coyote's words startled the siblings. Kai halted, and Hilly crumpled into his back. "My hands!" she wailed, holding her tortured hands in front of her. "My hands are on fire! Kai, please do something."

When they collided, Hilly had twirled away from Kai. He searched for her in the darkness, homing in on her moans.

"Where are you, Hilly?" he asked. He shuffled in short steps, and held his arms out straight, swinging them back and forth, probing the blackness for her.

"Ow!" Hilly cried as Kai bumped into her outstretched hands.

Kai pulled Hilly into his arms. Even though they faced each other, the gloom cloaked their features. "Give me your hands," he urged as he felt along her arms. When he reached her wrists, he gently cupped her hands and hummed a mantra.

Hilly softly sobbed. The relentless stinging stabbed at her spirit and eroded her fortitude. She detested being vulnerable. Dependent and fearless, she'd been able to overcome any adversity; and now, hundreds of hairy stingers were taking her to the brink of her tolerance.

A soft buzzing filled the air as Kai hummed the healing words, phrases that came easy to him. Although he had never spoken the ancient incantation before, his intuition pulled it forward accessing knowledge he possessed as a child.

A soft white glow surrounded their hands as a comforting warmth, which began in the tips of Hilly's fingers, spread along her palms and up her arms. The light's vibrant pulsing matched the heartbeats of the siblings, very rapid at first. But as the pain abated, the pulsating slowed and soon disappeared. Kai gently blew, propelling a misty puff of energy over their intwined hands.

"The pain is gone," Hilly whispered.

Kai leaned forward and kissed her hands. "I said I would take care of you, didn't I?"

A touching moment, Axel interrupted. *See, shaman, your natural gifts were eager to present themselves once you believed.*

"Believed what?" Kai asked.

You're awakening to who you really are. But I sense doubt still lingers under the surface. The final test will reveal all and bring you home to Mother Shasta.

A chill swirled through the glade. The temperature fell gradually as a fine mist encircled the clearing. The intense blackness morphed into a heavy milkiness as a fog billowed around Kai. The cool droplets felt like tiny fingertips caressing his cheeks. He peered upward into the inky night sky. Brilliant diamonds sparkled around the moon's silver lining.

Axel followed his gaze. *A new moon. New beginnings are within your grasp, shaman.*

Images of the past flickered in Kai's mind like frames of a vintage movie reel. Snapshots of scenes and places tugged at his memory. The surge of recollections shocked him, and he yearned for more.

You are remembering, aren't you shaman? You stand in the center of a magical place. It was here, in this exact spot, that we last saw you before your family spirited you away to join the other magicians in the human world.

Kai paced the clearing's perimeter, walking confidently in the familiar steps he recalled from his past. Bushy pine branches drooped low, offering pine cone gifts. He touched their aromatic needles and mouthed a silent *thank you* as he walked by. Despite the murkiness, Kai could clearly see all the elements around him—Axel, Hilly, and the entities that lurked within the forest. The dark veil had lifted leaving him with psychic sight.

"I've been here before," Kai admitted. "This glade, these trees, they're all familiar. But I don't recall being on Mount Shasta. How is that possible?"

Haven't you? Axel sat on the edge of the clearing. In the darkness, only his eyes were visible—two yellow torches with a flicker of red.

"I've never been on this mountain. But, yet, I have. As I touch the trees, they recognize me and I, them. Even the air is familiar. I've inhaled its essence before."

"Déjà vu," Hilly uttered. "I had that same sensation on Denali."

"Yes! Déjà vu." Kai strolled into the center of the glade and twirled around. "So, where are they, Axel? Where is the one who will conduct my final test?"

The coyote's ears twitched back and forth. *They are arriving, shaman. Open your ears. Open your heart. Open your mind.*

Kai closed his eyes and cocked his head, straining to hear any sounds. Beyond the denseness of the fog drifted a low buzzing. The thrumming grew louder as high-pitched trills mixed with low tones, creating a continuous melodic vibration that rolled through the forest in soft musical waves, gaining tempo and volume as it neared the clearing.

"My dream!" Kai shouted. "This is my dream." His nightly vision was unfolding before him. His insides quivered with the anticipation of what he expected next—the arrival of the orbs. He peered into the inky void, straining to see and hear the balls of light that always visited and sang to him while he slumbered.

He gasped. There they were. Pulsating lights descended from the sky and drifted through the forest. Six softly glowing orbs advanced toward him, moving easily around the trees and gently rising over the large rocks. They stopped a few yards away, hovering two feet above the ground. The six balls of light, each the size of a baseball, glowed a kaleidoscope of colors as they showered the forest in brilliant hues.

Moments passed before they advanced. Kai retreated into the center of the clearing as they maneuvered around him, encircling him in a ring of pulsating light. Electrical charges snapped and sizzled as the orbs rotated clockwise around the shaman. Kai swayed to the hypnotic voices.

Shaman, your third and final test is to sing the song of your people, Axel explained.

"The song of my people? What people?"

The coyote chuckled. *Shaman, you are surrounded by the Leohts. They are members of your birth family. They have come to take you home, but first you must prove yourself worthy by singing the ancient song of your people.*

"Leohts? How can I sing the song of my people when I don't know who they are?" Kai began to leave the center of the circle.

The orbs' radiance brightened as the Leohts corralled Kai back into the middle of the clearing with gentle nudging. They resumed circling Kai as their thrumming heightened with voices ranging from high-pitched squeals to baritone vocals, rising and falling like the waves of a tranquil ocean.

The bewitching tune and flashing colors lured Kai into a trance, and he moved in circles with the Leohts.

His mind quieted, and he ceased resisting the urge to escape. Kai opened his mind and released his ego. A wave of peace and contentment swept over him. He yearned to float with the orbs and to soar with them through the trees.

Feeling secure in the wash of the Leoht's positive energy, Kai closed his eyes and hummed a familiar melody from long ago. He had never spoken the words, but they fell easily from his lips. Familiar syllables from another time. Soon, the Leohts joined him, adjusting their pitch and tempo until their voices united in one melodic song. Kai slowly rotated in the middle of the circle with his arms outstretched to either side.

As the orbs and Kai performed their dance, Kai's feet lifted from the ground. Immersed in the lyrics of the song, he didn't notice that he steadily rose upward toward the stars. His arms still outstretched, Kai and his Leoht family spun wildly above the clearing.

The strobing lights formed a column of blurred colors; the song transformed into a powerful thrumming as though a million honeybees had joined the spiraling dance.

The performers whirled faster and faster until they vanished.

Silence.

The shaman has passed the final test. He has been taken to the other side of the veil.

Hilly walked into the middle of the clearing and scuffed the dirt where Kai once danced.

Your brother remembered the words to his family's ancient song. His Leoht brothers and sisters welcomed him to the other side to meet Mother Shasta.

"Those orbs were his family?"

Yes, your brother is a Leoht as were his father and mother. His parents chose to live away from Shasta and reside in your world. Although she knew they would be hunted down and killed, she allowed them to go. No one can stop the sacred word of the Prophecy. She had hoped Kai would find his way back to her. Today is a happy day.

"When will he return?"

He may not return.

"What? He's been taken captive?"

The shaman stands with his earth mother now. She will share the stories of his past, present, and future. The shaman may decide his future lies on these slopes with his magical family.

"I'm his family! I'm his sister!" Hilly shouted as she neared the coyote, fists clenched at her side.

Family can be an anchor that weighs you down so much you feel like you're drowning.

Hilly stopped. Her bottom lip trembled.

Axel repeated the words Kai shared with her at The Nine Muses when he told her about his journey to the estate, when Melvin Stanton asked about his family. At the time, Kai felt family weighed him down.

Axel studied the pain that lingered on her face. He knew his words wounded her. He intended no malice but had hoped his statement would prompt her to leave the mountain. The Cererian Prophecy had other plans for the witch and that did not include standing idly by on a remote slope while her brother met with Shasta.

You will not be able to follow your brother, witch. It's best if you leave and return home to Denali.

"Family doesn't leave family behind. I'll wait right here." Hilly crossed her arms, straightened her back, and squinted at Axel. "No matter how long it takes, I'll be here when Kai returns."

The coyote grinned.

Very well. If the shaman returns, he will appear in the middle of the clearing. Be careful. There are many magical souls that roam these slopes that are not as amicable as I or Troy.

The coyote pointed his nose toward the new moon, howled, and vanished.

Chapter 26

The Leoht Family

KAI STOOD ON THE magical side of the veil and watched Hilly and Axel.

They shimmered as though he viewed them through a watery window. The viscous membrane separating the worlds allowed Kai the privilege to see and hear everything in the human realm, but Hilly saw nothing of the magical dimension. Even though the siblings stood a foot apart, Hilly could sense nothing of her brother.

Axel's words infuriated Kai. He knew the coyote intended to anger his sister and drive her away. He shouted at Hilly, but she couldn't hear him. He telepathically reached out and was met by a wall of silence. He couldn't even sense her energy.

All communication with Hilly was removed.

You cannot link to your human sister on this side of the veil. The gentle words floated through Kai's brain, and he looked around. The six orbs hovered nearby many feet from the ground. Kai felt light as a dandelion seed drifting on the wind and looked down at his own body, which had transformed into a ball of light.

What happened to my body?

You are a Leoht. When you crossed the veil, you assumed your natural form.

Kai's brain swirled with questions and concerns, and the orbs drew near as if they sensed his confusion.

You have been gone so long. You have forgotten what it feels like to be a Leoht. But, like the healing words and the song of our people, your memories will return, and soon, you will understand your true nature.

What about my sister? Kai watched Hilly angrily approach Axel and knew the coyote was baiting her with his words.

Your human sister will be fine as long as she remains in the clearing. Axel will inform her of her options—to stay or to go.

But I don't want her to go! Kai's frustration elevated his energy, and the intensity of his emotions pushed the others away. The subtle action intrigued him. *What just happened?*

An orb approached. His blue colors pulsed brighter and stronger than the others. *Brother, you must control the energy of your thoughts. As you discovered, the human emotions you've developed while in the realm of man, negatively impact your energy on this side of the veil. Although you spoke telepathically, the force of your energy shoved us away.*

My apologies. I meant no harm. Kai had a lot to learn.

Having arrived in Shasta's world for a brief moment and Kai had already insulted his magical family and almost harmed them. Transforming into a ball of light was the last thing he expected. He anticipated standing in front of the earth spirit on his legs like Hilly did when she met Denali.

Instead, he arrived as an orb with no arms and no legs, full of human emotions that are unwelcome in this magical realm. He yearned to meet Shasta but confusion and doubt filled his mind. His sensibilities regarding his identity were scrambled once again—first at The Nine Muses and now in Shasta's world.

The Leohts floated around Kai and pulsed an array of softly glowing colors. The hues penetrated his skin and seeped to his core where the energy illuminated more memories. The flurry of images confused him. Kai cried out, *Axel said you were my family. How are we related? Do you have names?*

A tittering chorus echoed in his head as the Leohts giggled at his questions. The brighter orb replied, *Do you not sense who we are Kai? Are you not intuitive? Being human has dulled your abilities. Come with us, and we'll reintroduce you to your native family.*

The Leohts drifted away. Kai turned to follow but stopped and stole a glance at Hilly on the other side of the membrane. She stood alone in the darkened clearing. She was waiting for him. His heart soared. He knew he could count on his sister.

Kai, please follow us. The message tugged at Kai.

Buoyed by the assurances that his sister would wait for his return, Kai eagerly followed the Leohts, maneuvering his new body with great ease.

On the magical side of the veil, the mountain slope appeared the same as in the human realm except colors were brighter and the air was crisp and fresh, scrubbed of impurities. In this domain, fantastical beings walked freely about. Elves, fairies, trolls, and gremlins cordially waved as Kai passed. In the human world, they cloaked their existence and rarely appeared to humans.

The Leohts drifted by a stream where several undines sunbathed in their naked forms. Kai halted intrigued by the water nymphs. He had never seen such beautiful creatures before. The undines sensed the newcomer's presence and dove under the water. Several poked their heads above the surface and sneaked a peek at the stranger. Kai glowed a deep red, signaling his deep embarrassment, and departed.

An excited whinny snatched his attention, and Kai glanced up to the sky as a herd of winged horses flew overhead. They nickered and snorted as they passed, their white wings pumping effortlessly, carrying them toward Shasta's summit.

The Leohts led Kai to an immense cave which jutted from the slope underneath a massive quartz slab. The rocky mouth gaped almost thirty feet high and wide, its edges festooned with green vines and bushes which softened the appearance of the entranceway. The opening bustled with activity as magical entities entered and departed—some flying, some walking, and others slithering along the stones.

Troy and another bigfoot exited the cave. Troy waved as the Leohts flew by. Even though Kai was a ball of light, Troy intuitively knew it was his friend and welcomed the young shaman. "Welcome to the land of Shasta," he hailed in his gravelly voice.

Possessing no mouth, Kai could only mentally message his reply. *Thank you, Troy. I'm excited to be here.*

A pair of yellow eyes floated in the darkness and followed the tribe of orbs gliding through the entrance. *Axel!* Kai exclaimed.

The coyote yipped a welcome as Kai slid by and followed his family deeper into the cavern. Near the center of Mount Shasta, a network of pathways snaked throughout the mountain. These rough-hewn corridors led to the ancestral homes of Shasta's magical populations.

The Leohts maneuvered down a narrow shaft, barely a foot wide, which opened into an immense inner room. Kai entered the space and paused. Joy squeezed his heart as he witnessed thousands of orbs swirling within the room, all pulsating in different colors from vivid purple to pale yellow.

Here is your family, Kai. The bright blue orb stated.

Are they all related to me?

A chorus of sniggering resounded in his head, and Kai felt the heat of embarrassment.

Kai, we are all related. Think of it this way. Each member of the tribe of man is related in one manner or another, yes? Except for some natural variations, humans look the same. As it is with Leohts. So, that's why your sisters giggled. They laughed at your innocence.

Kai struggled to understand, but the differences between the worlds were vast. *Help me understand. I'm only familiar with the ways of humans, so I need to find a way to associate with that world. When you call me "brother" do you mean that as a term of familiarity or as a relation?*

The brighter orb gleamed. A pulse of blue scattered across its iridescent surface. *To use your human terms. I am your cousin. You can call me Lapis. My father was related to your mother. Your sisters who join you today are sister by association only. They are not related to you in human terms. But we use the terms "brother" and "sister" as a term of endearment. We are all one large family: the tribe of Leoht.*

Ah, I understand. Thank you for taking the time to explain it to me. Kai scanned the multitudes of orbs spinning within the three-story cave. A strong sense of belonging, of being part of something much bigger churned in his brain. *I'm honored and proud to be part of an amazing family.*

Kai glided further into the room, anxious to connect with other Leohts. As balls of light whizzed by him, many hailed him as "brother" and some called him 'Kai'. Profound happiness consumed him as he floated along supported on a cushion of positive energy. Even though he was part of a human family the Leohts represented that solid foundation on which he could hold on to and be secure. Like an anchor in a hurricane, he would never fear of being sent adrift or left behind. That deep sense of security had been missing for some time.

Except with Jeff. The name flashed in Kai's brain. Jeff had been Kai's rock for the last ten years—a decade full of passion, devotion and commitment. Lost and adrift after the incident at The Nine Muses, Kai found safe harbor in Jeff's arms. Kai regained his confidence and creativity thanks to Jeff's love and support. Jeff and Kai had created their own family.

Now, I have three families, Kai mused.

As Kai observed the other orbs, he realized that each one possessed a unique color variation. While they pulsed with the same colors of red, yellow, and blue, the sequence of colors, the strobing intensity or the speed in which the colors flashed were distinctly different for each orb. To his human eye, each ball of light had appeared the same, but as a Leoht, each individual was as different as a human.

Kai located Lapis and asked, *I overhead Axel tell my sister that my parents were Leoht but chose to live in the human world.*

A dark navy blue fluttered across the surface as he responded. *The coyote was reckless discussing Shasta's business with the witch. It is not his place to discuss those details with outsiders. Mother Shasta will inform you about your past, present, and future.*

When will I meet her? Kai couldn't contain his excitement. His outer skin pulsed through various shades of purple. He was anxious to finally meet the earth spirit that had visited his dreams and branded his chest with the shaman's mark.

I ense your eagerness to meet Shasta. She patiently awaits you in the main chamber. I will take you there now if you wish.

Yes, please. Let's go now. I've waited so long to meet her.

Lapis guided Kai out of the Leoht ancestral home and back into the main passageway. They journeyed farther into the depths of the great mountain. Initially, when they arrived, the Leohts traveled upward toward their family chamber. But now, Kai sensed his cousin was leading him downward, into the bowels of the mountain.

Multiple shafts crisscrossed like a honeycomb—some going up and down and others going right and left. The blue orb moved deftly, zipping through the dark tunnels while Kai followed close behind. Kai tried to remember the way, but his cousin traveled corridors seemingly without rhyme or reason. After many minutes, a long, snaking pathway deposited them into an immense room.

Constructed of white quartz and granite, the chamber soared thirty stories high. The floor shimmered orange-red as pure molten lava oozed through the fissures; and spit enormous flames upward toward a circular selenite platform perched fifty feet above the molten lake. In the middle of the platform, a quartz spiral staircase led up to a small observation room which glowed with a brilliant white light.

Mother Shasta awaits you. Kai's cousin gestured toward the shimmering white room. He floated back and forth with excitement.

Kai had intuitively noticed Shasta. He recalled how she appeared during her visit on the plane—an ethereal being bathed in brilliant white light and ice crystals.

Do I need a formal introduction? Kai asked.

His cousin patiently responded. *Kai, you are home with the mother. She already knows who you are. Now, it is time you become reacquainted.*

Lapis pulsed a happy sky blue and zipped away, leaving Kai alone. He stared at the room atop the staircase. Rays of white light engulfed the compartment, but Kai could see Shasta floating past the windows. An icy arm reached out to him, and she curled a finger gesturing for him to join her. *Come, my son.*

Kai was finally meeting Shasta. He had rehearsed this moment in his mind so many times. Now that the moment had arrived, he was paralyzed in fear.

He had been away too many years. *I understand your concern, Kai. But please join me, and let's talk about you and your family.*

Family.

That's what it was all about. Family awaited him in Sedona, family waited for him in the clearing on the other side of the veil, and family welcomed him in this magical world. He yearned to understand more about his birth mother and father and the Leoht tribe to which he belonged.

It was time Kai discovered who he truly was.

He drifted into the observation room and instantly felt a warm, welcoming energy penetrate his soul as Shasta spread her arms wide and folded him into her bosom.

Welcome home.

Chapter 27

Mother Shasta

THE OBSERVATION ROOM WAS small in comparison to the monstrous cavern which it was housed. The size of a small bedroom, the five-sided compartment featured an arch window in each of its walls, but instead of panes of glass, a shimmering membrane covered the openings. Shafts of light penetrated the thin barrier and illuminated the chamber. A selenite column connected each wall, and a quartz roof sat atop the magical space.

Shasta hovered in the middle of the room with white light radiating from every part of her body. To Kai, she appeared as a heavenly star. Despite the intensity of her brightness, Kai could discern Shasta's features. She gazed tenderly at him through eyes crafted of faceted emeralds set within a white quartz face. Her delicate mouth curved upward toward a petite, sharp nose. Her gown sparkled with thousands of uniquely formed ice crystals that formed a lacy fabric that draped to the floor.

When Kai joined Shasta, his colors brightened and hues of violet swirled within Shasta's aura as the two beings exchanged energy from their souls. A warm peaceful sensation consumed Kai. He didn't want the pleasure to end, but he needed answers.

Mother, I have so many questions. Kai floated out of her embrace and peered into her intense green eyes.

I anticipated you would want to know more about your family history and your lineage. Shasta drifted to a granite bench and lowered herself until she hovered above the rock. She gestured for Kai to join her.

The Leohts have existed behind my veil for thousands of years. They also have families on all the great peaks of the world. You were born right here on my slope. You were a special child, an individual who would impact our world in extraordinary ways.

A reddish-violet fluttered across Kai's skin. An awkward self-conscious-ness crept into his soul as he processed Shasta's word. *Mother, I'm humbled by your words. But how did I come to live in the world of the humans?*

Shasta's light shimmered as she sighed. *How you came to be in the world of the magicians is a frustrating tale, but The Cererian Prophecy dictated those actions. I disagreed with the predictions, but I am just an earth spirit and am subject to the Word like all other living beings.*

A thousand years ago, the world was thrown into chaos when Stygian and his followers began hunting and killing magical people. Magicians scattered throughout the world, cloaking their whereabouts, and protecting their family crystals.

The populations on my slopes yearned to join the magicians in their fight. The supernatural entities protected behind my veil begged to help the magi-cians vanquish the Yfel Brethren. A select few—those who were the stealthiest and cunning—were allowed to venture forth into the land of man. These included the coyotes, bigfoot, fairies, and the Leohts.

When they were old enough, your parents requested permission to join the magicians. But, unlike their kin, they asked to be allowed into the human world as humans and not Leoht. Their reckoning was that they would have more advantages in a human body than as a ball of light. Their argument was compelling, and I relented. I transformed them into the individuals they yearned to be.

Shasta stopped talking and drifted toward one of the windows. With her back toward Kai, she softly wept ice crystal tears. She twirled. *I regret that decision. I lost two amazing individuals who were pure of heart. But, despite that loss, I am fortunate to have before me, their son—a strong shaman and my champion. I don't want to lose you again, Kai.*

The spirit's words touched Kai's heart. This was as close as he would ever be to his birth mother—through Shasta's memories. *Was I born behind the veil or in the realm of man?*

You have a foot in both worlds, my son. You were born human. It was your parent's hope that they would return to me and bring you home to the tribe of the Leohts. They were killed on their journey home. They were murdered on my slopes.

Shasta raised her arms in anger, and a pulse of powerful energy buffeted Kai. *Their death angered me. The Cererian, Darrius, promised he would protect them from harm but reached them too late. He was able to spirit you away before Stygian could consume your power. When I demanded Darrius return you to your people, Darrius refused. He claimed The Cererian Prophecy dictated you be kept in the realm of man. You would be raised by humans and the memories of your previous life would be erased. He claimed it was for your protection.*

Shasta sat on the bench again, the energy beginning to calm in the room. *Only I know what is right for my people. When you were stolen from me, I wove a protection spell around my mountain. From that moment, Cererians were prevented from visiting my slopes. If they dared to set foot on my soil, they would disintegrate. They fear me now. They know my power.*

Kai's parents had intended to bring him home and deliver him into the loving arms of his Leoht family. Despite this poignant truth, his heart was filled with joy, and yet, he struggled with the matter of his other families: Jeff and the Kemps. Then there was his friend, Darrius. It was clear Shasta abhorred him.

His silence revealed his internal battle and Shasta spoke. *You struggle with knowing where you belong, don't you, my son?*

Mother, my heart sings with the love of my parents, and it beats with the lifeblood of my Leoht family, but I have two other families to which I belong. You mentioned you don't want to lose me again. But how can I resolve yearning to be with three families—one on this side of the veil and two in the realm of man? The Kemps are my human family, and Jeff is the love of my life.

Shasta embraced Kai. A sweet warmth engulfed him. *I understand the joy and agony of love. I'm not uncaring. However, you must decide. You will need to choose whether you join the magical beings on this side of the veil as your parents intended, or you will be part of the realm of man. You cannot have it both ways, Kai.*

Though he loved being in Shasta's peaceful aura, Kai pulled away and stood by the wall. He was not prepared to make such a hard decision: choose the Leohts or his siblings and Jeff. There had to be a way to exist in both worlds. Kai had a mission to find his crystal and reunite it with the Guardian boulder. Nobody, not even Shasta, could stand in the way of The Cererian Prophecy.

Mother, I understand your concerns, but there is my destiny to consider. I am one of the four who will restore peace to the world. Hilly has completed her part. Now, it is my turn. I must find my family's crystal and return it to its Guardian boulder. I must travel into the realm of man for this. There has to be a compromise with my existence in both worlds.

Shasta nodded knowingly, pleased with Kai's assertion. *Yes, my son. I am aware of your mission and will support you. Peace must be restored to the earth. Your family crystal resides in your ancestral home. Lapis will show you where it is located. I caution you; the crystal is fragile. In this realm, it is solid, but once you cross into the human world, it becomes pure energy and will live in that form for only three months. If you are not successful uniting it with its Guardian within that timeframe, the crystal's energy will disintegrate and be lost forever. And peace will never be restored to the world.*

Three months. To some, that is a long time. But to a magician who has no idea where the Guardian boulder resides, three months is not long enough. Kai shuddered with the enormity of the task. Hues of light purple skittered across his skin.

Shasta noticed the hesitation swirl over Kai. *You are full of doubt. But you are a Leoht and a child of Shasta. You have powers and abilities unmatched by others. You can accomplish this task. I have faith in you. And, you have friends in the realm of man who will help you in your journey.*

Kai brightened at her words. In his fear, he had forgotten about Jake. *Mother, thank you for reminding me about my friend. He will assist me in searching for the Guardian. The Sentinel Boulder provided him with the location of the remaining three receptacles. With Jake as my guide, I will be successful in restoring the crystal to its seat of power.*

Shasta beamed. *You make me proud. I look forward to your victorious return. But don't forget, Kai, one day you will need to decide. You will need to choose whether you live with your Leoht family behind the veil or stay with your human family. If you choose the land of man, you will never be able to penetrate the veil again. It's a serious decision not to be taken lightly.*

Chapter 28

Bromus

KAI LEFT THE OBSERVATION room and glided toward Lapis who pulsed a steady aquamarine as a warm welcome to his cousin.

Kai responded with shimmering hues of violet. *You overhead our conversation?*

No, Kai. Shasta's words are private, audible only to the intended party. However, I could see the emotions roiling through your skin. Did she upset you?

Kai gazed lovingly at the brightened chamber where Shasta's brilliance glimmered and danced. *No, she didn't upset me, but she gave me a lot to consider.*

Yes, Shasta is known for her deliberate conundrums in which there are no right or wrong answers. Lapis fluttered with various blue hues as a light giggling echoed in Kai's head. *All visitors leave in various states of wonderment after meeting with her.* Lapis giggled again.

Kai mused on his cousin's bewildering response. Was Shasta testing him again? Was there yet another answer to the earth spirit's demand that he must eventually make a choice between the two realms? He hoped the answer presented itself soon. *Lapis, Shasta mentioned that you will guide me to the location of the Leoht family crystal. It's my responsibility to unite it with its Guardian boulder in the realm of man.*

Yes, Shasta notified me of your quest and asked me to assist you in any way I can. Follow me back to our ancestral home, and I'll introduce you to Bromus, the elder of our Leoht tribe. He is a fascinating soul who has lived longer than any other Leoht. He is the storyteller of our family history.

Lapis led Kai through the maze of narrow passageways snaking through the mountain. The twists and turns were too numerous, and Kai struggled to remember the way. *Cousin, how do you know which way to go? Though we passed this way earlier, the corridors look entirely different—these rocky tubes appear like the miles of other passages we've traveled.*

Lapis flashed a bright blue. *Cousin, once you remain permanently in the world of Shasta, you will learn to employ the essence of your life force. Your soul's light will guide you through the channels of our rocky lair.*

Kai quivered with excitement and purple hues skittered across his skin. The Leoht powers were numerous. He wondered if he would retain his human magical abilities if he stayed behind the veil. Combining his psychic skills with his innate Leoht capabilities could possibly make him more powerful than any of his kin or any other magical entity.

Kai shuddered, but not in a pleasant manner. Thoughts of power and control shot through his mind so easily, yet he was not a person who thirsted for these qualities. He was a man of peace and loved to make others laugh. The notion that he might dominant others crept effortlessly into his brain and that disturbed him.

We have arrived. Lapis' announcement jerked Kai from his reverie. The two Leohts floated into the ancestral home. The massive room swirled with a multi-colored glow as thousands of orbs glided by, pulsing their unique hues. *Follow me, Kai. I will take you to Bromus.*

They approached a large niche carved into the side of the cavern. Located near the midpoint of the chamber, the rocky cavity was only a foot wide and tall and appeared as an insignificant hole in the granite. As they drew closer, six larger orbs—the guards of the crystal—pulsed a warning of dark crimson while closing ranks in front of the entranceway. In unison they ordered, *Halt! This area is off limits. You must turn around immediately.*

We have permission from Shasta to seek the wisdom of Bromus. Lapis flashed a calming blue hue to demonstrate he meant no harm.

A red orb advanced toward Kai and demanded, *Who are you? Your inner light pulses with strange hues. You are not from our world.*

I am Kai. I am human by birth, but I am a Leoht descendant. My mother and father lived in this ancestral home. Lapis pulsed a nervous bright blue at Kai's boldness and watched angry shades of burgundy flutter across the guard's skin.

Tense moments passed before the guard spoke again. *You are Shasta's champion. We heard you entered the veil earlier. I've just communicated with the Mother, and she vouches for you and your cousin. Follow me.*

The tiny entrance opened into a ten-foot-high chamber constructed of luminous, white quartz. Crystalline shards jutted from the ceiling like rows of glittering teeth. In the middle of the spacious room, sitting atop a rocky alter, blazed a brilliant quartz gemstone. The crystal was barely three inches in length, but the minuscule gem brightened the space with an intense power.

Kai trembled in its presence. The crystal's energy poured through his body and tenderly caressed his soul. A flurry of violet hues fluttered across his skin.

She recognizes you.

The foreign voice surprised Kai, and he whirled to find another orb had joined them. The hazel-colored Leoht pulsed earthy hues of greens and browns. The mottled surface of the orb's skin reminded Kai of marbles he'd own as a child.

The crimson guard floated forward. *This is Bromus, the Keeper of the Crystal, the elder of our tribe, and the storyteller of our history.*

I am Kai. I am a shaman and Shasta's champion. I am Keeper of the Keys and a member of the Family of Air. Kai proudly stated his accomplishments. Since Troy's admonishment for omitting his achievements during the second test, Kai remained conscious of his attitude during introductions.

The red guard spoke sharply. *Bromus, Shasta has requested that you meet with Kai. He seeks information on you and the family crystal.*

Bromus flashed a warming mossy shade. *Yes, Captain. Shasta has made me aware of Kai's quest. You may leave us now.*

The red guard hovered for several seconds and scanned Lapis and Kai for any negative intentions before he darted back into the main cavern.

The three orbs floated around the family crystal, lured by her beauty and mesmerized by her power. A tranquil stillness filled the room.

Uncomfortable with the prolonged silence, Kai uttered, *Bromus, Lapis informs me that you are the oldest Leoht. Is that correct?*

Before Lapis could explain his cousin's brusqueness, Bromus responded. *You are like your mother, Kai. She, too, was a restless soul. She was anxious to make a difference in both worlds. Your impetuous nature may garner you results sometimes, but it can also create animosity.* Bromus moved away from the crystal and continued, *Why don't we start at the beginning?*

A chill raced through Kai's soul. Those words were so familiar. Hilly spoke the same sentence when she advised Kai about how to locate his family crystal. Was that purely a coincidence?

Bromus flashed a bright green. *Let me start with who I am. I am the oldest, living Leoht. I have existed in this world for over two thousand years. Leohts have long lifespans, however there are several factors that might impact how long an individual will live. I have never been in the realm of man but many Leohts have crossed over often—some out of curiosity, and others to perform missions for Mother Shasta. To them it's an exciting adventure full of new sights, sounds and smells. But they risk shortening their natural life with each visit to the other side of the veil. Each journey through the membrane degrades their cellular structure. Eventually, they will be too weak to travel to the world of man or they will lose their light and die.*

Kai pondered Bromus' words. *I think I understand. Humans know drinking and smoking shortens their life, but they find these habits pleasurable and continue to do them despite the consequences.*

Bromus flashed a bright green in agreement. *Follow me, and I will share the tales of your family.*

Bromus hovered near a corner of the room. As Kai and Lapis drew near, they pulsed with excitement as they scanned a wall studded with colored crystal nuggets. The decorated wall soared vertically up to the ceiling of the chamber. *Behold, the history markers of each Leoht family. There are hundreds of families represented on this wall. Each nugget contains the names and history of a family's ancestors.*

The trio drifted upward until Bromus halted at a stone swirling in an iridescent purple. Kai knew the nugget represented his family, and anxiously blurted, *This is my family. What can you tell me about them?*

Bromus pulsed a happy bright green. *You are correct. This gemstone belongs to your family. Over one thousand years of history is contained within this stone. Some of your ancestors witnessed the creation of The Cererian Prophecy. The forefathers of your human friends do not share that privilege.*

Bromus approached the purple nugget until he touched the stone. An electrical charge skittered at the connection and ancient history flooded into Bromus. *Your mother and father met in the ancestral chamber. It was a perfect match between the strong blues of your mother's sacred clan and the bold reds of your father's warrior family. Together, they forged a powerful, magical union. But they desired to do so much more than perform their duties behind the veil. They knew of the magicians' plight in the realm of man with the murders by the Yfel Brethren. Shasta's children watched in horror as magicians were killed for their magic. With the combined powers of your mother's and your father's families, they were confident they could make a difference and help the magicians kill the evil soldiers.*

Alas, their brashness attracted Stygian who hungered for their unique powers—the same abilities you possess. The earth spirits of the world implored the Cererians to intervene and stop the killing, but they were too late.

Bromus paused and studied Kai's glow which shuddered lilac with bursts of deep purple. *I know it is painful to hear of your parent's deaths, but although their lives ended, yours had just begun. Darrius saved you as was preordained by the Prophecy. Darrius was aware he would not be able to save the entire family. Shasta, too, had the same knowledge. Still, it angered her that Darrius kept you in the realm of man to be reared a human along with the other three magical children who would restore peace to the world.*

Kai had remained quiet throughout Bromus' story. But his emotions flowed across his skin in waves of sadness and regret. His parents' selflessness and desire to make a difference in the world impressed him; he wondered if he would ever measure up to their ideals and accomplishments.

Bromus, do I have any living relatives here behind the veil?

The orb glowed a brooding deep forest green as he pondered Kai's question. *You don't have any direct brothers and sisters. You were an only child, but you have Lapis and other cousins that are related to you. And don't forget, you have all the brothers and sisters of the Leoht family.*

In the land of man, Kai had a finite number of relatives. In the land of Shasta, Kai had thousands of kin who would treat him as one of their own without prejudice. The thought of so many relations overwhelmed his senses. He was more comfortable with a few individual souls interacting with his energy. The thought of many individuals claiming him as their brother, prompted Kai to conjure an image of himself as a lonely soul in a colony of ants.

Troubling dark purple fluttered across Kai's skin. *Bromus, I am fortunate to have the support of so many loved ones, but I also have family on the other side of the veil. Those individuals are just as important to me as those in the land of Shasta. It will be my human family that will sustain me as I embark on my quest to join our family crystal with the Guardian boulder.*

And it will be your Leoht family who supports you as you carry our prized family jewel to the other side. Bromus had no bitterness in his voice but spoke deliberately to reinforce the importance of all the entities who have a vested interest in Kai's success.

You are right, Bromus. I meant no disrespect.

You have only been on this side of the veil for one day. We cannot expect you to behave like a fully-fledged Leoht in this short amount of time.

Bromus chuckled. Bursts of brown and green streaked across his skin. *Come, Kai. It's time you became more acquainted with the family crystal. The magical populations on Shasta's slopes are anxious for you to embark on your quest and restore our prize jewel to its seat of power. You don't want to disappoint them, do you?*

Chapter 29

The Crystal of Air

Lapis, Bromus, and Kai gathered around the family crystal that sat upon the granite alter. The gemstone gleamed a rainbow of colors. The hues cascaded around the room and bounced off the jagged quartz jutting from the ceiling. The refracted light radiated miniature rainbows throughout the chamber.

I always imagined the family crystal would burn with a light blue flame since it is associated with the Family of Air, Kai remarked as he gazed upon the jewel. *My sister's gemstone flamed a pale-yellow glow, which represented her alliance with the Family of Fire.*

Bromus flashed a bright green. *You will find that all the crystals respond differently depending on the family from whence they came. The Leoht crystal is unique. As you see, it pulses all the colors of our tribe—red, yellow, blue, and all the shades in between. It is a stone of inclusion and demonstrates this unity by pulsing all the colors. But once you unite it with its Guardian boulder, it will burn a steady blue flame, representing the element of air.*

Kai hovered closer to the crystal. A low tone thrummed throughout the room as the gem recognized and welcomed him. *I feel so peaceful in her presence.*

Bromus pulsed a comforting mossy green. *She knows you are the chosen one, the Leoht responsible for carrying her to her final destination. It is an immense responsibility, a task reserved for the most holy of shamans.*

A flurry of lavender hues fluttered across Kai's surface. The word shaman was still uncomfortable for him to hear. He had never felt the slightest inkling of being a holy person until Shasta branded him with the Shaman's Eye and again, when Axel addressed him by the title. Now the elder, Bromus, proudly stated it, and Kai felt that familial connection once again.

As Shasta has told you, our precious jewel cannot survive in the world of humans for very long. Once you carry her through the veil, you have three short months to accomplish your mission, or she will dissipate into the ether and peace will never be restored to Earth. Bromus moved closer to Kai as he continued in hushed tones, *The family crystal is solid in Shasta's world, but will transform into an ethereal being on the other side of the veil. She will need to become one with you by fusing to the Shamans' Eye brand on your chest.*

Shasta advised me that merging with my essence will ensure her safety until I unite her with the Guardian boulder. Kai paused, considering his next statement. *Of course, if I'm found and killed by the Yfel Brethren, not only will they consume my magic, but they will also claim the power of our family crystal.*

Dismayed by Kai's words, Bromus flashed dark browns across his skin. *Thinking negative thoughts will gain you nothing, Kai. You must embrace your abilities and believe in your success. For only through having faith in your mission, will you be successful.*

Like Shasta, Bromus, had privileged knowledge of The Cererian Prophecy. He was aware of the future events but was bound by the Word to not share the information with anyone, not even Shasta's champion. Bromus could only observe as the future unfolded as it was preordained.

The gemstone pulsed a dazzling array of bright colors. *She is ready to be united with you, Kai.* Bromus flashed a bright, grassy green. His brilliance brightened as he conjured magic to levitate the gemstone from its rocky altar to Kai. Slowly the stone lifted upward, and drifted toward Kai who pulsed a flurry of purple hues in excitement.

The crystal nudged him and lightly fastened to his surface as Bromus completed his magic incantation.

The gemstone and you are now united, Kai. When you cross the veil to the land of man, she will fuse into the brand upon your chest. The crystal will naturally meld with your abilities. Your combined life forces will heighten your innate magic and grant you the powers you need to see the gemstone safely to the Guardian boulder. She will support you as you encounter the hardships along your journey.

What hardships? Kai asked, as an uneasy gray flicked across his surface.

Bromus pulsed a happy green to calm Kai's nerves. *One does not embark on an important quest such as yours and not expect the journey to be treacherous. There are those who wish to see you fail. Hilly, Fen, and Chance will combine their magic with yours to strengthen your defenses, but be wary, for things are not always as they appear.*

What do you know, Bromus? What will happen to me?

I have shared the words that can be spoken to you. I can say no more. Allow the strength of your abilities to lead the way and always trust your intuition.

The crystal thrummed against Kai's skin. The pleasant vibration rippled throughout his body and generated a tranquil state that he'd not felt in a long time. The gemstone assuaged Kai's fears and silenced his concerns.

Come, Kai, it's time to cross the veil and complete your quest, Bromus said as he led Kai and Lapis out of the small room, and into the ancestral chamber. The six red guards surrounded the group the moment they emerged. Activity in the cavern ceased as all the Leohts stopped swirling and pulsed their individual colors in recognition of Kai's sacred mission.

Your brothers and sisters bid you a safe journey, Kai, Bromus observed.

Kai slowly twirled as he absorbed the significance of their light show—his family paid tribute to his critical undertaking. In return, Kai pulsed a series of purple hues, his humble way to thank the Leohts for trusting him with the precious jewel.

Follow us, ordered the captain of the guard.

Two soldiers assumed the lead and guided the entourage out of the ancestral home and into the narrow passageways. The group followed the winding channels as they proceeded toward the exit from the great mountain. As they neared the gaping mouth of the cave, the guards encircled Kai, Bromus, and Lapis, ensuring the crystal and her sacred carrier were protected as they glided toward the veil.

The membrane that separated the realms of Shasta and of the human world shimmered like a gentle waterfall. Kai pulsed a happy violet when he saw Hilly on the other side of the glistening wall. His heart quickened with joy upon seeing his sister patiently waiting for his return.

He telepathically reached out to her. *Hilly, I'm here. I'll be joining you soon.* But his thoughts slammed against a barrier.

Bromus noticed Kai's frustration. *Your human sister cannot hear you. Once you crossed the veil, your psychic connection to Hilly was severed. When you walk in the world of man, your sister will no longer receive your thoughts.*

What? Nobody told me that would happen! Kai yelled his displeasure. Bromus and Lapis were buffeted by the emotional assault.

As Shasta has told you before, Kai. You cannot have it both ways. You will either live the life of a Leoht or be a human.

She said I had a choice.

Yes, you do have a choice. If you stay in the realm of man, your psychic connection to your sister is forever lost. Remember, you are transforming into the being you were meant to be. So, is your human sister. You may have lost one power, but you have gained so many more abilities. This is the way of the world, Kai. There will always be compromises—sometimes happy and sometimes not so pleasant.

Hilly cocked her ear toward the veil. Although Kai could no longer mentally talk with her, something deeper must've have alerted her to his presence.

The Leohts watched her actions with interest.

Fascinating, Bromus observed. *Your sister appears to be aware that we are nearby.*

Kai giggled softly. Dots of violet flickered across his skin. *Never underestimate the intuition of a firewalker witch.*

One day I will meet your sister, Bromus said as he hovered closer to the veil and watched Hilly peer directly at him. *She possesses a keen insight, indeed.*

Bromus changed the subject. *Kai, how will you find the Guardian boulder in the vast realm of man?*

My friend, Jake, knows where they are located. He is not allowed to speak the information, so he will accompany my siblings and I on our journeys.

Very good. I am familiar with the shaman named Jake. All magical entities have heard the tales of the Sentinel Boulder's son. He is an excellent ally.

The family crystal thrummed a message to Kai. Her words vibrated within his body as she conveyed her excitement to cross the veil.

It's time for me to go, Kai announced. *The crystal is anxious to meet my friends and to be united with its Guardian boulder.*

Lapis drifted closer and pulsed a sad dark blue. *It's hard for me to say goodbye. You just arrived and now you must leave. I look forward to the day you return to your ancestral home, and the day I can introduce you to the rest of your relatives.*

Lapis, I look forward to that day as well. I promise I will return. Kai drifted closer to the membrane separating the worlds. He hesitated. He stared at Hilly and then traded glances with Bromus and Lapis who flashed their colors in his honor.

How would he be able to choose between the families?

Kai pulsed violet hues and then pushed through the veil to the land of man.

Never forget who you are! Bromus shouted after him.

Chapter 30

Realm of Man

"My chest!" Kai screamed as he emerged from the veil. He collapsed onto his knees and clamped a hand across his chest.

"What happened, Kai?" Hilly knelt by his side and tried to peer under his shirt, but Kai pushed her away.

"There's nothing you can do. Damn, it stings so bad!" Kai rocked and stared at his sister. Agony filled his teary eyes. "It will be okay soon. I hope."

After several moments, Kai released a breathy groan and fell onto his side into a fetal position. He blankly stared forward as his fingers teased the shirt above his left breast.

Hilly rubbed the small of his back to comfort him. "Where's the pain, Kai?

He jerked his thumb at his chest.

"Shasta's brand?"

Kai nodded and closed his eyes.

"Let me see." Hilly grappled for Kai's shirt, but he slapped her hands away.

"Don't, Hilly. I don't think you're allowed." Kai pushed away from her, scooting backward in the dirt until he leaned against the boulder. He lifted his shirt flap and studied the Shaman's Eye. The burning eased, signaling the union of the crystal and brand was complete. Various hues danced across the marking, and Kai exhaled audibly with relief. "It hurt like hell, but this is one of the most beautiful things I've ever seen."

Hilly sat on her haunches observing her brother. "After saying that, do you really expect me to just sit here and *not* see it?" Hilly jumped to her feet and joined Kai. "Come on, let me see it," she demanded.

"Wait a minute," Kai countered. "I need to confer with my confidant."

"What the hell? What confidant?"

"I'll tell you in a minute. I need to get my bearings."

Kai closed his eyes and reached out to the crystal whose essence hovered below the surface of his consciousness. She thrummed a welcoming, and the vibration tickled up his backbone causing him to giggle.

"Are you okay, Kai? You're acting very weird."

"I'm better than okay," he replied as he struggled to stand. "First things first. Give your brother a big hug. I missed you."

Hilly pulled Kai into her arms and squeezed him hard. "I thought I had lost you, Kai. You've been gone two days."

Kai pushed back. "Two days? No, you're wrong. I was only gone about ten hours."

Hilly frowned. "Seriously, Kai. You've been in Shasta's world for two entire days. Believe me, I should know. I've been huddled by this boulder the entire time. Axel warned me against venturing off anywhere. He said unfriendly creatures inhabit the slopes and wouldn't be as kind to me as he and Troy."

Kai walked away, raking his fingers through his hair. His brain churned with the sequence of events in Shasta's world and the loss of time. Nothing made sense. He whirled toward his sister. "You wouldn't lie to me just to get your jollies from making me suffer would you?"

Hilly crossed her arms and glowered at Kai suspiciously.

"Why have you blocked your thoughts?" she asked.

"What do you mean?"

"I tried to probe your mind and encountered a massive barrier."

"Oh, yeah." Kai sat on the boulder and gazed off into the forest.

"Kai, are you okay?" Worry edged into Hilly's voice.

"Honestly, I don't know. My mind is scrambled right now. I do need to tell you something." Kai patted the boulder. "Come sit with me, Hilly."

Hilly obliged. But she squinted at her brother questioningly.

"A funny thing happened on my way to Shasta's world." Kai grinned, hoping to keep the mood light, but Hilly scrunched her face at his attempt of humor. He cleared his throat and continued. "I discovered when I crossed the veil, my psychic connection to you was permanently broken. It's the price I had to pay to visit Shasta." Kai winced after delivering the news, expecting Hilly to react badly.

Hilly stood calmly and walked to the edge of the clearing. Deep in thought, she fiddled with pine needles hanging on a low bough, twisting them between her fingers as she stared at Kai. "So what you're saying is that I can't reach you telepathically anymore. Is that right?"

Kai nodded.

"And that special bond we shared where I could feel your emotions and you could sense mine is gone. Is that correct?"

Kai nodded.

"So you and I will no longer have nightmares of each other's skirmishes and conflicts?"

Kai nodded. "Are you upset?"

Hilly bit her lower lip as she pondered his question. "I will definitely miss the convenience of mentally messaging you instead of calling. But I won't miss all those feelings and visions that weren't mine. Honestly, there were days I thought I would go insane."

Kai jumped to his feet. "Me too!" He ran to Hilly and grabbed her hands. "I love you, Hilly, but managing my life is hard enough without your crazy emotions mixing with mine."

"Agreed!"

The siblings danced around the clearing celebrating their new found freedom. For a moment, all their troubles had disappeared.

Then Hilly stopped. "But something is very different about you. I can't put my finger on it, but you've changed. What happened when you came through the veil?"

Kai smirked. Hilly's intuition was too good. "About that." Kai paused, unsure if he should share any more information about his travels to Shasta's world.

The crystal sensed Kai's quandary and vibrated warmth throughout his body. Kai slipped into the relaxation the gemstone offered. She gently coaxed Kai to tell Hilly everything.

Kai stared at the ground as he gathered his thoughts. A generous grin filled his face as he turned toward Hilly. "Do you recall your family crystal?"

"Yes, but what has that got to do with anything?"

"Be patient. Well, I found my crystal while I was in Shasta's world."

"Congratulations," Hilly said. She scanned his arms for the gem. "Where is it?"

"That's the interesting part. In the land of Shasta, my family crystal is solid, but in this realm, it transforms into an ethereal being. So I can carry it safely to its Guardian boulder, it has been fused into the brand on my chest." Kai unbuttoned his shirt and peeled back the left side.

Hilly's eyes widened as she gazed upon the Shaman's Eye which was no longer a red welt. Now that Kai's crystal had merged with his essence, the marking shimmered in iridescent colors—the multiple hues of the Leoht family.

"May I touch it?" she asked.

"Go ahead. It hurt like hell when I crossed the veil, but now there's no pain at all."

Hilly lightly brushed the brand with her fingertips. The colors glimmered and changed wherever her finger trailed. "It looks as though your brand is responding to my touch."

The crystal's essence acknowledged Hilly and churned a series of vibrations throughout Kai's body. He quivered from the interaction and gasped.

Concerned about his reaction, Hilly asked, "Did that hurt?"

"No, it was *very* pleasurable." Kai leered at Hilly and she punched his arm.

"How do you unite it with the Guardian?"

Kai glanced to both sides, searching for the answer. "That's a good question. I suppose we'll figure that out when we find the boulder. I'm sure the crystal will let me know."

"The crystal?" Hilly's forehead creased in wonderment.

"Yes. When she merged with my brand, we became a part of each other's life force. We are joined together until the moment she unites with the Guardian. She is the confidant I spoke of earlier." Kai's eyes sparkled. The thought of sharing the same space as the family crystal excited him and made him more determined to carry out his mission.

"Interesting development," Hilly noted. "It must feel odd to have another voice inside your head." The moment the words fell out of her mouth, Hilly blanched.

"I don't notice a separation. It's as though we've always been joined. It feels quite natural, actually." Kai gazed off into the distance. His eyes softened and the muscles in his jaw relaxed as he mused about his trip to Shasta's world.

"I imagine you have many stories about your visit with Shasta. If it was like my trip to Denali, you will need a full day just to catch me up on what happened."

"I have a story or two," Kai responded. His eyes flashed with mischief as he wiggled his eyebrows. "But I'll save those tales for when we have all the Kemps together. The more pressing issue is traveling back to Aningan so I can talk to Jake. I only have three months to unite my crystal with her Guardian. So I must leave on my journey as soon as possible."

"Three months? What happens if it takes you longer to find the boulder?"

"The crystal will dissipate into the ether and peace will never be restored to the world."

They stared at the ground as they considered the consequences of failing to restore the Crystal of Air onto its seat of power. A somber mood swirled as they envisioned the Yfel Brethren ruling the earth.

Kai broke the tension. "I have a more pressing matter."

"Oh? What would that be?"

"I desperately need a shower and clean clothes." Kai sniffed his armpits and grimaced.

Hilly chuckled. "I was going to say something."

"Do you happen to know where a guy like me could find a portal?"

Hilly laughed. After two days of worrying about her brother, it felt good to have Kai back and to be laughing again. "Sure thing, mister. I can hook you up with Hilly's Portals. Guaranteed to ferry you to anywhere in the world."

"Sign me up, please." Kai snorted with laughter.

On the other side of the veil, Bromus and Axel observed Hilly and Kai.

Humans are interesting to watch, Axel noted.

For a thousand years, I've watched humans come and go as they played the roles The Cererian Prophecy outlined for them. These two and their siblings, are critical in restoring peace to the earth. Follow them, Axel, and keep me apprised of their progress. We must be successful in uniting all the crystals with their Guardians.

The coyote nodded and bounded through the veil into the land of man.

Chapter 31

Return to Aningan

JAKE SAT ON THE steps leading to Aningan Properties. He peered into the street and fingered the amulet around his neck. Before leaving Shasta, he used the talisman to cast a protection spell over Kai and Hilly. Now the ancient artifact furiously vibrated, alerting Jake to the imminent return of his friends.

The gateway opened in the middle of the dusty street and kicked gravel against the bottom step of the stairs. Hilly emerged first pulling Kai behind her. Kai covered his eyes with one hand, hoping the portal's dizzying effects wouldn't be so bad on his second trip. Once the siblings had jumped clear of the entrance, the portal silently closed.

"How you doing?" Hilly asked as she led her brother toward Jake.

"Not so bad this time." Kai lowered his hand and was relieved that he didn't spin into the dirt like before.

"Welcome back!" Jake hailed them. "You took longer than expected."

Kai flashed his brilliant smile. "Hi, handsome Jake. Hilly and I have a dispute. I was only in Shasta's realm for ten hours, and Hilly seems to think I was gone for two days."

"Hmm," Jake murmured. "Hilly's right."

"I *knew* you would take her side. You disappoint me. I thought we had a thing going on."

Jake's eyebrows arched in surprise. "A thing?" He flashed a confused glance at Hilly.

Kai snuggled beside his friend and curled an arm around his waist. "You know. That cold night we shared a seat on the boulder when you wrapped me into your arms." Kai laid his head on Jake's shoulder and fluttered his eyes.

Jake bolted into the street. "Now, hold on, Kai. There's been a big misunderstanding."

Hilly and Kai burst out laughing.

"Wait. Is this one of your shitty jokes?" Jake shot piercing looks at the snickering siblings.

Kai bounded down the steps. "Jake, I love you like a brother. But, honey, I can't resist taking advantage of you because you are so damn gullible." Kai snorted loud which launched another round of laughter.

The tips of Jake's ears flamed red. He bit his lower lip and narrowed his eyes as he backed away from the siblings. He hated being fooled.

"Jake, it was just a joke. We didn't mean any harm," Hilly cajoled.

"See if I ever wait for you again." Jake turned his back and huffed. He knew if he pretended to be hurt, at least one, if not both of the siblings would come to his aide.

Hilly took the bait. She tilted her head and frowned. "Have you been sitting on those steps for *two* days waiting for us to return?"

Jake hung his head.

Hilly gripped his arm and turned him around. Jake's bottom lip pushed out in the biggest pout he could muster. "I'm sorry you waited all that time. We're both sorry, aren't we, Kai?"

Kai squinted suspiciously at Jake.

"Kai? You're sorry, right?" Hilly frowned at her brother who stared impassively back at her with a hint of a grin on his face.

Jake's pout transformed into a wide smile, his white teeth glinting in the sunshine. "Gotcha, firewalker. I didn't wait on those steps for two days. I had privileged knowledge that you were coming home a few minutes ago."

Hilly's cheeks flushed crimson. "Oh? And where did you get your privileged info? I didn't tell anybody we were coming home."

"An elder never discloses his sources," Jake smirked as he rubbed the amulet.

Hilly glared at her friend.

Jake held her gaze. Determined not to break the silence first, he thrust his chin out and narrowed his eyes.

"Good lord!" Kai exclaimed. "You two are so damned stubborn. Hilly, give Jake a hug."

Hilly exhaled loudly through her nose. "Okay, Jake. You got me. Now come here." She wrapped her arms around his neck and planted a kiss on his cheek. "It's good to see you again." She shook her head. "I don't know who's more evil, you or that butthead," she said as she jerked her thumb at Kai.

"Hey, now. Be kind. I am your brother," Kai said as he joined them. He elbowed Jake in the side, "I need to talk to you. It's about the location of the Guardian boulder for my crystal."

"You know I can't tell you anything," Jake said as he marched toward the stairs.

"I know. I know. But I only have three months to unite my crystal with the Guardian or it will be lost forever."

Jake stopped. "You found your crystal? Where is it?"

"Well, if you insist." Kai seductively unbuttoned his shirt. Jake peeked at Hilly, his eyes full of concern as Kai gyrated in front of him. "Ta-da!" Kai peeled the left side of his shirt open, exposing the Shaman's Eye.

"Wow! Look at the colors," Jake exclaimed. "But where's the crystal?"

Kai grinned a mischievous smile. "You're looking at her."

"What?" Jake leaned closer to inspect the marking. "I don't follow you. You're saying the brand is the crystal?"

"Well, you might say we had a meeting of the minds," Kai teased.

"Good grief, Kai, we don't have all day," Hilly blurted. "Jake, the crystal is an ethereal entity in the human world, so she had to fuse with the Shaman's Eye in order to travel to this side of the veil."

"That was my surprise, Hilly. No fair," Kai complained. The brand shimmered like an oil slick and lured Jake closer. Kai noticed his interest. "Go on, Jake. You can touch her."

Jake's eyes jumped in anticipation. He reached forward until his fingertips lightly skimmed the surface of the marking. The gentle action caused the colors to swirl in response.

A chill flew up Kai's spine. "Hey, that tickles," he giggled.

Jake stepped back. "I am impressed, Kai. That is some extraordinary magic."

"And you only know half the story."

"What else happened in Shasta's world?"

Kai casually brushed the dirt off his clothes, prolonging the anticipation. "That's a long story that will demand a stiff drink and much more time than what we have right now. Speaking of time, I don't have much of it to find the Guardian boulder."

"Stop, Kai. You know I can't tell you. I can only guide you to the location."

"I know you can't tell me. But I need an idea of where the Guardian is so I can plan a trip there as soon as possible. I'm sure Jeff is already mad at me so I might as well make him furious with my prolonged adventure. Can you hint at where we need to go?"

"What adventure?" The group swiveled to find Darrius standing outside the office door. His brilliant green eyes flashed a warm welcome.

Hilly sprinted up the steps and engulfed him in a hug. "Darrius, it's so good to see you again. The journey to Shasta has been interesting, but it's nice to be back in Aningan."

Overjoyed at Hilly's return, Darrius lifted her off the ground and twirled her around, which made her squeal with delight. He gently set her down and turned toward Kai. "How is Mother Shasta, Kai?"

"Well, she doesn't send her love." Kai chuckled as he mounted the steps toward Darrius.

The emerald green in Darrius' eyes grayed. "I see she shared some history with you."

"That and a lot more," Kai added as he hugged Darrius.

Jake announced, "Kai found his crystal and has an urgent need to find the Guardian boulder. The crystal will only survive in this world three months."

"I see," Darrius said as he brought his hands together in contemplation. After several moments, Darrius spoke. "I think our meeting today will bring clarity to your situation, Kai and will enlighten all of us on the events concerning Aaron."

Kai interjected. "You don't understand, Darrius. I need information now so I can talk to Jeff. He expects me back in Sedona today and that's not gonna happen." Worry lines wrinkled across Kai's forehead.

A gentle breeze kicked gravel across the dirt street. The disturbance snatched everyone's attention. Seconds later, Benedict and Fen materialized in the middle of the dusty road.

"Fen!" Hilly yelled as she ran down the steps toward her sister. Kai followed and the three siblings hugged in the middle of the street while Benedict joined Darrius.

Benedict politely nodded at Jake before mentally messaging Darrius, *Brother, I would have brought Chance back first, but he has already embarked on his journey.*

That's disconcerting. Do you know to where he traveled?

His wife explained that he departed for England three days prior. He has embarked on his quest to locate his family crystal. Having failed to reach Chance in a timely fashion, I immediately located Fen at her home and brought her here.

Hilly called out, "Darrius, Fen told us that Benedict brought her here for her protection. What's going on? Is Chance coming too?"

Darrius glanced up and down the street and psychically scanned the area to ensure no unfriendly entities had crept up on them. "Let's go inside. There's much to be shared, but not out here."

"Are we in danger?" Kai asked as he mounted the steps. "I need to call Jeff right away. If I'm in danger, he needs to know."

Darrius laid a calming hand on his shoulder. "Be patient, Kai. We have a plan for everything."

Darrius held the door open and invited everyone to enter. As each person filed by, Darrius searched their eyes, and probed deep into their minds. Concern and worry filled everyone's thoughts as they passed him.

Benedict lingered behind the others so he could have private words with Darrius. "I fear Chance is in peril. If our brothers on Ceres are correct, Aaron's appearance in England would have coincided with Chance's arrival."

"Yes, Benedict. The Cererian Prophecy spoke of this moment, but we are not privy to Chance's current situation. We must have faith in the Word, brother."

"Agreed, Darrius, but do the Kemps have faith?"

Chapter 32

The Plan

"Hiya!" Sammy called out as everyone shuffled into the back office. "I'm making coffee. Who wants some?"

Silence.

Jake, Hilly, and Fen eased into their seats and brooded, lost in their private worlds. Gloom settled around them like an energy thief.

Kai collapsed into his chair and chirped, "I'd rather have something with a little more kick, Sammy."

"You mean like a double espresso?"

Jake was in no mood for babbling nonsense and cut the conversation short. "Sammy, come sit by me. Nobody needs coffee." Jake glared at Kai for his inane request.

Sammy jumped on the wooden stool behind Jake's chair. His eyes nervously darted around the room. "Everyone seems mad. Is everything okay?"

"Everything is fine, Sammy," Darrius interjected. The Cererian hovered in the doorway and surveyed the room. The notion of condemned individuals awaiting their fate fluttered through his mind. Hilly chewed her bottom lip, Fen rubbed her temples, Kai fiddled with the brand on his chest, and Jake glared at Darrius.

Benedict had silently entered and stood near the window. Because of his pale coloring and extreme height, he appeared to float behind Hilly like a ghostly apparition.

Darrius exchanged a quick glance with Benedict before shutting the door. The two Cererians had chatted earlier, and had developed a plan for capturing Aaron, but the concept demanded everybody's cooperation.

Jake was aware of the plan to find Aaron. He wasn't pleased with all of the details, but he knew he had to trust Darrius.

Darrius grabbed the swivel chair from behind the desk and sat down. He studied the Kemps and remarked, "Your faces are etched with hopelessness and sadness. Are you already admitting defeat?" Darrius hoped his words would prick someone's pride.

"There's a lot to consider," Hilly began. "Aaron's free and furious. We have no idea how many other Cererians have joined him. And let's not forget that Chance is somewhere in the world unaware of Aaron's escape. Our brother's life could be in danger."

Darrius nodded. "Yes. The situation is serious but not insurmountable."

"Wonderful. Why don't you enlighten us, Darrius?" Hilly regretted the sarcasm the moment the words tumbled out of her mouth. "I'm sorry. I didn't mean to sound so bitchy," she added.

"Yes, you did," Kai remarked. "It was warranted. Frankly, I'm fed up with the trouble caused by these rogue Cererians. Since having our memories restored, we've been the targets of their brutality and we've been responsible for cleaning up their messes."

"Silence!" Benedict's demand surprised everyone, even Darrius. Usually quiet and mild-mannered, the gentle Cererian trembled with anger as he addressed the room. "Your comments are disrespectful and insulting. You behave like spoiled children and not like the powerful magicians you've become. Cererians have given their lives so that you may live. We have made sacrifices so that you can flourish and restore peace to the earth."

Hilly and Kai shrank away from Benedict who towered over them. He peered directly into their eyes. Pink splotches dotted his pale face, and he puffed from his explosive tirade. Known for being direct with his thoughts, Benedict had always delivered his comments without emotion—until now.

"Brother, your words were rich with truth," Darrius commented. "But your fury tainted their value." Darrius laid a hand on Benedict's shoulder, hoping to calm his comrade. "Come Benedict. We have much to share with the Kemps, and I need your assistance."

Benedict had recovered from his outburst—his breathing had eased, and his face had resumed its pasty white appearance. He lowered his eyes and backed away from the Kemps. "Yes, Darrius. You are correct. My apologies for the disruption. I meant no disrespect."

"All is well, brother. No harm has been done. Let's focus on why we are all here today."

Darrius cleared his throat, signaling the end to Benedict's interruption and the beginning of the main discussion. "Let me start at the beginning since all of you possess bits and pieces of the story, except for Fen." Darrius politely nodded at her.

"Aaron Aningan escaped his Cererian prison four days ago."

"I have a question," Kai interrupted. "Aaron has the same last name as this town? What's that all about?"

Jake muffled a groan and rolled his eyes toward the ceiling.

"Jake," Darrius admonished. "Please, a little decorum. Not everyone knows of this town's history. In order for everyone to plan for the future, we need to ensure we understand our past."

"Sorry, Darrius. You're right," Jake whispered as he shifted uncomfortably in his seat.

"Over a thousand years ago, this town was known as Pierson."

"What?" Hilly gasped. She stared wide-eyed at Darrius and then Jake who grimaced at her reaction. "I wasn't aware of that tidbit."

"During that time, Cererians arrived on your planet to explore and meet the inhabitants. Ours was a peaceful mission. But the longer we remained in your world, we realized changes were occurring within our bodies. Our host bodies were generated by merging our Cererian energy with the DNA harvested from human cadavers. What we couldn't predict was that we would adopt the emotions and behaviors of the individual who contributed their DNA. This evolution worked well for the majority of us and we maintained a peaceful coexistence with Earth's populations. But for some of our brothers, the transition was disastrous."

"What do you mean disastrous?" Fen asked.

"To our disappointment, we realized, much too late, that many of the donor cadavers were the remains of brutal individuals. As our brothers evolved, their emotions grew more volatile, and they eventually broke from our peaceful mission. Stygian is an example of a good soul inside a bad body. We later learned that his donor body had belonged to a disgraced warrior who relished killing others for sport."

Darrius paused to gather his thoughts before continuing. "Aaron also fell prey to greed and control. In exchange for betraying his human friends the Yfel granted him full control of the town including changing the name from Pierson to Aningan. So, to answer Kai's original question. The town was named after Aaron because he demanded the change. Now, that the town is back in the hands of the people, it will be their decision to revert back to the name of Pierson or keep it as it is."

The air in the room thickened with emotions.

The bleak mood was not lost on Benedict who reached out to Darrius telepathically. *I sense an overwhelming amount of negative energy in the room.*

You are paying attention to human emotions. Unlike you and I, they need time to process unsavory news. We have four strong magicians in this room. Once they've had adequate time to filter the information, they will endorse our plan.

Benedict nodded his agreement.

"Before I continue, does anyone have any questions?" Darrius paused and brought his hands together in front of him, the fingertips lightly touching. He peered at each person as he scanned the room and contemplated his next steps.

Silence.

"Very well. I will continue. Aaron escaped with the help of three individuals—two Cererians and a human magician who bargained for his life with Stygian directly."

Jake cringed. When he looked up, Darrius peered directly at him.

Darrius messaged Jake. *Do you want to tell your friends about your father or shall I?*

Can we omit that detail right now. I'm not in the mood to discuss personal issues.

But they will find out eventually. It's better if it comes from someone they trust. But it's your decision.

Indecision clouded Jake's eyes. If they were planning a way to catch Aaron, everyone involved needed to know what, and with whom, they were dealing.

Okay, Darrius. Go ahead and share the information. I'll prepare for any fallout.

Darrius shifted in his seat and began again. "The Cererians who aided Aaron are new converts to Stygian's Brethren. The human is a convert from the killing that occurred here in this town when Jake was a toddler. In exchange for information on local magicians that were in hiding, Stygian granted the human the opportunity to feed on his friends' magic like his Cererian followers. This human is known as Ryan Pierson."

"What?" Hilly blurted. She glanced at Jake who chewed his bottom lip and stared at the rug. "Are you related to him, Jake?"

Jake's boot heel thumped the floor nervously. Answers raced through his mind but none seemed right. No explanation seemed adequate. His jaw muscles flexed as he chewed on the proper answer. Then he looked up at Hilly. Tears of frustration watered his eyes.

"He's my father." Jake said nothing else. He glared at everyone, daring anyone to ask another question.

Hilly saw the suffering in Jake's face and redirected a different question to Darrius. "Do we know their whereabouts?" She sneaked a peek at Jake and offered him a friendly smile.

Jake leaned back and closed his eyes.

Darrius replied. "We have an idea of where Aaron has gone. When he and his cohorts teleported from Ceres, the psychic register of their launch indicated they hopped to England. We are not able to pinpoint the exact location, but he arrived somewhere around the southwest region of the country, near Salisbury."

Fen gripped the arms of her chair so hard her knuckles whitened. "That's where Chance went," she said in a shaky voice. "Chance was heading to Amesbury to chase down his family crystal."

Fen's words troubled Benedict, and he blurted, "Darrius, it is as we assumed. Aaron is hunting—"

"Not now, Benedict," Darrius cut him off.

"What?" Hilly demanded, "What was Benedict going to say?"

Darrius drew in a long breath and slowly exhaled. After many tense moments, Darrius continued.

"Once we learned that Chance and Aaron arrived in England at roughly the same time, we theorized that Aaron may be planning to kidnap Chance to use him as bait for Hilly. Jake has messaged magicians around the world to cloak their whereabouts and to prepare for a possible war with the Yfel Brethren."

"Is war imminent?" Fen asked, her soft voice barely audible.

"Once Hilly placed her crystal into the Sentinel Boulder, a message was sent around the world. While the communication was intended for magicians and supernatural souls, the Yfel Brethren are very capable of intercepting these messages, especially with Ryan in their midst. With one crystal restored, the Yfel are anxious to prevent the other three from reaching their intended destinations."

Jake squirmed at hearing his father's name again.

Darrius cautioned, "Time is not on our side. Our every move will be monitored. All of you are in danger. Now that Kai has located his crystal it is imperative that we unite it with its Guardian boulder as soon as possible. I can only hope that Chance has evaded Aaron and his followers. Be assured that we have already deployed friendly Cererians to England to hunt for Aaron and Chance. Chance's inability to receive messages telepathically is an unfortunate disadvantage, but he is a clever man. And, as Keeper of the Records, he also possesses knowledge from the ancients that might assist him in this situation."

Darrius paused and studied the room. He sensed the wheels were turning in everybody's minds. The Kemps and Jake had shifted into warrior mode and were considering options and determining strategy.

"Now, the plan to capture Aaron."

The room fell silent as all eyes turned to Darrius.

"Our best strategy is to use Hilly as a lure," Darrius announced as he nodded at his friend.

Hilly gazed at Darrius, a bemused smile on her face. Of course, this was the perfect plan—bait the snare with Stygian's kin. She was the most powerful magician on the earth. If she could imprison Stygian, she could easily apprehend Aaron. Once again, her abilities would be pushed to the limit and that excited her.

Darrius' tone became serious. "We will travel to England immediately and search for Chance."

"What do I tell Jeff?" Kai asked as fear edged into his voice.

"Kai, you cannot talk with your husband. We can't risk the Yfel intercepting your calls with Jeff."

"He needs to know I'm alright. He's expecting me home today." Kai confronted the Cererian, standing face-to-face with him as he demanded, "You can't keep me hostage."

"I understand, Kai. But would you want to endanger your husband by talking with him?"

"No, but—"

"Would you risk the lives of your family and friends to speak with Jeff?"

"Darrius, you know how important he is to me."

"Everyone in this room has a friend or loved one that is just as important to them. If I promised to get word to Jeff about your situation, will you do as I ask?"

"Do you promise he'll be safe? Do you promise no harm will come to him?"

"I can only promise that I, and my fellow Cererians, will do our best."

"Darrius, we must leave," Benedict interjected.

"We have to leave *now?*" Hilly asked.

Darrius sighed. "Aaron has a three-day lead on us. We must move fast to save your brother. We need to find Chance before Aaron does. Benedict and I will teleport together if you'll transport Jake and your siblings through a portal. I will send you the coordinates telepathically to the location in England where we will assemble. Does everyone understand?"

Events were moving swiftly. Too fast to even think. The Kemps and Jake reacted by instinct. Moments ago, they celebrated their reunion; and now, they prepared to go to war. A strangled silence descended over the group.

Hilly stepped forward and looked around the room. "We have a job to do. Chance's life is in peril and the lives of all magicians are in our hands. We must act now." She grabbed Fen's hand and then took Kai's hand. "We are three of the four who will restore peace. We must leave now to find the fourth. Who's with me?"

Kai and Fen exchanged glances, and cried out in unison, "We are!"

Jake added, "Don't forget me!"

Darrius mentally messaged Benedict, *Inform our brothers in England that we will arrive soon. Send an emissary to Jeff to inform him of Kai's whereabouts. He will need to stay with Jeff to protect him from the Yfel Brethren until we return from our mission.*

The new moon bathed Stonehenge in gray and silver shadows. The massive sarsen stones jutted into the inky night sky which had churned over them for thousands of years.

Chance stood before a bluestone in the inner circle, his hand gliding over the surface as his intuition searched for remnants to a long-forgotten past. The ripples were slight but not strong enough to convince him the family crystal was near the monolithic structure.

"Hello, Chance."

The unexpected voice startled the magician, and he whirled to meet the danger with his hands raised, ready to fight. Four men stood before him. Their darkened faces were cloaked in the shadowy night.

"It's time, Chance," a man said.

"Time for what?" Chance growled in response. He sensed a battle was imminent.

"Time for the past to meet the future."

Thank You

Thank you for taking the time to read **Shasta Beckons**, book 3 of Chronicle of Ceres.

Please take a moment to write a review.

It's so important for a book to have social proof, and I'd love your help sharing this series with others who embrace their magic.

Leave a review or star rating at your favorite book retailer

For new releases, giveaways, and fun info, subscribe to my newsletter by visiting www.cllavigne.com

Acknowledgements

To the readers who embrace their magic.

To my husband, Chris, who joined me in the waters of fantasy and magic.

To my siblings for providing the inspiration to write about the Kemps.

To Super Jimmy who sits beside me in spirit and who drinks beer in my fictional Flanagan's Irish Pub.

To Brittany's amazing editing. Your thoughtful questions and suggestions made this story brilliant.

About Author

Born in Alaska and raised in England, CL is an Elemental Specialist who writes magical realism novels that have witch fantasy overtones. Her stories feature real people and natural magic, all controlled by the Spirits of Nature and otherworldly beings.

Residing in the Sunshine State with her husband, four cats and four goldfish, CL incorporates elements of magic, mysticism and mythology into her writings. It's not unusual to encounter dragons, elemental spirits, Leotes (glowing orbs) and even Big Foot as you follow her characters on their adventures.

Her current fantasy series is Chronicle of Ceres, which will feature 6 books. Fantasy fans loved Book 1 (Beginning of Tomorrow), Book 2 (Denali Rising), and Book 3 (Shasta Beckons). Book 4 (Bluestone Shadows) will release in 2024.

A collection of horror short stories titled Tales From the Crows will release October 2023.

Embrace your magic!

Find the magic and stay informed about special deals, giveaways, new releases and other great updates by subscribing to her **NEWSLETTER**.

Discover CL's magic:

www.cllavigne.com

www.facebook.com/CLLaVigneAuthor

www.instagram.com/cllavigneauthor/